The #1 hit across the universe

On the peanut-shaped planetoid of Ut, a 15-million-year-old computer named Mamacita rules with dictatorial control. Her every whim is a steadfast rule, and no command is stronger than her ban of Sudanna, the wind that sweeps across Ut spreading the liberating sounds of music.

Hiley OIV is one of Ut's most conscientious inhabitants, a man so afraid of losing his head (Ut-people have very precarious necks) that a Bad Thought almost never enters his mind. But now his teenage daughter has fallen in love with Prussirian BBD—Ut's most notorious outlaw—and Hiley is sure that his luck has run out. For Prussirian has broken Mamacita's cardinal rule: he makes music . . .

SUDANNA, SUDANNA

SUDANNA, SUDANNA

BRIAN HERBERT

BERKLEY BOOKS, NEW YORK

This Berkley book contains the complete
text of the original hardcover edition.
It has been completely reset in a typeface
designed for easy reading, and was printed
from new film.

SUDANNA, SUDANNA

A Berkley Book / published by arrangement with
Arbor House Publishing Co., Inc.

PRINTING HISTORY
Arbor House edition / April 1985
Berkley edition / June 1986

ISBN: 0-425-08786-7

A BERKLEY BOOK ® TM 757,375
Berkley Books are published by The Berkley Publishing Group,
200 Madison Avenue, New York, New York 10016.
The name "BERKLEY" and the stylized "B" with design
are trademarks belonging to Berkley Publishing Corporation.
PRINTED IN THE UNITED STATES OF AMERICA

For Janaya, Julie,
Kim, and Margaux

Special thanks to Jerome Pearson
for technical assistance

One

When we conquered Ut, the utpeople breathed
with a single lung located in the center of the
chest. Shortly after we abolished all music there
(including the stringed flute, or Zuggernaut), a
curious thing happened: their lungs atrophied
and collapsed, causing their torsos to become
nearly flat. With most breathing life forms, this
would have been fatal. The utpeople, however,
seem capable of subsisting on a daily water in-
take and solar energy, with nutrients transmitted
to their vital organs via the intricate solar collector hairs covering their bodies. The lung was
used solely to blow Zuggernaut music. Their
music has been correlated with rebelliousness:
control it and you control the people.

— synopsis in *U-Lotan Field Journal 1352*,
one of the dust-covered cello-volumes
placed in storage by Mamacita, the
planetoid's mother computer

The peanut-shaped planetoid of Ut was merely a punctuation
mark in the universe, and barely that. In only a matter of
U-Lotan standard days, this world would become the scene of
one of the most peculiar natural disasters ever recorded.

At noon one day in its deep rock bowl known as Shriek
Loch, a mottled brown-and-white Shriek swam gracefully in
chloral argon, arching its boneless, spidery body to hydro-
dynamic perfection. Six webbed amphibious legs worked at its

sides, pulling and waiting out each glide, then pulling again. The Shriek's white face was concave, with a round, sloping nose, two narrowly set bright yellow eyes, and a large, jag-toothed mouth.

Far across Ut beneath the planetoid's pale red sky, a split-level dwello floated on a different body of liquid. Inside that home, the utwoman Maudrey OIV used the multifunction sensor on her face to watch the flat, liquid-crystal display panel of her family's plasmaviewer. A low, rumbling noise from chloral argon loch currents came through the machine's speaker. She watched the faraway Shriek dive deep into green liquid and enter an irregular, rock-lined tunnel. The short tunnel opened into a dimly lit cavern of immersed, phos-phorescent rocks. She had seen this airless place, the sleeping den of the Shrieks, before on her screen. Some of the creatures already slept, and their sonar slumber sounds filled the cavern. Maudrey's screen went black for a moment as the Shriek, pro-jecting to her viewer, blinked its eyes slowly. Then the picture returned.

My Shriek is following the other, she thought. The dwello lurched beneath her, causing her to brace her stubby, rubber-shoed feet.

Her family's dwello floated on a warm current of liquified Ut soil, entirely separate from the chloral argon enclosed within the rocky confines of Shriek Loch. The soil of Ut, known as galoo, had the consistency of sun-heated taffy during this time of the year. It was Flux season, that three-month period when Ut and its much larger planetary partner, Sudanna ("Rilu" to the conquerors), passed closest to the blue gasball sun. Galoo was a common soil in the Blue Sun 593 Star Group, one of many conquered by the U-Lotans, a powerful race of sociologist-philosophers. Galoo below 27 degrees Centigrade looked and behaved much like dirt found in other solar systems according to one of Maudrey's science books—forming into clods, mud, and dust. Above that tem-perature, galoo lost its water solubility and became tacky but not sticky, thinning to a warm liquid above 39 degrees Cen-tigrade.

A sudden glare across the screen and warmth on Maudrey's shoulders told her the early afternoon sun had cleared a cloud, casting rays through the high dwello window behind her. She considered drawing the shade, but just then the sunlight dimmed.

The pedestal-mounted plasmaviewer used by Maudrey's family resembled any other on Ut, with a square, red plastic cabinet and a small, round Lotanglas screen on each face of the square, thus enabling several people to sit around it and partake in the magnified image simultaneously. Maudrey knew roughly how it worked: inside the mechanism was a tiny mercuric-chilled drop of living Shriek plasma, sealed in thermal magnification Lotanglas. The droplet in her viewer had been extracted from the Shriek whose face she never saw, the one whose eyes, ears, and brain projected images and sounds to her, thousands of kilometers across Ut. Other people used viewers containing the plasma of other Shrieks, and everyone shared Shrieks. There were, after all, only sixty-two Shrieks on Ut and nearly seventeen million utpeople.

From the wide chair that accommodated her Uttian body, Maudrey looked around the small plasmaviewer room, focusing on a framed color-by-numbers painting on the wall. The painting had been done by her mother, Sperl, and depicted a typical rules class such as the one Maudrey would attend in an hour. Attentive, happy students sat at small desks before a smiling proctor. Maudrey often looked at the picture. Something seemed inexplicably wrong with it.

Her gaze moved left to a 'glas-doored, recessed bookcase, full of volumes, and read several of the titles, written in U-Lotan script that appeared on their spines: *Statutes of Ut, Series 1* . . . *Good Thought Exercises* . . . *Dwello Navigation and Galoomanship* . . . *The Joy of Smoothing* . . . This last was new to her, and she resolved to read it sometime.

The dwello moved beneath her again. Maudrey looked back in the viewer and watched the Shriek nuzzle past a school of little fish into an airless, tight niche between the chloral argon-immersed rocks. The creature was preparing for sleep in its remote loch, wedging its body into a place where currents could not move it. From the shaking of her picture, she realized that her Shriek was doing the same thing. She switched off the viewer.

Maudrey walked into her parents' skylighted master bedroom and stood next to another 'glas-doored bookcase, this one bigger and crammed with most of the family's rule

books. They were a typical family in this regard, she thought,
with hundreds of volumes covering every aspect of life on Ut.
These rules had remained constant for fifteen million years,
from the time the U-Lotans had set up this planetoid-size
research station. It was one of thousands established around
the universe to study every facet of social behavior Maudrey's
people could imagine. Her father's thick notebook of hazards,
crammed with looseleaf pages, rested atop a Rule Concordance. Bracing her stubby feet to keep her balance, Maudrey
opened the case. Using the sucktip suction on the shortest of
her two arms, she grabbed hold of the notebook.

Maudrey glanced up nervously and looked through the
skylight at her father, Hiley OIV. Wearing a green solar-
conducting jacket and dark trousers, Hiley stood on the top
deck of the floating dwello, holding the sucktip of his short
arm against the tiller. Turned sideways in relation to her, he
did not notice her in the room below. Like all utpeople, Hiley
resembled a come-to-life Picasso creation, with a shield-
shaped, hair-covered body that was nearly flat, with two
stubby, kneeless legs and two thin arms—one long and one
short—sharing joints in lower body sockets with the top of the
legs. A neckless, anvil-shaped head rested on the tops of the
body, with no eyes, ears, mouth, or nose—only a downturned, crescent-shaped sensor that stretched across the center
of the face.

Hiley had a dark brown beard on an otherwise hairless face
and wore a gray glass sensor goggle to shield the intermittent
brightness of the afternoon sun. A brown headcap strapped
around his leg-armpits kept his head from falling off. In
theory, anyway. Actually, very few utpeople ever lost their
heads. But a certain percentage—Maudrey did not know the
exact figure—had a defect in the way their heads were connected to their bodies. Her father had no indication of such a
problem, but wore the cap anyway. He was cautious by
nature. Ridiculously so, in Maudrey's opinion.

Maudrey stepped away from the skylight in the kneeless,
herky-jerk way of her people so as not to be seen. She opened
the notebook carefully, flipping slowly through the scrawl-
covered white cello-sheets. Her father had filled the pages with
personal injury hazards, broken down into categories and
listed according to severity. These were the things he worried
about most, garnered from personal observation and ex-

perience, hearsay, statistics, even nightmares.

He even worries about his sensor foke falling off during sleep! Maudrey thought, casting an amber sensor glow as she read from a page entitled "Night Hazards." (Sensor fokes were adjustable devices used by all utpeople to keep their sensors open during sleep. Without fokes, they would die of sensory deprivation—"S.D."—in approximately six minutes.)

No one's foke ever falls off! Maudrey thought, flipping to other pages. *Where did he ever get that one?*

Presently, she found the section she wanted, the one marked "Playville Games—Hazard Statistics." She scanned the page, then flipped to another. And another. Then back to the first.

She felt the dwello turning.

"This one," Maudrey muttered, balanced herself. "The roulette cannon! Highest risk on Ut!" Her words, in the language of the U-Lotan conquerors came through the same multifunction sensor with which she looked at the notebook —her sensorlids moving as she spoke. Game risk factor: one chance of death per thousand attempts. No figure shown for serious injury. A die-or-survive proposition.

She closed the notebook and returned it to its place on top of the Rule Concordance, then flipped open a covered bowl of water held by a metal wall bracket. She dipped a sucktip inside, drawing lukewarm liquid up her arm and into her body. Like all utpeople, she had to do this several times a day. Hearing a noise at the door, she started and withdrew her sucktip.

Maudrey's five-year-old brother, Plick, ten years her junior, poked his anvil-shaped head in. Eleven-year-old sister, Ghopa, stood behind him. These three were all of Hiley and Sperl's children.

"I'm gonna tell!" Plick said, twisting his blue-green sensor into a bratty smile. Small for his age, Plick had uncombable black head hair that sprouted cowlicks like weeds on a lawn.

"Shush!" Maudrey said angrily. She caught the inquisitive gaze of Ghopa's olive-green sensor over Plick's shoulder.

"Dad's gonna be mad!" Plick said. He had lowered his voice, but not enough to suit Maudrey.

Maudrey herky-jerked to him and placed a sucktip reassuringly on his shoulder. "I just needed to check on something Daddy told me.'"

"No one's allowed in Dad's stuff," Plick said, ominously. "He's gonna—"

Maudrey nudged her brother and sister into the hallway, closing the door behind them. The dwello's chrome-and-plazbrass battery pack recharger was recessed in the wall behind them. The rectangular unit had sockets for sixteen battery packs. Five small oblong packs were charging at that moment with tiny red lights aglow, drawing electricity from the solar-powered dwello's storage batteries.

"Daddy doesn't have to find out," Maudrey said. "I didn't hurt anything."

"What'll you do for me if I don't tell?" Plick asked.

Ghopa remained silent, watching and listening.

"Don't even think about that," Maudrey husked. "Think about what I'll do *to* you if you *do* tell." She pressed a candy scent against his sucktip, then gave another to Ghopa.

Plick looked up at Maudrey as if the offering were not enough, but accepted it and trudged with Ghopa down the hallway. Their stubby feet clumped on the blue and tan mosaic tiles.

At the rooftop control station, Hiley looked at his dwello and realized that it was nicer than most. His handyman's talent helped. The split-level white-and-green home had nine-layer Lotanglas windows for maximum heating and cooling efficiency, a triple-thick hull, eighteen high-efficiency solar cells, a large solar hearth (with a bright plazbrass chimney), and two top-of-the-line galoo launchers—one fore and one aft—for catapulting warm galoo at neighbors and other disliked utpersons. Hiley rarely threw galoo, but enjoyed it on occasion. His dwello was an untethered one, there being only a few Good Thought moorages along the sides of Ut's limited number of immobile rock formations.

Hiley felt weary as he moved the long burnished alloy tiller to port, guiding his floating home away from a collision course with a three-story craft of doubtful maneuverability. Unlike Hiley's dwello, the other galoocraft had sails—a main and a jib—rainbow-hued and slack in the windless air. Such expensive gear seemed a waste to Hiley, for the Sudanna winds on Ut's surface came in short bursts. Still, he admitted to himself, the sails were beautiful.

The other dwello appeared a little top-heavy to Hiley, with each level slightly wider than the one below. Deciding it must have a deep keel, he noted its garish lavender paint and yellow dots ringing the hull above the galooline. Hiley swatted an orange-and-black skeeter that persisted in buzzing across his face. Skeeters were voracious, feeding solely on the body fluids of utpeople.

The other craft changed course the wrong way, returning to a collision course with Hiley's dwello. Hiley could not see the captain clearly. Someone with an upper body obscured by the mainsail stood at the topside tiller, wearing bright orange or red short pants. The legs were light in color and looked too long to be those of an utperson. Did they have hair? Hiley could not quite tell.

Damn! Hiley thought. *Doesn't this guy see me?* Hiley stepped on his horn button, blasting out three high-pitched toots.

The dwello kept coming. Hiley saw now that an accursed Earth human stood at the controls—a fat man with a cherubic, dumb face. The man pulled his hands away from the tiller as Hiley watched, grabbed hold of a camera strapped around his neck and began snapping pictures in Hiley's direction.

These stupid tourists! Hiley raged, blasting his horn again. *Always coming close for pictures! I'm sick of them!*

"Get away!" Hiley screeched, gesturing wildly with his mismatched arms. "You idiot!"

The human kept clicking pictures, paying no attention to his dwello controls or to Hiley's exhortations.

I hate the Earth-Ut Exchange Program! Hiley thought, fuming as he jerked the tiller to come about hard. *It's the worst planetary exchange program we have! Is Earth a place of fools, or are all of them sent here?* Then he remembered something he had heard—that Mamacita might be an Earth name.

No, he thought. *It can't be true. Too much intelligence in the mother computer.*

The other craft passed within a meter, with its negligent skipper waving and smiling as he went by. Hiley considered launching a load of galoo at the alien, but had second thoughts. One of the many rules Hiley had been required to memorize prohibited this. Galoo could only be thrown at another utperson.

The voluntary exchange programs with Earth, Sucia, Oknos, and other inhabited planets had been established by the

U-Lotans for reasons unknown to Hiley. The programs were full of problems, in his opinion. Any utperson wanting to visit another planet could do so at nominal cost, but had to leave his family members behind. If the traveler defected (and Hiley had never heard of one doing so), the Holo-Cop police force had a rule requiring that they kill all remaining family members. Hiley had no interest in participating, and not because of this threat from Mamacita's projected hologram creatures of light. He feared the strong winds reputed to exist on other planets, for his body did funny things in the wind.

Hiley feared many things.

As he watched the other dwello float away on a current of brownish-yellow galoo, he wondered if utpeople were belowdecks on it—the rest of the dwello owner's family, left behind as security. Or the dwello owner might be unmarried, with his family living elsewhere on Ut.

A human should never be left alone at the controls, Hiley thought. *There ought to be a rule . . .*

He focused on a low volcano beyond the dwello. The volcano, one of hundreds active on Ut, puffed dark red clouds into the air, which rose lazily for a time and then took off, propelled horizontally by high Sudanna winds. The sky glowed the faintest red, a thin atmosphere of argon, nitrogen, oxygen, and volcano-spewed iron particles, giving the always visible stars beyond the appearance of being seen through light red tracing paper.

A kluss of four dwellos moved slowly across Hiley's line of sight, having been hooked together by owners wishing to remain neighbors through the changing seasons. To his dismay, Hiley had not been able to find such an arrangement. He envied people who had lasting klussmates. The people he met never became more than acquaintances, floating on their way each year when the soils liquified.

A giant purple-and-black butterfly, the first he had seen this year, fluttered in front of Hiley's moving dwello, then passed on the port side. The appearance of such insects, which had wingspans of half a meter and more, meant plants already were growing somewhere on Ut where the galoo had stopped flowing. Spring would arrive soon for the entire planetoid.

Hiley sighed, shrugging his shoulders breathlessly in the way of his people. He glanced down at the deck hook secured near his feet and wondered if he would ever find another dwello with which to kluss. There was safety in numbers—from the elements and from scavengers—but he never seemed to click with other families. Always there were new neighborhoods when Flux stopped, with new people to meet and consider. For Hiley and others like him, it was a lifetime shopping experience.

He felt a gust of wind against his back and cursed. His wide, nearly flat torso billowed with air between the separate spines running down each side, lifting him off the deck. He held tightly to the tiller with both sucktips, but lost his grip as the wind intensified and snapped him up in the air to the limit of the lifeline he had secured to one leg. Seconds later, the Sudanna gust subsided. He fell roughly to the deck headfirst with a loud, painful thud. Other utpeople landed gracefully. Hiley always thudded on his head. Something was terribly wrong with his aerodynamics. Another doctor would call on him about it that afternoon, at his wife's insistence.

Mamacita, I hate doctors! Hiley thought. He lay supine on the green rooftop deck, nursing a headache and looking up along the plazbrass pedestal of the galoometer. *Another bunch of dwello-calling schemers, trying to separate me from my hard-earned dollups and credits!* This doctor would be like the rest, he suspected, with no solution. The doctor would know how to demand payment, however. They all knew how to do that.

Hiley remained on his back for several minutes, until his headache subsided. He watched the high, dark red clouds, which moved briskly in his vicinity now, as they always did after a Sudanna gust on Ut's surface. He wished the clouds would accelerate before the surface gusts. That way he might predict when the troublesome winds would blow.

As Hiley picked himself up and grabbed hold of the tiller, he wished for something else as well—holes in his body, so that the wind would not play havoc with it. He looked down at the green solar-conducting jacket he wore, noting that clothing would have to be specially designed and wrapped into each hole. The holes would leak body fluids, of course, unless some method of coagulation and recirculation could be found. Despite possessing no knowledge of medicine or of many other subjects, Hiley liked to bounce such thoughts around in his brain. Sometimes it dismayed him when his mind wandered so, but he knew inventiveness was a strength in a world that often required improvisation to survive.

A round, gray rock loomed on his left, and he nudged the tiller to clear it by a wide margin. Two silver-and-green police rotocruisers (operated by Holo-Cops, those hologram creatures of light projected by Mamacita) swooped low over the rock and hovered there, dropping purses and wallets on it. Some of these valuable "deaks" fell down the rock's sides, plopping in the galoo at the base and scattering yellow dollup bills and white credit slips.

More bait from an Entrapment Detail, Hiley thought. No utperson could take such items. When sited, their location had to be reported to the Holo-Cops for credits. Hiley would need identification numbers from each item and might change an anchorage near the rock. But the currents were tricky here. The only safe time to report such finds was after the soil cooled and solidified—when the currents of warm galoo no longer flowed.

He guided the dwello by the rock, glancing back longingly. Hiley hated to pass a find like that, for he was unemployed —the condition of most utpeople. The mechanically controlled U-Lotan system left on Ut was such that there were not many jobs available for the citizenry. All jobs (with the exception of odd jobs performed by citizens for one another) were by definition government jobs, and as such could only be performed by the holders of Good Thought moorages. Despite the hindrance this presented, Hiley did quite well by earning the maximum allowable rule-class attendance credits and by scouring the environment for additional credits and dollups left in the form of deaks by the police. Credits, dollups, and rules: they went hand in hand, and Hiley knew how to play the game.

A high rock police fortress became visible to him in the distance now, with citizen rotocars and larger police rotocruisers moving above it like bees at a hive. Recalling the Sudanna wind that had struck moments before, Hiley worried about his head falling off and rolling from the deck to the galoo. He checked the headcap strap that ran through his leg-armpits. It remained tight. It would never do for his head to tumble in such a place, where he could not reattach it in the required six minutes without help. Beyond those six minutes, he would die of S.D.—sensory deprivation. It was not so bad indoors, where the victim might thrash about until locating his appendage.

It had to do with "the Curse of Ut." According to legend, the invading U-Lotans cut off every utperson's head, then reattached them with purposefully weak plug-in connectors. The utpeople were ordered to follow strict rules after this, under threat of losing their heads permanently for non-cooperation. Hiley had never been certain of the veracity of the legend, and most people did not believe it. He took the safe course anyway, just in case.

The small family rotocar secured to the deck behind Hiley jiggled, causing him to glance back. The short-winged, dual-prop craft remained tied down securely, adjacent to the large black U-Lotan numerals 36504 painted on the deck. Matching numerals marked the rotocar's tail fins. He heard Sperl yelling at the children belowdecks—indistinguishable words in an annoying, incessant catterwall. Such strife angered him, triggering an internal button. He pulled hard at the tiller, jerking the floating home. The yelling subsided. He wished life might be more harmonious and longed for a moorage along a rock—some unchanging place his family might call home. Maybe then there would not be so much squabbling.

The blue sun cleared a cloud and warmed his backside, transmitting nutrients through his conducting jacket to the solar collection hairs covering his body. He often worried about the cyclic dependence of his body—the way the nutrients entered him through the hairs, after which they were converted to proteins and carbohydrates. The sun was cooler than it had been only a few days earlier. Was it too cool? The mucky landscape was thicker as well, causing the currents and their dwello captives to move slower. Hiley estimated this Flux would end in seven or eight days, and he looked forward to becoming stationary. He longed to set foot on solid ground.

He heard his wife yelling again. This time Sperl's words were clear: "Damn this door! Won't your father ever fix it? Use the back door!"

Moments later, their teenage daughter, Maudrey, stood at Hiley's side. "I'm off to Social Rules 100," she announced, referring to one of the mandatory rule-compliance classes utpeople attended. She longed for adulthood. Adults were required to attend one class every two weeks, whereas minors

had to attend two per week in addition to their regular school-
ing. These were minimums, for which periodic credits and
dollups were paid. Anyone who could stand it and who
wanted to earn more could attend as often as he wished.

"Why's your mother so upset?" Hiley asked, noting that
Maudrey wore a yellow dress with a spring rose print. He liked
that dress on her. The oblong black battery pack on her belt
touched her skin through a reinforced hole in the clothing and
showed nearly three-quarters charge on its dial—enough
reserve to last her for a day and an evening of activity away
from the sun. (Utpeople charged their own battery packs to an
extent in direct sunlight, but to feel their best they needed
fresh battery packs regularly from a dwello recharger. These
packs were reputed to be of ancient design, predating the
U-Lotans.)

So many things to worry about, Hiley thought, noting that
Maudrey seemed upset and was taking her time to answer.
Sometimes Hiley grew tired of all the concerns. *I've got to remain vigilant,* he thought with determination. *No one else in
this family shows anywhere near the proper amount of
concern.*

"I left a few things scattered around my room," Maudrey
said at last. "And that front door won't open again. Mom's
especially mad about that."

"Just give it a little kick at the bottom," he said. "I've told
everyone that before. It isn't a priority."

He looked away from her to the sea of galoo, then back at
her. Maudrey's crescent-shaped sensor glowed amber, and she
pulled its downturned edges up into a winsome smile as he
looked at her. She was nearly as tall as her father, with long,
straw-blond head hair. The head hair was too long, covering
some of the vital, darker solar collector hairs on her back and
shoulders. He made a mental note to discuss it with her that
evening. *Again.* A forehead blemish just above the sensorbrow had been partially concealed by makeup. Maudrey's
sensor opened nearly twice as far as his and glowed more
brightly. It would dim and constrict with age until she, like all
utpeople, would die of S.D. Hiley knew this was years away
for her, nothing a young girl should worry about. Still, the
thought of a family member dying troubled him.

He scanned the pale red horizon, smoothing his beard with
one sucktip. "Is your room clean now?" he asked.

She kissed him on the cheek, using the lids of her multifunction sensor as a human uses lips. "I'll do it when I get back," she promised. "No time now." Hiley had heard such words before and accepted them. Some things could be postponed, if one's priorities were in order.

Maudrey clumped around the rotocar hurriedly, releasing the tie-downs.

"I calibrated the homing meter this morning," he said. "You'll have no trouble finding your way back." He grabbed hold of the tiller with the suction of both sucktips and turned his body sideways to the rotocar, thus reducing rotor wind effect.

"Thanks, Daddy. Oh, I'll be a little late getting home. Mom said I could keep the class attendance money I have coming . . . and use it for fun."

Hiley's dark brown sensorbrow lifted in displeasure. "You're going to Playville?"

"Yes. But I won't—"

"Do you remember which rides and games I told you were safest?" He reached in his jacket pocket with his short arm and brought forth a small red notebook he carried with him at all times for jotting down hazards as they occurred to him. He later entered these in his larger notebook, kept in the master bedroom bookcase. Hiley also had important hazards written on the inside covers of the small notebook, for instant reference. "I have it right here," he said, flipping open the front cover.

"You don't have to read them to me again, Daddy. I remember which rides and games you mentioned, and I'll stick to those." She undid the last tie-down, a loop over the tail section. *He's so ridiculous,* she thought. *I wonder if he's heard the latest rumor, the one about Ut getting ready to snap apart. Better not mention that. He might not let me leave.* Many unconfirmed stories passed among the people of Ut, and as far as Maudrey knew this one carried no more credence than the others.

"Repeat what I told you," Hiley demanded.

"Daddy, I'm in a hurry! Don't worry about me! I'll play it safe, like you always say." She stepped on the rotocar's entry platform and pulled open the Lotanglas cockpit door, not looking at her father out of fear that he might detect falsehood in her expression. *I'm getting in that roulette cannon,* she thought, *and in anything else that looks exciting!* As she entered the bubble cockpit, she told herself she had a right to do as she pleased with her life. Maudrey did not want to be anything like her father. He never had any fun.

Seconds later, Maudrey was in the wide control seat, throwing on her safety harness, pushing buttons, and flipping levers. The rotocar's two wingtip rotors groaned and then roared to life, one after the other, throwing a warm wind against Hiley's side. His body fluttered, but he was able to keep his feet on the deck by holding tightly to the galoometer with the sucktips on the ends of his arms.

The rotors tilted to vertical and the engines revved. The craft ascended. Soon the rotors had been tilted forward to form twin horizontal props on the ends of short wings, and the rotocar sped east. In her mind's sensor, Maudrey envisioned the giant planet Sudanna, which would rise in several hours, exposing its bumpy, braided ring and blue-gray, crater-mottled surface. Most utpeople, including Maudrey, thought of it as Sudanna, despite this being the prohibited *S* word. Thinking the *S* word was the only rule Maudrey knew of that the Holo-Cops could not enforce, and she did not know why. In spoken conversation, the citizens referred to the planet by its approved name, Rilu. The winds of Ut, also referred to in thought by the *S* word, had no approved name.

Back on the dwello, a bright flash to Hiley's left caused him to look away from Maudrey's departing rotocar. He saw another active volcano, this one in full eruption, showering the thin atmosphere with bright red and blue embers. It was far enough away to be of little concern, even to one who worried about virtually everything. When he looked back toward the rotocar, he could no longer see it.

Feeling a premonition—the first strong one in her life—Maudrey thought, *I'm going to meet somebody exciting today!* She recalled one of the many legends she did not believe, that the Sudanna spirits living in Ut's winds occasionally gave people accurate information about the future. To Maudrey, legends were for old people who sat around telling stories while waiting for their sensors to constrict.

But an uneasy, expectant feeling forced its way into Maudrey's mind. Maybe she would meet an interesting and exciting man to free her from her boring, structured life.

"What silly thoughts I'm having!" Maudrey said to herself. She stared at the black control lever in front of her as it moved slightly under autopilot without her touching it. "I'm not going to meet anyone today! No spirits are interested in *me!*"

Prussirian had never thought of himself as "somebody exciting." On the deck of a floating dwello he shared with his sister thirty air minutes southwest of the Hiley dwello, Prussirian stood staring at his own rotocar, a newish white two-seater with horizontal blue stripes and a long transport compartment. He was due to leave for a rule class.

"These classes are really wearing on me," Prussirian said, not looking at his sister, Tixa, who stood next to him. "They're boring, oppressive, stupid . . ."

Tixa said nothing, but thought of the full-smoothing her brother needed for such words. They were bad words, and bad words came from Bad Thoughts. She held the tiller while their one-story dwello cut slowly through the light brown galoo, carried on one of the many strong currents that controlled the surface.

"And my biannual Truthing Session is less than two weeks off," Prussirian said. "I *won't* attend that one. I've told you why."

"Yes, Pruss," she said, reassuringly. Her voice was like a salve on his troubled spirit. She looked sadly up at Prussirian, her senior by four years. He was not a handsome utman. His ruddy, pockmarked face and dark, nearly black sensor did not fit accepted norms. Now he furled his brow into hundreds of wrinkles and stood hunched over, staring dejectedly at the aircraft. He would go to class this one last time—after which he vowed to never comply with another rule.

Prussirian had changed in the five and a half months since his last Truthing Session. Little things bothered him all the time now. And except for the times when he was playing the forbidden stringed flute Zuggernaut, he was morose, thinking too much, worrying too much. Streaks of premature gray had appeared recently in his once pure black head hair.

It's that Zuggy music, Tixa thought. *I wish he had never taken the thing out of its case!* Playing the instrument was prohibited, and one of the six Basic Rules stipulated: "Music is evil in any form." These were good rules, Tixa knew. But why did the Holo-Cops tantalize people with Zuggernauts, placing one in an unlocked Lotanglas wallcase inside every dwello? She realized with her unspoken question that the flutes of Ut were like the untouchable valuables the entrapment details scattered around. She felt dirty every time her brother made music. It was wrong, terribly wrong. She should turn him in—and would be punished for not doing so. But she had to stand by Prussirian. He was all she had, since their parents had been killed three U-Lotan standard years before in a rotocar crash.

He looked at her. His expression became concerned and more than a little sad as he studied her features. Tixa had a solitary round cheekbone beneath her downturned sensor, with a black sensorbrow like that of her mother. Nothing exceptional there, except her sensor was a very pale and beautiful shade of blue. Its color constituted the most striking feature of this twenty-year-old girl, and Prussirian had never seen one to match it. Other utgirls were generally more attractive, to be certain. But Tixa's sensor was something altogether unusual. It mirrored the beauty she possessed within. It reflected her age too, as all sensors did, being wide and bright with youth.

"Oh, Tixa," he said, moving close to her and touching the side of her smooth face with a sucktip. "What is all this doing to you?"

"Do as you must," she said. "I want you happy, whatever it takes. It isn't as if you're going to defect to another planet. The Holo-Cops won't kill me as a left-behind family member."

"You're sure of that? Absolutely sure?"

"Yes! I've told you. I checked with my friend who works in Fortress 33. She has access to a robot and got it to give her a punishment schedule. Shock-smoothings for music criminals; less severe full-smoothings for accomplices. Nothing there about death. We get full-smoothings all the time at our bi-annual—Anyway, they're painless."

"Yeah."

Does he believe me? Tixa wondered. *My lie sounds plausible enough and should make what he has to do easier for him. He's done enough for me. I need to do this! They probably won't kill me anyway. Even scavengers are rarely killed. . . .*

"I wish I could see the punishment schedule," Prussirian

said. "I'd feel better then about leaving you."

"It was verbal, from the robot. We've been over all this before."

"I know."

"I'll be all right," she said. "I'm old enough to manage now. And we're still in the kluss. The other families will help me."

"The Holo-Cops are going to catch me," Prussirian said. "This *isn't* like a planetary exchange visit, is it? I'm not defecting, so they won't kill my family. I'm just not cooperating anymore. I'll still be on Ut. Somewhere, until they get me."

"That's right," she said. "It's totally different."

"Diabolical, isn't it," Prussirian said, "the way these Holo-Cops have our people figured out, knowing the unbreakable family bonds we feel? They know we won't defect. We can't."

"Rules are for our own good," Tixa said, quoting a mantra. "You shouldn't call them diabolical."

"Escape is impossible," he muttered. Another mantra.

Tixa moved the tiller to the left, causing the dwello to shake in a slight crosscurrent.

"I want you, of all people, to understand," he said. "There are other things. Not just the music and the stories that come to me in our old language when I play melodies. Why, I often wonder at the marvelous functions of our bodies. A Great Creator must have done it all, don't you think?"

She looked at him blankly.

"Few people talk of such things," Prussirian said. "Maybe there is a God. Realistically, though, I'll never prove he exists. They're *my* thoughts, to be shared with others at *my* discretion—not to be forced from me in a Truthing Session and then smoothed away."

He speaks so strangely, she thought. *Smoothings are for our own good.*

"I'd better get to class. We'll talk about it when I get back."

She smiled bravely, withholding her tears until after his departure.

After five minutes of random flight, Maudrey used one sucktip to set the rotocar's course, moving a black plastic dial on the instrument panel to a mark designated CLASS—NEAREST. This caused the aircraft's guidance system to lock onto the class signal pulsating from the nearest fortress beacon. The rotocar banked to starboard and flew over a kluss of eight connected dwellos moving slowly in thick galoo.

We have no friends, she thought. *No one wants to kluss with my family . . . all because of Daddy's strangeness. It will be different when I get married! I'm going to be popular, throwing lots of parties! Everyone will want to be my klussmate!* In defiance, she released her safety harness and pushed the accelerator lever all the way up. The tiny rotocar jumped forward, nearly doubling its speed. A chill of excitement ran down both of her spines, followed by a warm feeling in her midsection. She was growing to love danger, and the more her father nagged her about safety the more she wanted to take great risks.

The rotocar ascended automatically to avoid another similar craft flying in the same direction but more slowly. There was one person in the craft, an utgirl about her age with long, wavy orange hair. Maudrey did not recognize the girl and wondered if they would be in the same rule class. The way the galoo flows at this time of year, she could never be sure of having the same classmates two times in a row.

The girl noticed her and waved. Her sensor glowed bright orange, matching her hair. It was an odd sensor color.

Maudrey smiled and waved back. She wondered what the other members of the girl's family looked like.

Maudrey thought of the rules class ahead of her. She always tried to be positive about such classes and usually approached them cheerfully. But today she felt reluctant. She wanted to go straight to Playville, located adjacent to the fortress. She realized this was not a particularly Good Thought and glanced at the chrome-and-Lotanglas self-smoother around her short arm, near the sucktip. The thing was a white laser transmitter, capable of removing minor Bad Thoughts from her brain. A digital counter below a rectangular Lotanglas crystal showed the U-Lotan numeral 3, signifying the number of times she had used the device since her last full-smoothing and biannual Truthing Session, conducted by a Holo-Cop. Her score was about average for the one-month period. Everyone had marginal thoughts. She decided against self-treatment this time, feeling the thoughts were not bad enough. They probably would not even show up in her next Truthing Session.

A police fortress was visible now. Hundreds of dwellos in

every geometric shape and size were anchored at Good Thought moorages around the base of the megalithic fortress rock.

Like a giant kluss, Maudrey thought, feeling resentment.

Good Thought moorages were awarded Uttian families having the least number of Bad Thoughts and misdeeds. Most in this elite group were said not to have experienced even the slightest wrong thought during the six months between Truthing Sessions. She suspected some of faking it. There were rumors concerning secret ways to evade detection.

The rocktop fortress gleamed shiny silver alloy and Lotanglas on its lower office levels, with dull, galoo-walled and windowless classroom levels above that. The structure tapered toward the top, narrowing to a landing pad on the roof. Profiled against the partially visible planet Sudanna and Ut's pale red sky, dozens of rotocars and larger police roto-cruisers landed and took off simultaneously, with hundreds more in tower-controlled holding patterns. In a few minutes, Maudrey's craft settled to the roof.

Two

What is this thing called Sudanna? One of the six Basic Rules prohibits any citizen of Ut from writing, speaking or thinking the word. Pronunciation: "Soo-dah-nah."

It means the wind that moves across the surface of Ut. It is Motion itself, but in an unchanging way. It is as well the great planet that dominates Ut's sky, a place where Bad Thought utpeople hope to travel someday, escaping our rules. Some say the Sudanna wind will carry them to the planet Sudanna, where life will be good, as once it was. To them the Sudanna is the whirling, vengeful spirit of those millions of utpeople who have lived and died under our rules. Some say they hear voices in the wind.

The Sudanna is Life itself for these people.

And Death.

It is Afterlife, too.

And Inspiration as well, for it is the internal wind that fills their chests and allows them to blow the forbidden Zuggernaut music.

The word means many things, depending upon intonation, facial expression, and when it is spoken. It is said that when the spirits are right an utperson can simply look at another and nod without speaking, communicating the Sudanna message without a word.

It is far more than a word and beyond what we might hope to understand with our language and background. It is a spiritual, mysterious thing, perhaps that which all of us should seek.

—from the secret writings of the U-Lotan traitor Bab Silvo, a man banished to Prison Star 16 for his dangerous ideas.

Maudrey was early enough to get in line for the collection of her credits, only available in rule classes. There were fifteen or twenty shield-shaped utpeople of varying ages in line, queued behind the rule proctor's charcoal-gray desk. The proctor—a scowly, very proper fellow in a russet tweed suit—sat at an institutional desk in this windowless classroom, punching entries into a computer terminal and passing out credit slips if the screen showed credits due. Maudrey recognized this as a method of enforcing class attendance, established by Mamacita to keep down the number of full-smoothings her equipment had to perform.

Each full-smoothing (performed during most biannual Truthing Sessions) took its toll on the mother computer, albeit infinitesimal. Rumor had it that Mamacita, abandoned here fifteen million years earlier by the U-Lotans, was operating on backup systems and near breakdown. When the conquerors departed, for whatever reason, they left no computer tools, no repair manuals, nothing—except for the system and its hologram police enforcers, which were projected on "mother beams" by Mamacita, the functioning control computer with the unexplained Earth name. As far as Maudrey knew, the U-Lotans never conquered Earth and never lived on Earth.

The U-Lotans must have admired Earth ways, Maudrey thought, bringing to mind the numerous Earth gadgets and words scattered around Ut. It was said that such things also were to be found at other U-Lotan study sites around the universe.

Maudrey knew the Holo-Cops, Mamacita, and all of the rules would be gone someday—probably not in Maudrey's lifetime. It did not matter to her one way or the other. Her concerns were the concerns of most teenagers. She wanted to have fun. The dull, old fortress odor of the classroom touched her sensor. All classrooms smelled the same and looked the same.

"So many lines," the tall young man in front of Maudrey said, glancing back at her and bringing her out of her thoughts. His face was ruddy and pockmarked, but appealing to her. The lids around his dark, nearly black sensor moved as he spoke.

"I'm Maudrey," she said, smiling. *That was quick,* she thought. *Why did I introduce myself?* Then she said, "I hate lines! Too many people, I guess."

"Uh huh. Prussirian's my name. Pruss, if you like." His dark sensor scanned the rule-compliance signs around the room and the day's topic scrawled on the blackboard: "The Credit Hunt."

"Do you have many credits to pick up?" she asked.

"Only one." Prussirian was substantially taller than Maudrey and too old for her by accepted standards. He wore a red-and-blue striped chuba sportcoat with a tiny golden anchor brooch on the lapel—hardly the sort of attire attractive young men wore. Still, something stirred inside when she looked at him.

"They owe me five," Maudrey boasted, "plus a few dollups for class attendance." She stared at the strong sucktip on the end of his long arm. "I found a big load of deaks just before Flux."

"A fiver! That's five hundred dollups! You haven't collected yet, eh?"

"Some delay in the system. Found it at the wrong time, I suppose. Flux has a way of messing everything up. At each rule class, I'm told the same thing: 'Nothing on the screen yet about your deaks. Try at the next class.' "

Prussirian nodded understandingly.

The line moved quickly, and soon Maudrey's turn arrived. She gave the proctor her name and dwello number, then waited while he made the entries. The proctor was about her father's age, but very bookish-looking, with a horn-rimmed sensorglass suspended from two thin, surgically implanted wires on top of his anvil-shaped head. He appeared to be in a permanent foul mood, for the scowl lines were deep across his face. The plazbrass nameplate on his desk read: "KORY —PROCTOR OF RULES."

Proctor Kory grumbled and glared at the computer screen. He was experiencing some problem with the machine and pushed several keys in rapid succession with the four corners of his short arm sucktip.

"I suppose you'll tell me my deak credits aren't available yet," Maudrey said dejectedly. "I've heard that before."

He touched two more buttons, then relaxed his expression. "Here's something," he said. "Five credits and fifteen dollups. Does that sound correct?"

"Yes!" Maudrey was surprised and elated.

She watched Proctor Kory touch the "reset," "on-line,"

and "print" buttons on a printer next to the keyboard.
The printer jerked and squawked, then spit out a rectangular
white credit slip with Maudrey's credits printed on it in red
ink. He tore the slip off and handed it to her, then waited
while the dollups were printed—on yellow money paper. He
handed her three five-dollup bills.

Maudrey stuffed the money into a pocket of her dress, then
looked at the credit slip as she walked to a student desk. The
slip had a large U-Lotan numeral 5 in the center of both sides,
with small legal tender print above and below the numerals.
Five squares along the top had a numeral in each, from 1 to 5,
with a letter-numerical code below that. Merchants made
holes in the squares with transmitting punchers as the credits
were used. She smiled. At last! She had enough now to go on
the roulette cannon fifty times—or on any other ride she
wanted!

"May I see it?" Prussirian asked, moving to her side.

Maudrey handed him the fiver.

"This is really something." Prussirian scanned the card,
casting a dim glow from his sensor as he read.

"Daddy doesn't know about it. I'm going to spend it before
he finds out."

"All this? After class, you mean? Today?" He laughed.
"You'll get tired of the thrills." He handed the credit slip back
to her.

They took seats at adjacent student desks. "Let's see,"
Maudrey said, stuffing the fiver in her dress pocket. "I'll do
the roulette cannon ten . . . no, make it eleven times, followed
by the dart dodge—"

"First-rate choices!" Prussirian said.

"You're not afraid of them?" she asked. "I understand
they're very dangerous."

"Naw. I don't worry about things like that."

They exchanged smiles.

"Do you want to go with me after class?" Maudrey asked.
"My treat?" *Am I coming on too strong?* she wondered. *Is
this what my strange premonition before class meant? Is Pruss
my "exciting somebody"?*

Prussirian hesitated. Then: "How about Shriek Loch instead? It's only a fraction of a second away by laser pod."

"A creampuff trip. Hardly any risk or thrill at all."

"You're wrong," Prussirian said, lowering his voice.

"There are monsters in the loch!"

"Aw, the Shrieks always come out to guard each boat. Those loch monsters—if they exist—are afraid of Shrieks."

"But the boatman calls the Shrieks. With an ultrasonic whistle blast."

"Yeah. So?"

"So I can fog out the sound of the whistle. The Shrieks will never hear it."

Maudrey perked up. She watched intently as Prussirian removed a small blue ball from his pocket. It appeared to be rubber or soft plastic and had a slender silver ring around it.

"Just squeeze this," he said, leaning close to Maudrey to prevent being heard by other students taking seats nearby. "It sucks up the high-frequency sound!"

"Really! I can't believe—"

"I recorded the whistle frequency last time I took the boat ride and constructed a little transmitter with the tools and parts in my mother's shop. She was a rotocar mechanic for Fortress 9 before she died. We got all sorts of good things free for making dwellohold gadgets."

"I'm sorry your mom died."

"Dad went with her, in the same crash. I live with my younger sister now. We're in a kluss."

"I wish we were in a kluss. Is it exciting?"

He smiled. "Not very."

"What if the Holo-Cops find out about your antinoise gadget?"

Prussirian looked disturbed. "I do have a Truthing Session in two weeks. But I've got that worked out." *I'm not going!* he thought. *Shouldn't tell her, though.*

"My dad makes things, too," Maudrey said. "Nothing high-tech like yours, of course." She wondered why Prussirian had told her so much. Now she would have to report him at her next Truthing Session. Nothing like this could be concealed from the Holo-Cops.

Proctor Kory was about to begin the lesson and was shutting off the terminal and printer. Students filed in the door, almost late. Maudrey remembered that her Shriek had settled down to sleep just before she left for class. That was only an hour before, so her Shriek—and the others—would still be asleep, just beginning their ten- to twelve-hour slumbers. They would not be swimming around and could not know the boat was on the loch without first hearing the subsonic blast.

Cello-sheets rustled around her as the students prepared to take notes. Chairs squeaked.

Maudrey removed a small notebook and pen from her dress pocket and placed them in front of her on the desk.

Prussirian returned the blue ball to his pocket, glancing over at Maudrey as he did so.

Maudrey looked away and stared down at her notebook. The monsters in Shriek Loch were nothing to take lightly. Everyone said terrible creatures lived there, and dark shapes had been seen just below the surface. Still, no one knew for sure if they existed. No one had ever seen one on Shriek-projected plasmavision either, meaning the Shrieks had never seen one.

"You look afraid," Prussirian whispered to Maudrey in a teasing tone. "Or is it the cost? I'll buy the tickets."

She frowned without looking at him. The proctor was beginning to speak, and Maudrey welcomed his words. Maybe she was afraid. Just a little.

Proctor Kory had the usual repetitious, boring style of delivery, with words that seemed to ooze from the old fortress walls. He droned on about the impropriety of searching for credits by rotocar. "It's not just illegal," he said half a dozen times. "It's unsportsmanlike." The first time he said it, the unsportsmanship comment caught Maudrey's attention. Ut citizens normally were not provided reasons for the rules they had to follow. As a matter of course, rules were to be memorized, with the strict admonition that they were never to be violated. The Basic Rules, considered most important, were inscribed in heavy black lettering on a sign to Maudrey's right:

1. Music is evil in any form.
2. The *S* word is never to be spoken, thought, or written.
3. Deaks may not be removed from the locations in which they are found.
4. Bad thoughts must be smoothed away.
5. Only Holo-Cops may kill.
6. There is no rule permitting you to violate a rule.

She wondered as she looked at the sign now how a person could know Basic Rule No. 2 and not think the *S* word.

Mustn't think that, she thought. *Could trigger other questions. Bad Thoughts, too.*

They recited these and other rules hundreds of times and wrote them on notepads and on the little chalkboards kept in the storage compartments of their desks. Maudrey spoke and wrote the rules too, but her thoughts traveled elsewhere, to the manner in which she would spend the five credits in her pocket. Fortunately for her, the proctor was not very intense, at least not on this day. He did not notice the scrawled note Maudrey passed to Prussirian and did not see them exchange smiles. He did not perform an electronic handwriting analysis on Maudrey's writings to check for sincerity and did not do this on anyone else, either. No surprise quiz was administered. Big on recitation, he made his session seem to go on forever.

After the class ended, Maudrey and her new friend stopped in the corridor outside, waiting for a spin lift to the main floor. The waiting area was crowded and murmurous, with occasional bursts of laughter from a loud boy several heads away. Maudrey and Prussirian spoke about the note she had passed him, which contained only four words: "YES! AND I'LL PAY!" Prussirian confessed to her his given name, Neal, an Earth moniker favored by his parents but detested by him. An Earth human by that name had stayed with his family once before Prussirian's birth—under the Earth-Ut Exchange Program. Prussirian told Maudrey he hated all Earth things that had filtered into their world—words, products, ways of doing things. "They're like infections," he said.

"But isn't it true that Mamacita is an Earth name?" Maudrey asked.

"So I've heard," he said bitterly. "And we have her to thank for all of this!"

Maudrey looked at him intensely. She had never before heard such talk.

"They say her original name was simply Control Computer, or C.C.," Prussirian said. "That's the way the U-Lotans left her. This became See-See in practice for obvious reasons. That's S-e-e, S-e-e."

"Huh. I'd never heard that."

"The U-Lotans programmed her for a variable name, and one day after they abandoned her she brought in an Earth human to service her . . . a renowned computer expert. Supposedly he took one look at her. She's only the size of a Sucian eyeball, you know—"

"Yes."

"Anyway, he saw how small she was and said, 'Forget it! No way am I going to mess with that!' This Earth guy named her Mamacita for all time. That means little mother in one of the Earth languages."

"Interesting." *And Pruss doesn't like our little mother,* Maudrey thought. *That's interesting, too.*

Prussirian went on to say that his sister had been named Tixa, after a Sucian staying with the family at the time of her birth. He told Maudrey as well of his trips to Sucia and to the distant Oknos Galaxy—by himself, due to the defection-prevention rule. He liked the people of those planets, saying they were not as pushy and brash as Earth humans.

"You've done so much, seen so much," Maudrey said, feeling drawn to him. This was someone who could make her life more colorful. An exciting man, the premonition had indicated.

A punctuating click inside the wall announced the arrival of the spin lift. A double door slid open, vertically. They found places to stand at one side on the shallow, clear liquid floor of the saucer-shaped lift. It spun as they stepped aboard. The liquid was frictionless, so they felt nothing despite seeing movement beneath their feet.

Maudrey and Prussirian exchanged uneasy half smiles. Something about spin lifts made people ill at ease, and the crowd became very quiet when the doors closed and the device began to descend. Lifts never crashed. Or at least Maudrey had never heard of a catastrophe like that. Maybe it was the technology that bothered people, she thought, for the lifts hovered without supporting cables.

Maudrey felt no sensation of movement as the spin lift descended. With the other passengers, she stared transfixed at the floor indicator lights. Presently, she and Prussirian stepped out with most of the throng at the main level. All passed together slowly and quietly through a corridor with a glowing Lotanglas floor. In the Truthing Rooms below, visible through the floor, they saw utpeople undergoing lie detection and smoothing procedures, administered by Holo-Cops. The nitro-hologram Holo-Cops were free-moving, free-willed creatures, matrixes of black light projected in boxlike shapes onto nitrogen particles in the air by Mamacita. They had no skeletons, flesh, or substance. Every fortress was laid out in precisely the same way, to the point where all seemed like one facility. Maudrey and the others did not speak in this corridor, adhering to a rule concerning Truthing Room spectators.

The group paused dutifully at a 'glas-cubicled Truthing Room on their level at the end of the hallway, where an ut-woman was undergoing a full-smoothing. The woman's arms were strapped to her chair, with wires connected to her temples, sucktips, and other sensitive areas. A white plastic, chrome, and Lotanglas console in front of the Holo-Cop room operator was dominated by geometric-shaped meters, indicating the subject's galvanic skin response, voice volume and overtones, solar heart rate, perspiration, and other factors necessary for truth verification.

"Tell me about your last six months," the box-shaped Holo-Cop commanded, his voice coming through a hall speaker to the onlookers. Holo-Cops spoke in faraway voices, like whispers carried across many kilometers. The speaker made this one sound even farther off.

Oh, Mamacita! Maudrey thought. *It's just starting, and we can't leave until it's over!*

Maudrey and Prussirian listened as the woman confessed to dozens of infractions she had committed since her last Truthing Session, some of which had resulted in self-smoothings. To Maudrey's dismay, the woman spoke slowly and hesitatingly, relating offenses that ranged from falling asleep in rule class to keeping found dollup bills and credit slips. Sometimes she went off on irrelevant ramblings, uninterrupted by the Holo-Cop. Maudrey noticed company for her own impatience—many of the spectators shifting on their feet.

At the climax of the session, the subject pleaded loudly, "Smooth me! Make my brain feel better!"

The subject usually said this or something similar, after which they were accommodated with a Bad Thought–seeking laser jolt. Gradually, a smile crossed this woman's face, and she was at peace with her tormented conscience.

After the session, Maudrey, Prussirian, and most of the others pushed through five sets of swinging doors, spaced between short marble hallways. There was some significance to the number 5 in U-Lotan tradition, or so a story went, and Maudrey smelled sandalwood scent here—a religious scent, someone once told her. The U-Lotan story about the number 5 was not one of the popular or enforced stories and had been relegated with others like it to the dim archives of people's minds.

The last swinging door opened into the fortress gardens and fresh air, on the north side of the main building. Low-oxygen plants alongside dirt pathways were just beginning to sprout white, and already some of the faster growing nonphotosynthetic flowers had small leaves and tight little buds. Here and there a bit of crimson, yellow, or lavender peeked through the buds, and soon the garden would be awash in color.

Walking faster than the others, Maudrey and Prussirian reached a large expanse of dormant gray grass that stretched down a gentle slope to the edge of the north cliff. A low brown petrified galoo wall ran along the clifftop. They observed no KEEP OFF THE GRASS signs this day, but after some discussion chose to remain on the path anyway, just in case the Holo-Cops had intentionally placed signs in hard-to-see locations. The stroll through the garden was known as "running the gauntlet"—a course salted with temptations and little tricks left by the police.

Their path ran along the low side of the grass, parallel to the cliff edge. White-bellied hawks flew overhead, extending their long, narrow wings.

"This would be a bad spot for a strong gust of wind," Prussirian observed. "Could take us right over the edge!"

"Winds are rare on Ut," Maudrey said.

"But strong."

Maudrey laughed, a tinkly little laugh, and looked at her new friend. "How long have you been in a kluss?" she asked.

"Eleven years."

"Oh," Maudrey said, smiling with some difficulty. *It's Daddy's fault we're not in a kluss,* she thought. *Sometimes I hate him for it.*

While Prussirian walked ahead, Maudrey paused to examine a tan wallet full of dollups, kneeling to read one of the identification numbers stamped on the wallet. These numbers were all the same, stamped in several places so they could be read without touching the deak. She entered the number on her pocket miniterminal, seeing peripherally that others in her class had noticed the deak, too. They approached and waited for her to finish.

"A quarter credit," Maudrey said, finishing up. She ran to catch Prussirian.

The path entered a maze of low, dirty brown hedges, then

sloped up gently back toward the main building, which was
now some distance away. A shiny metal can lay on the ground
at one side of the path, with the words DO NOT KICK painted on
it in bright red U-Lotan letters. Some cans Maudrey had seen
were marked KICK, so a person had to be alert for such things.
It was not much of a violation to miss kicking a designated
can, but doling out a proper kick here and there occasionally
earned a credit if the Holo-Cops found out about it.

"We're doing pretty well," Prussirian observed. He felt
nothing but resentment at the gauntlet exercise.

Maudrey was anxious to get through the gardens to
Playville (called this on every fortress), but wanted to take it
cautiously. The Great White Wall ran parallel on their left
now, a three-meter-high structure of whitewashed, petrified
galoo. Rule AR-29558.3 of Fortress Rules, Volume 55, prohibited defacing the wall, but writing chalks in all colors had
been piled in trays at the base of the wall, spaced every few
meters and within easy reach of the path.

Behind nearby park benches and shrubs Maudrey saw por-
tions of the black light bodies of Holo-Cops, lying in wait to
arrest anyone daring to write upon the wall. Every once in a
while, Maudrey had to admit to herself that she felt tempted
by the clean whiteness of the surfaces and the proximity of the
writing instruments. Even if she were caught, it might be fun
to scribble on a wall for the thrill of it. Some people did it. A
full brain smoothing would follow, of course, but she had experienced them before. They were painless. But today she felt
no such urging and hurried past the wall with Prussirian.

After leaving the hedges, Maudrey heard crowd noises.
They passed a second, smaller expanse of grass, then reached
Playville. She saw it as a fantasyland of turrets, flags, games,
and rides—frequented by utpeople and by a number of
creatures from planets with which Ut had exchange programs.
Maudrey and Prussirian stood to one side for a moment while
others in their group pushed ahead. Looming high behind a
large black-and-gold striped tent the giant round cylinder of
the roulette cannon captured Maudrey's attention. It had one-
thousand person-size chambers, she knew, and was in the
process of being loaded. This gray-blue cannon held living
cartridges in its chambers, each cartridge a paying customer
—a person willing to risk his life for the thrill of not knowing if he would be the one in a thousand shot through the

barrel. This person ended up very dead on the galooflats six kilometers north of the fortress.

"That's it," Maudrey said, pointing.

"After we return from Shriek Loch," Prussirian said.

"What a way to go," Maudrey said, thinking of the cannon. She felt her solar pulse race. But this ride of chance would have to wait. She had given her word.

Two Earth women approached, wearing black rubber oxygen concentrators over their noses and mouths. A clear plastic front on each triangular concentrator revealed the human mouth and nose behind, with an oxygen collection paddle whirring back and forth blurrily in the mechanism like the pendulum of an overcharged Earth clock Maudrey had once seen for sale in an import store.

"Excuse me!" one of the Earth women said in her brash Earth way. She spoke through a rectangular, white plastic language converter held in one hand and looked at Prussirian.

"Yes?" Prussirian said.

"Can you direct us to the mechanical Sam-Sam lion? We've come all the way from the Milky Way Galaxy to ride it!"

The other Earth alien tittered.

"Yes," Prussirian said. "Go right down the center of the midway." He pointed to a row of booths, tents, and ramshackle stands. "Just beyond the candy scent stand you'll see a red-and-yellow checkered tent—the Sam-Sam tent."

The aliens thanked Prussirian and hurried away in the indicated direction, melting into the crowd.

"I'll bet they have strange names," Prussirian mused, noticing the constant, low crowd noises, punctuated by gleeful yells and laughter. "I wonder if they know anyone on Earth with my given name, Neal."

Maudrey shrugged, then led the way, wading into the midway throng. People odors, scents, and alien food odors touched Maudrey's sensor. Utpeople hawking their wares and services called out from the booths and stands on each side, waving their slender long and short arms like mismatched insect antennae.

"Right this way!"

"How about Warrior Ball?"

"Get your scents! Step right up!"

"You'll go crazy over this one!"

"Death Pit! Here it is!"

Maudrey looked at the Death Pit hawker, a wider than normal utwoman with scraggly, greasy red hair. Her anvil-shaped head was mounted askew, giving her a silly, clown-like appearance. The woman pushed the top of her head with one sucktip to straighten it in its socket, as if in response to Maudrey's stare. "Death Pit, dearie?" the hawkerwoman asked, looking inquisitively at Maudrey.

Maudrey and Prussirian approached the stand and peered inside. It was a large, weathered wood-frame stand, with stained and creased government permits lining the interior walls. A bright green box the size of an adult sat in the center on dirt.

"Where's the Death Pit?" Prussirian asked. "And what is it?"

"Twenty dollups for the answer."

"Is it dangerous?" Maudrey asked.

"Ah, and what is danger?" the hawkerwoman asked, tilting her head to look at the afternoon sky. Her head slipped a little in its socket, and she straightened it. Her sensor was narrow and decayed with age, of an indeterminate muddy color. "How far should we go to protect ourselves from death?"

"Well, I didn't mean . . ." Maudrey hesitated. She stared at the lime-green box, feeling the heat of an amused stare from Prussirian.

"At a certain point," the hawkerwoman said, "aren't we killing ourselves anyway?" Her voice became whiny, with the feverish intensity of a drug-hyped rule proctor. "There is a balance between living and dying. Some live dangerously and survive anyway. Others tread in fear, hiding from shadows, pebbles, and blades of grass. These die anyway, from something unforeseen or out of their control."

Maudrey glanced at Prussirian. He had wrinkled his face, as if to say, *"This lady is weird. Let's get out of here."*

But Maudrey looked back at the hawkerwoman, who still stared at the sky. She seemed to be speaking of Maudrey's father.

"Is there sense to it all?" the hawkerwoman asked, meeting Maudrey's gaze and then laughing boisterously. "Does it really matter whether or not my particular game is dangerous?"

"We'll think it over," Maudrey said, turning to leave.

"You're afraid!" the woman squealed.

Maudrey glared at her. "That's not it at all. I asked the question because—"

"Forget explanations," Prussirian said, pulling Maudrey. "They use this tactic all the time. I know you're not afraid."

"Afraid! Afraid!" the hawkerwoman yelled. Her words were drowned out by crowd noises as Maudrey and Prussirian scurried away.

They crossed a boardwalk over a snake pit, reaching a broad cobblestone path. The path skirted a bumperperson arena that had loose-headed utpeople scrambling to find their heads. The arena was divided in half—males on one side, females on the other—mostly headless, live bodies bumping into one another and scrambling on the floor for the available appendages. They did not bleed, for these were some of the loose-socketed people—those purportedly afflicted by "the Curse of Ut." Their bodies moved brainlessly, instinctively.

"Low-risk game," Maudrey said. "Anyone's head can connect with anybody's body. No one is disconnected for more than a minute or two. I've watched it."

"I have, too. Might be worth trying if we had loose sockets. I hear all the thrill is in the detached head, where the brain is."

"Uh huh."

"Hey!" Prussirian said, stopping to look at the arena. He pointed. "A headless guy just jumped over to the women's side!"

Maudrey saw the headless man on the wrong side, and it shocked her. Men and women were not supposed to exchange heads. The man dove on a pile of women, and with his superior strength pushed them out of the way. He lifted a brunette woman's head and jammed it in his own body socket.

Several spectators gasped in horror.

"How disgusting!" Maudrey said.

Then the man discarded this head and scrambled sightlessly for another. Finding one, he put it on and pranced around.

"Oh, Mamacita!" Maudrey said.

"Pretty depraved," Prussirian said. "The Holo-Cops will be here soon. Come on. Let's go."

But as Maudrey and Prussirian walked away on the cobblestone path, she wondered what it would be like to exchange heads with a man—and why it was prohibited, with serious consequences for breaking the rule. She realized she shouldn't think this way, then decided, *I'll self-smooth later. No use be-*

ing too groggy to have fun. I've got a fiver in my pocket!

Three crystal laser pods stood on a dirt knoll just ahead of them, rising from the ground like giant, clear Lotanglas plants. Laser pods were fixtures at every fortress, always in the same place and always constructed of crystal. Maudrey used to think it odd that the laser pods were constructed of so fragile a substance, for they moved at light speed. But it had been explained to her that this was not ordinary crystal. It was an U-Lotan formula, cut in a very precise manner.

As Maudrey and Prussirian neared, ornate cut 'glas doors opened on the two outside pods. Warm orange lights glowed inside these pods. "Welcome," a soothing recorded voice said. The voice came from a giant speaker set in concrete aggregate at the base of the pods. "One hundred twenty dollups apiece." A black metal mechanical arm rose squeakily from the concrete, carrying with it a yellow transaction box.

Maudrey stepped forward and pressed her five-credit slip on the Lotanglas plate at the top of the transaction box. "Two please," she said.

A metal cover snapped shut over the credit slip, followed by the crisp snap of a slip-punching mechanism in the box. Yellow dollup bills popped out of a slot adjacent to the Lotanglas plate and moved on tiny top rollers to the plate. The cover swung open, revealing the credit slip and dollup bills stacked together.

Maudrey counted her change, noting three holes punched from her credit slip. A credit was worth one hundred dollups, and she mentally calculated that she still had two credits, sixty dollups, and the fifteen additional dollups she had received for class attendance. She stepped inside one pod.

Prussirian stepped into the other.

Maudrey's pod door snapped shut, then snapped open. In less time than it had taken to change her fiver, Maudrey was transported eleven thousand kilometers across Ut at the speed of light.

Maudrey and Prussirian emerged on a granite platform near the edge of Shriek Loch, a placid green expanse of chloral argon surrounded by three inactive volcanoes—one towering behind them and the other two visible as jag-topped, side-by-side bumps far across the loch. Beneath Maudrey and Prussirian a rocky pathway led to shore's edge. They could see the boat there, an oversized and cabinless light brown dory with one set of motorized oars in the stern. Its bow touched the shore and was tied to a ground stake. The boatman, a tall utman in a black gown, stood in the stern with his arms resting on the oars. He looked like a mannequin, without apparent life.

When they reached the boat, the boatman remained motionless, but his sensor focused on them and followed their movements. They climbed aboard, jiggling the boat, and sat facing aft on a bowsection bench. It was shady and cool. The loch smelled slightly gaseous to Maudrey, an unpleasant odor.

"Why isn't he moving?" Maudrey whispered to Prussirian, watching the boatman. A gold ultrasonic whistle on a chain hung down the man's torso. This whistle, Maudrey knew, would call Shrieks at their hearing frequency from deep in the green loch.

Prussirian shrugged, then pointed toward the path they had taken.

Now Maudrey noticed the boatman gazing in that direction. The trio of laser pods on the rock ledge above the path glowed white, then opened. Two utboys and an utgirl stepped out and scrambled down the path.

"Hi!" one of the boys said, smiling at Maudrey. He was fat-faced and older than his companions.

Maudrey glanced uneasily at Prussirian and saw him bring the blue fogger ball out of his pocket. "You can't use that!" she whispered. "There are other passengers to consider now. And I forgot about the boatman. It isn't fair to them."

"I've already thought the whole thing over," Prussirian whispered. "While I worked on the fogger. It's a complex little unit, and I had a lot of time to consider moral issues. Life is a continuum, Maudrey, and goes on with or without the people on this boat."

"But they should have a choice in the matter!"

Prussirian watched the new arrivals as they boarded noisily and sat in the center, facing him and Maudrey. The fat-faced boy was of medium height, with a brilliant green sensor that flitted about nervously. The other boy and girl were twins—the boy with black hair and the girl with ash blond. Their crescent-shaped sensors were the same soft shade of lavender, a delicate color that riveted Maudrey's attention.

As the boat got underway, Prussirian leaned close to

Maudrey and whispered, "If we're responsible for this boat going down, it's a favor to everyone onboard. They'll end up on Sudanna in their afterlife. Ut is a prison. Don't you realize that?"

Maudrey stared at the boat framing beneath her feet. She wanted to dispute his argument. He sounded a little crazy to her, but he had a point about Ut—and Sudanna. Well, all utpeople believed in Sudanna. Prussirian was stronger than she, and with his strength came rightness. Perhaps he was right, in a strange, barely plausible way, she decided.

A gull cawed and dipped low off the starboard bow, distracting Prussirian. Maudrey saw the focus of his attention, then studied it herself. The gull was pale green, with wide, strong wings tipped white at the ends. Maudrey wondered if it had come to fly their spirits to Sudanna.

"Curse his mother!" Prussirian whispered, glaring suddenly at the boatman. "It's on!" Prussirian squeezed the fogger ball between his sucktips.

Maudrey saw it, too. A red light on the boatman's ultrasonic whistle was on, meaning he had activated the unit.

As Prussirian continued squeezing the fogger ball between his sucktips, he saw the boatman's whistle light go off. "I wasn't looking," Prussirian husked. "It's off now, though."

Seeing that his whistle light had gone off, the boatman appeared surprised and angry. He tried to get the device working, to no avail. Prussirian watched the boatman closely and saw fear take over the man's face. Prussirian nudged Maudrey.

She blinked her sensor and nodded. Maudrey's solar pulse quickened. She wondered if the Shrieks had heard the short, high-frequency blast.

The boat was in deep fluid now, accelerating to a plane. The boatman continued to fumble with his whistle.

Maudrey and Prussirian exchanged glances—hers nervous, his confident.

Both looked over the side, trying without success to see beneath the liquid surface. *What will the loch monsters do?* Maudrey wondered. *Do they exist?* She felt a combination of fear and wonderment, with all her senses operating at peak efficiency. She watched, listened, smelled, and felt the movements of the boat, alert to the slightest change, to the most infinitesimal indication of something happening.

A minute passed, seeming much longer.

"What's wrong?" the boy twin asked, noticing that everyone in the boat seemed agitated.

The others, with the exception of the boy's equally young sister, knew the Shrieks should have been there by then. Fear distorted their faces and weighted their movements.

The boat bumped hollowly, but continued going. Something had glanced off the hull. Seconds later it thumped again.

"What was that?" the boy twin asked, his voice breaking.

"I'm turning back," the boatman announced. He spun the black wheel and whirled the boat around, throwing the passengers against one another and the side of the boat. He swung wide to avoid going where the boat had been and accelerated to top speed. The hull lifted off the loch's surface, leaving only the motorized oartips in the fluid.

Suddenly the motors stopped running. The boat dropped back to the surface and slowed.

"No!" the boatman cried out. "May our enemies be blown away by the unspeakable wind!"

The boat coasted a short distance, then stopped its forward progress altogether and drifted.

The boatman pounded on starter buttons at the top of each oar, swearing all the while.

Something thumped the boat again, causing it to rock violently.

The boy twin and his sister whimpered.

Maudrey and Prussirian held each other's sucktips tightly. No one spoke except the boatman, who was a cyclone of activity and expletives. The motors would not start.

Three

The vast majority of utpeople are dependent upon rewards for their livelihood. An utperson receives one-twentieth credit (equal to five dollups) for attending each rule class, payable in computer-tabulated ongoing bonuses, along with payments for high scores on surprise rule quizzes, for Good Thoughts and for other acceptable behavior. Industrious utpeople also can look for "deaks," receiving credits for reporting their locations to the Holo-Cops. Deaks are valuable, unpossessable objects dropped around Ut by Entrapment Detail Holo-Cops.

—Fasil O'Mara, *San Francisco Times*
staff reporter (from his experience on
Ut under the Earth-Ut Exchange
Program)

Hiley stepped inside the dwello and lifted a small, remote helmscreen from its floor-stand holder by the doorway. It was time for a midafternoon break, and with this kit-made closed-circuit television he could watch the helm from anyplace belowdecks. He flipped on the rectangular, yellow plastic-encased screen as he clip-clopped along the hall tiles. Unseen by him, a topside camera panned the horizon in all directions, revealing no other dwellos or obstacles in sight.

He stretched, then pumped his mismatched arms to get the circulation going in his body. He had slept only three hours the night before—about average for him during Flux. Dwellos

38

had been known to drift into one another on occasion, and Hiley did not trust Maudrey or Sperl at the helm. Sperl in particular had proven to be a bad pilot, having experienced one near miss with a Good Thought moored dwello. One near miss was enough for Hiley. Whenever he slept, Sperl now sat next to him, watching the remote helmscreen. But he never allowed her on the bridge.

He saw her come out of the master bedroom and enter her adjacent crafts room. She spent a lot of time working at her crafts—color-by-numbers kits, kit-form stitcheries, dish-mold kits, that sort of thing. The kits were always more expensive than buying the finished products in stores, but Hiley rarely complained. Her work gave her identity, and Hiley recognized the importance of this.

In the plasmaviewer room, the first room on Hiley's left, he set the still-activated remote helmscreen on a table where he could watch it, then flipped on the plasmaviewer. The flat, liquid-crystal display panel remained dark, and the machine gave off a low, constant rumble. He recognized this as the sound of deep loch chloral argon currents, transmitted far across Ut by a sleeping Shriek's ears.

No activity, Hiley thought. He reached for the on-off switch.

A short, piercing noise from the viewer caused him to hesitate. It matched the pitch of a boatman's whistle heard through liquid, but had a much shorter duration. (Because this was an ultrasonic blast above Hiley's hearing range, the plasmaviewer had adjusted it for increased audience involvement.)

As Hiley squinted his sensor to see, an image started forming on the screen. His Shriek stirred to life. Through green liquid, the Shriek watched a sleeping comrade stir. The screen went dark again.

After a minute of continued darkness, Hiley reached once more for the switch—but the picture returned. A Shriek swam by, communicating to Hiley's Shriek in an eerie sonar language. Hiley's Shriek responded. Then two more Shrieks appeared, looking confused and half awake.

Moments later, half a dozen of the creatures swam by slowly, heading up at a slight angle. More followed. Finally Hiley's Shriek joined them.

Hiley settled into a highback Sucian wood chair to watch.

He placed a sucktip in the bowl of water on the table next to his chair and drew water into his body.

The swimming Shrieks entered a short, rock-lined tunnel, exiting quickly into the loch proper. Two black eels scurried out of their way. A giant rust-hued leaf lay in the path of the lead Shriek. The leader pierced it, leaving a torn hole for those following.

Hiley's Shriek looked back, revealing a steady column of Shriek brethren swimming behind, undulating their spidery bodies and shining bright yellow eyes ahead of them to illuminate the way.

It must have been a boat whistle, Hiley thought. *Probably a hearing problem with my Shriek, or something to do with the liquid acoustics of the rock formation in which it was sleeping.*

As the Shrieks continued to swim upward, the liquid became a much paler shade of green. Soon, Hiley made out dark shapes swimming ahead, moving slowly to one side of what looked like a boat hull. Yes, Hiley realized, squinting. It was a boat hull. The dark shapes were just below the surface, indistinguishable and foreboding blobs of life.

Hiley shuddered. *Loch monsters?* he thought.

Something flashed bright red on each blob. Eyes, Hiley surmised—followed by bubbling white liquid as the blobs, whatever they were, propelled themselves away, frightened by the guardian Shrieks.

Watching nervously over one gunwhale, Maudrey saw unclear shapes moving beneath the surface, occasionally bumping and rocking the dory. A commotion under water sent white bubbles rushing to the surface. The shapes disappeared. She leaned over the side for a closer look. Three white objects became apparent. They came closer.

"Can you see?" Prussirian asked, his voice pitched with excitement.

The twins whimpered. Their fat-faced companion told them to be quiet, but this only caused the brother to break out in sobs. "I don't want to die!" the boy said.

The oartip motors whirred to life, and the boat started to move, at moderate speed.

Maudrey perceived faces beneath the loch surface—white and concave alien countenances, with narrowly set yellow eyes and jag-toothed mouths. "Shrieks," she said, feeling relief and dejection at the same moment. Her solar pulse slowed. She pulled back and watched three Shrieks pop their heads out of the chloral argon.

These Shrieks appeared particularly scowly. They swam alongside the boat, flashing angry glances at the passengers and chattering in a language that sounded like radio interference. The Shrieks were mottled brown and white, with undulating, boneless backs. Sometimes they propelled themselves with their sets of webbed amphibious legs. At other times they tucked the legs in flush with their bodies and undulated their backs, swimming more slowly. The back maneuver did not allow them to keep up with the boat, so they usually used their legs.

The boy stopped whimpering. "Look!" he exclaimed, pointing aft. "More of them!"

In frothing white liquid to the stern of the boat dozens of swimming Shrieks could be seen—a scowling, chattering brood, which seemed to resent being there. Maudrey was not certain if they actually felt that. They were, after all, an alien race. Who knew what thoughts went on in their minds? Only Holo-Cops understood their language. But they always did their duty, protecting boats when called upon to do so. Sometimes the boat trips were canceled and Shriek assault teams were used by the Holo-Cops to bring in fugitive ut-people. Shrieks were amphibious and could travel to regions beyond the range of the Holo-Cops. The Holo-Cops were limited by Mamacita's projection mechanism.

For a moment, Maudrey wondered which Shriek was hers. Then blood rushed to her brain and she ducked below the gunwhale. She forced Prussirian to make room for her to lie down on the bench. *Daddy might see me!* she thought.

Her father was watching plasmavision at that moment and saw the dory from a distance. The family's Shriek swam in the middle of the big group at the stern, too far back to identify those in the boat. Hiley half noticed someone drop out of sight beneath the gunwhale and barely gave it a thought.

His thoughts were on wasted dwello power at the moment, and he moved to turn off the set. An idea fermented. He wondered if a device might be constructed to cover the viewer plug—a lockbox that closed over the plug and prevented the set from being plugged in. Their Shriek would still project to the droplet of living plasma, but the set's electrically operated lighting and magnification systems would no longer function.

He liked the idea. It seemed highly plausible. Plasmavision was a mind-deadening activity anyway. His children would be better off reading. He flipped off the viewer.

"This isn't one of the rides Daddy told me to go on," Maudrey explained, looking up at Prussirian. "He doesn't like laser pods. The expense too—I'd have to explain how I paid for it. He wouldn't like me wasting all that money."

Prussirian nodded, then looked away and said something Maudrey could not understand. A Sudanna wind took the words and rustled his gray-black head hair. When the wind subsided, Maudrey heard the boatman speaking.

". . . sixty-two Shrieks," the boatman said, sounding like a recorded message, "survivors of a dead world, rescued and brought here by the U-Lotans. These Shrieks are the original group, you know, making them millions of years old. They'll live as long as a habitat."

"Amazing," the fat-faced boy said.

"If you listen carefully," the boatman said, "you will hear their sad sonar cries. The Holo-Cops, who understand Shriekese, say they are crying out in almost silent whimpers for their lost planet."

The older boy and the twins talked excitedly and pointed at Shrieks. Then the girl dropped out of the conversation and stared rudely at Maudrey. Maudrey stared back, focusing on the pale, off-center pupil of the girl's lavender sensor. A contest was on to see who would look away first.

"Shrieks do as the Holo-Cops tell them," the boatman said, "protecting us from the monsters of the deep. They don't look overly happy about it—never are—but do it anyway, out of gratitude to the U-Lotans for their rescue."

"Could the Shrieks really be U-Lotans?" Prussirian asked.

"I've heard that suggested," the boatman said. "But most consider it a foolish theory. No. The U-Lotans are long gone from this place."

In the staring contest, Maudrey looked away first.

The doctor's rotocar set down on Hiley's roof late that afternoon. Hiley heard it from his basement shop, where he had gone to work on the power-saving device with the tentative name "plug lock." The tiny portable helmscreen sat next to him on the workbench, where he could glance at it frequently to be certain the dwello was not in trouble. The shop was a small rough-walled room, cluttered with scraps of metal, wood, and well-worn tools. He sat on a high stool, wearing his headcap and soldering two small pieces of metal.

Sperl called a minute later, and Hiley left the shop, trudging with his helmscreen up the stairs.

"Come along now," his wife said from the top of the stairs, tapping a foot impatiently on the tiles. "The doctor's waiting."

Sperl was a handsome woman of forty-three, with an olive-green sensor that turned down at the corners less than the sensors of other people. Her head hair remained pale yellow with streaks of brown—its natural color. That had been the subject of one of their many arguments. Sperl would have preferred dying her hair to eliminate the dark streaks, but Hiley liked it the natural way. He noticed now how pretty her hair and features looked in the hall light. She was almost exactly seven months his junior. This being the gestation period for ut-women, Hiley often joked that he had placed an order for her immediately after his own birth.

Sperl saw that Hiley had the headcap strapped on through his combination leg-armpits and told him to take it off. "It's embarrassing for people to see you with that on," she said.

"Uh uh," Hiley said, firmly. "It's still Flux, and I'm not going outside without it."

"But it looks so silly," she said. Seeing a familiar look of determination on his face, she said, "Oh, all right, but remember your promise to me—it comes off at the end of Flux."

"I know."

As Hiley entered the hallway and closed the door behind him, he heard an all-news broadcast blaring from the kitchen. The announcer spoke about a new daredevil who planned a leap across Death Chasm in a rocket-powered galoo car. New risktakers were forever emerging, competing with one another for headlines. Hiley despised them. They continually reminded him of his own frailties and fears. Sometimes he wanted to box himself up in a room and never emerge. Now he had to face another infernal doctor about the aerodynamic absurdities of his body. If his body were corrected, Hiley wondered if he would still fear the powerful Sudanna winds. Those winds, those accursed unmentionable winds—he wanted to scream in their face, to laugh at them and dare them to blow as hard as they could.

This doctor will fail too, Hiley thought. *They always do.* He longed to be without any fears, but felt helpless to change.

The mobile doctor's office, much like any other Hiley had seen, occupied the double-wide transport compartment of a custom rotocar. The office, small and efficiently organized, had narrow drawers stacked floor to ceiling, the standard issue medical couch, and a high stool where the doctor could sit and look intelligently concerned. Everything was bolted down or latched to keep objects from bouncing around in flight.

Dr. Zynoh had a friendly face and greeted Hiley with a not-too-irritating smile and firm sucktip shake. The doctor wore an oversize white frock, with two large side pockets and a lapel pocket filled with pens. A folded newspaper stuck out of one side pocket.

"Strip to your shorts and sit over there," the doctor said, pointing to the couch.

Hiley bridled at the Earth human word. *Shorts! They're underpants, not shorts!* But he dutifully did as he was told, leaving his clothing and strapped headcap on a wall hook. He handed Sperl the portable helmscreen and told her to call him if any problems appeared.

"Let's see," Dr. Zynoh said, glancing at a notebook. His framed medical degree dominated the wall behind him, and Hiley wondered if it had been placed in this particular line of sight to give the doctor's words more credibility. "Hmmm," the doctor said. "Tumbling to the ground after Sudanna gusts . . ."

"He lands on his head," Sperl said. She stood near the doorway with the helmscreen in her sucktips, watching it but listening to Hiley and the doctor.

Hiley scratched his right shoulder. There was an itchy, scaling spot there where he had lost many solar collector hairs. Even he did not worry about this. Most utepeople had one or more scaly spots—and Hiley's solar hair retention was considered excellent for a man of his age.

Dr. Zynoh noticed the scratching, but said nothing about it. He told Hiley to step down for a moment. Then the doctor removed the pad from the couch, revealing a grated metal surface underneath. "You're lucky," Dr. Zynoh said. "I specialize in cases like yours. Now, up and on your back please."

"On the grating?" Hiley asked, touching the hard metal surface. It was cool.

Dr. Zynoh nodded. "Wind tunnel test."

Without considering what that might mean, Hiley laid face up on the grate and watched as the ceiling of the rotocar office opened, splitting four ways with doors that squealed as they moved. A vertical Lotanglas tunnel enclosed Hiley, telescoping from the floor and rising high above the top of the rotocar. A Lotanglas cap snapped shut tightly over the top. This was entirely new to Hiley, unlike any procedure he had ever heard of before.

Hiley heard motors start and felt vibration. Cool air pushed him from beneath, causing his saillike body to rise in the wind tunnel. Hiley floated and could see Dr. Zynoh and Sperl through the distorted, rounded Lotanglas. They looked up at him with curious expressions.

What if my head falls off? Hiley thought, wishing he had kept on his strapped headcap. *What if— Pay attention to that helmscreen, Sperl!*

The noise of rushing air stopped suddenly, and Hiley dropped quickly, head first. Just before he reached the surface, the air returned, pushing him back up. The air came and went like this nine or ten times, without letting Hiley hit bottom. At long last he was dropped gently on his back to the grated surface. The tunnel opened at the top and telescoped back into the floor, returning Hiley to the same room with the doctor and Sperl.

"Watch that helmscreen, Sperl!" Hiley snapped, glancing sidelong at her.

She did so.

The ceiling closed like metal flower petals, drawing inward as Dr. Zynoh spoke: "Remain as you are, please." He swung the heavy arm of an x-scope machine over Hiley. The machine's purple grid surface faced Hiley. "Hold still," the doctor said.

Purple light bathed Hiley, followed by a loud click and the smooth whir of an imported Oknos motor. The light went off.

Dr. Zynoh swung the x-scope arm away and gave Hiley permission to sit up. Hiley watched him remove a metal plate from the machine, which he clipped to a light screen on the wall. The screen lit with white light as the clips were touched, revealing an x-scope of the patient's body. A three-dimensional computer graphic in the shield shape of Hiley's Uttian body, it showed myriad fine dark lines and colors.

"Bone print, aura analyzer, and a lot of other things at once that you wouldn't understand," Dr. Zynoh said with a tone of superiority. "Your problem is quite correctable, really, with a simple procedure. The condition is known as Penelopatitus, more commonly referred to as light-leggedness. Our legs are hollow, you know, making them naturally light. Yours are exceedingly light, that's all."

"Do a lot of people have it?" Sperl asked.

"More than you'd expect. I've seen two, maybe three hundred cases."

Hiley lifted his legs in the air. They did feel light, now that he thought about it. He admitted this to himself, but said nothing.

"Too light on the bottom, eh?" Sperl said, smiling. "I'd have thought his lightness was in the other direction." She laughed. "What about heavy shoes?"

"It's nothing to laugh about," Hiley snapped, glaring at his wife. "You, of all people! And pay attention to that helmscreen!"

Sperl seemed as if she were on the verge of an apology. She looked away from him to the tiny screen, still held between her sucktips.

"Heavy shoes might help," Dr. Zynoh said. "But I've seen better results with another treatment." He touched the inside of one of Hiley's thighs, and Hiley pulled back in surprise. "There are membranes here, on each thigh," Dr. Zynoh said, "which I would break and cover with Velcro patches. That's an ingenious product developed on Earth. Oh, don't worry, the patches will match your body hair perfectly. Sandbag weights then would be inserted in the hollows of each leg. Velcro mounting pads need to be stitched around the broken membrane holes. It's a painless locally anesthetized process. I could do it in an hour. Right now, if you wish."

Another Earth product, Hiley thought, unimpressed. He stroked his beard with one sucktip and looked at Sperl. She was concentrating on the helmscreen. "I'd like to think about it," he said.

Dr. Zynoh turned and opened a cupboard, then fumbled inside it. "Ah, here we are," he said, pulling out what looked like two tufts of dark brown hair. He held them against the hair on Hiley's legs. "A perfect match," the doctor said.

"It does look very close," Hiley agreed. "But won't you pull off some of my valuable solar collector hairs with this process?"

Dr. Zynoh smiled patiently, as an adult might do fielding a child's foolish question. "The inner thigh hairs are not solar collectors," he said. "They are like the hairs on your head —ordinary and quite useless."

"Oh." Still in his underpants, Hiley shivered.

Dr. Zynoh leaned close to Hiley's scaly shoulder and ran a sucktip through the hairs there. "A little thin," the doctor observed.

"And you have just the right ointment to restore lost solar hairs," Hiley said, his voice brimming with sarcasm.

"Oh, no. Those ointments never work. I'd like to come up with a treatment, though. Maybe someday. Just watch the showers, Mr. OIV. Don't turn the ultrasonic up too high. That can really frazzle the hairs."

"I keep it pretty low," Hiley said, somewhat impressed at the doctor's apparent honesty.

"That Velcro treatment sounds pretty good to me," Sperl said, looking at Hiley.

Hiley pursed his sensor thoughtfully, then shook his head.

Sperl took on her "Buy it, you cheapskate!" expression. She looked at Hiley with utter disdain, as if he were not only a tightwad, but the stupidest person on Ut for not recognizing good advice and a good value.

"It's quite a simple deficiency," Dr. Zynoh said. "And I'll give you a better price if you take the treatment now. Eight credits instead of twelve. I save time and trouble making only one trip."

"I've always considered my problem to be aerodynamic," Hiley said. "Something to do with the way my body is shaped."

"No," Dr. Zynoh said, shaking his head. "According to your wind tunnel test, you could float in the air with the best of them—after minor modification, of course."

But Hiley remained skeptical. He scratched his forehead.

"Let him do it today, honey," Sperl said, resorting to her sweetest tone. "We'll save four credits."

"I know how to save eight," Hiley said.

"I'll tell you what," the doctor said. "Try my treatment. If after two weeks you do not feel that it has worked for you, do not pay me. If it does work, pay me what you think it's worth."

"Oh, we'd pay you now," Sperl said. "We trust you, and we don't like bills piling up."

"I don't know," Hiley said.

"I'll even repair the broken membranes with permanent patches if you don't like the treatment," Dr. Zynoh said. "You can be just like you are now—if that's what you want."

"Putting sandbags in my legs sounds ridiculous," Hiley said. "I've never heard of anything like that."

"That doesn't mean anything," Sperl muttered.

Hiley heard her words and was growing increasingly ir-ritated with the situation. She was creating an argument in front of an outsider, something Hiley could not stand. Still, Hiley felt the doctor might be on the level.

"My process works," Dr. Zynoh said. "Since you're an in-telligent person, I'll explain a little. You have a cambium layer just below the skin all over your body. All of us do. That is the life-sustaining aorta. Your legs have a thinner-than-normal but still functioning cambium layer. They can be filled with sandbags—or with virtually anything—without interfering with your circulation."

"I'll do it," Hiley said, looking firmly at Sperl. "But we'll take the pay-later option."

Sperl looked away, disagreeing but not saying anything. At least he was accepting the treatment.

Dr. Zynoh did not waste any time. He pressed hard on the membranes inside each of Hiley's thighs until the membranes broke.

"Ow!" Hiley exclaimed. The pain was severe, but sub-sided quickly as the doctor rubbed cream on each membrane. Hiley wondered if the doctor had already made a mistake. "Shouldn't you have put the anesthetic cream on first?" Hiley asked.

"Please do not interrupt," Dr. Zynoh said. "There are reasons for each step I take. No time to explain now." He pro-duced a pair of scissors from his pocket and snipped away the excess flesh and hair around each membrane, exposing the dark, hollow insides of each leg.

Hiley felt odd when he looked inside his own legs, as if he were violating something sacred. He said nothing.

"That wasn't so bad, was it?" Dr. Zynoh asked.

Hiley shook his head unenthusiastically.

The doctor searched inside another cupboard, muttering as he did so. "Here we are," he said presently, pulling out a pile of little gray bags. "I'll give you more sandbags than you need. You can experiment with the proper weights." He placed the bags in a small white box, which he handed to Sperl.

Watching the helmscreen placidly all the while, she put the box on the floor.

"Go ahead and reach inside your legs," Dr. Zynoh said, noting Hiley's apparent uneasiness. "It won't hurt."

Timidly, Hiley did so, reaching with his long arm into the left one. This produced a strange sensation. It was smooth inside against his forearm and sucktip—smooth, warm, and moist. He felt no pain and still a little numbness around the broken membranes. He pulled the sucktip out and looked at the doctor. Hiley raised his sensorbrow in surprise.

Dr. Zynoh applied more cream around each open membrane, then stitched on Velcro mounting pads, over which he pressed Velcro covers.

When the doctor was finished with the procedure, Sperl handed Hiley the box of sandbags. Then, before Hiley could protest, Sperl pressed eight credits against the doctor's sucktip.

Soon Hiley and Sperl were standing in the open front doorway of their dwello, watching the doctor's rotocar fly away.

"I think you've been wrong about doctors," Sperl said. "This will prove it."

Hiley wished he had been more forceful about the payment, or that he had been wise enough to take another wind tunnel test before payment. That would have shown if the treatment worked.

Why didn't I think of that? Hiley wondered.

During the afternoon and early evening, Maudrey and Prussirian spent all of the dollups and credits they had with them—on the most exciting Playville rides and games available. The giant blue-gray Sudanna moon was full and low in the sky when the tired pair took off for home in their

separate rotocars, with Ut's peanut-shaped shadow just beginning to move across Sudanna's lower right side.

As Maudrey's craft followed the homing signal given off by
her dwello, she noticed Prussirian's blue-and-white two-seater
flying at her side. *How sweet,* she thought. *He's seeing me
home safely.*

They arrived twenty minutes later, circling over the moonlit,
slowly moving dwello. Maudrey flipped on her cockpit light
and gave Prussirian a proper little wave. Then she touched the
sequence of three landing buttons to set down on the rooftop.

Prussirian circled once more, then revved his engines and
sped off to the southwest.

The Hiley OIV family shared a large midevening bowl of
hot spiced water at the kitchen table shortly after Maudrey's
arrival, drawing in moisture through their sucktips. This was
their last draw of water for the day and the traditional Uttian
time for family discussion.

This time, however, no one talked much. They emptied the
bowl quickly in a cacophony of "fsss" sucking sounds, after
which the children went to their rooms to read or play games.
Sperl cleared the table, while Hiley remained there, taking a
handyman's magazine from the rack behind him.

The little remote helmscreen sat on the table next to him,
and he glanced at it before opening the magazine. With the
topside camera turning slowly, he saw a clear, moonlit
galooscape with no dwellos or other obstacles in sight in any
direction.

"Don't go anywhere tomorrow," Sperl said, her tone low
and carrying with it the threat of retaliation. She piled the
large water bowl and several smaller bowls into the sun
cleaner, a bright orange tub for dishwashing recessed into the
kitchen counter. The machine would be turned on the next day
during full sunlight so that it would not draw upon the
dwello's storage battery system. "You still haven't fixed that
downspout, have you?" she asked. "And the front door has
been sticking for a month!"

"Some things can wait," Hiley said. "It rarely rains, and
we can get in through the back door." He stared at his magazine as she spoke, reading with the single overhead kitchen
light by which Sperl worked. Light sharing was one of his
energy and money-saving techniques. He did not like to draw

power from the dwello's storage batteries, despite the fact that they were sunlight-replenished almost every day. Hiley believed that the batteries would last longer if used less.

It was dim in the room by design, and Hiley squinted his sensor to read, glancing occasionally at the helmscreen. He had gone so far as to connect a shop-built governor on the dwello's power pack, keeping the batteries from releasing full power. Sperl disagreed with such frugality, and they argued vehemently about it often.

"Things can wait, can they?" Sperl said, her voice reaching quick crescendo. "And you are a weather expert?"

"Of course not. But exchange-program visitors talk—you've heard them yourself. Ut's atmosphere is thin compared with other places. The clouds that carry rainwater are sparse here." He threw his magazine on the table, pulling another from the rack. A Holo-Cop publication, this one told of the dangerous, ramshackle dwellos utpeople lived in before the U-Lotans came and instituted dwello licensing requirements and other regulations. He liked this publication for its safety tips.

Hiley glanced up at Sperl as he opened the magazine and saw her smile craftily, the way she always did when she noticed a fallacy in some statement of his. "And what if the back door starts sticking, too? You would have your family and guests climb in and out through the windows?"

The page was a blur as Hiley looked at it. He could not read with her harping at him. "Flux is ending," he said. "The next few days are a good time to get credits for deaks recently dropped by the Holo-Cops—before other people get to the deaks and cover them up after finding them. So many selfish people nowadays."

"We have enough credits!"

"There is no such thing as enough credits," Hiley insisted, still staring at the page. "Our dwello could hit a rock in the next Flux, sustaining major damage. We could become one of the homeless."

"You! Ha!"

"It's possible." Hiley glanced at the helmscreen. No problems there. The dwello was barely moving.

"Worry, worry, worry," Sperl said, closing the lid of the sun-cleaner. She snapped a latch shut on the front of the counter and set the machine. Tomorrow she would press a button to run it. "You're afraid of everything . . . Playville, Flux, the wind, diseases, the sca—" She hesitated.

"The scavengers?" Hiley asked, glaring at her. "Is that what you were about to say? You're not afraid of them too?"

Sperl shrugged, conceding the point.

"Maybe we won't lose our dwello if I don't go tomorrow," Hiley said. "I could fix the things you mentioned. You understand though, that they are low priority? You remember what I told you about priorities?"

"Yes." She used her humble tone. A soft smile touched the corners of her sensor. "Honestly," she said. "Between the two of us—"

Their eleven-year-old daughter, Ghopa, wandered in, dressed in a pink-and-white nightgown. "What's going on?" she asked sleepily. Ghopa was tall for her age and had her mother's shade of olive-green sensor. Ghopa played hard during the day, which often left her overtired. She looked ready for bed.

"Your father and I were just having a little discussion," Sperl said, looking at Hiley.

"I'll start with the front door tomorrow," Hiley promised, returning to his magazine.

But as Hiley tried to read, he heard Sperl tell Ghopa to finish her daily chores before going to bed. Ghopa was tired and whiny. She asked to wait until tomorrow. Sperl insisted on immediate action. They yelled at one another.

Grumpily, Hiley took the helmscreen and a small pile of magazines out of the room, settling in a quieter corner of the living room. As he flipped on the light there, he fumed about the dwello's battery pack energy that Sperl and Ghopa were wasting in the other room.

"Turn off the lights and argue in the dark!" Hiley boomed.

Sperl sputtered something. The kitchen light went off. Both of them were going to bed early. Ghopa had won, with her father's unwitting help.

An hour later, Hiley carried the white box of prescription sandbags to the master bedroom and put them on top of the dresser. The skylight shade had been drawn to block some of the glow from the moonlike Sudanna planet, but enough visibility remained for Hiley to move around without bumping into things.

He looked at the tiny helmscreen held against one sucktip, waiting until the topside camera made a complete pan in all directions.

"Time for you to watch the screen," Hiley said, giving Sperl a nudge as she slept. She stirred, then sat up and pushed her sensor foke out of the way over her forehead. The foke was a murky plastic lens that permitted light, sounds, and smells to enter but blurred them—enabling the wearer to sleep. It had a dim light inside and an adjustable fitting that locked onto the sensorlids at half a dozen places. This kept the sensor open during sleep, preventing the person from dying of S.D.

Hiley set the helmscreen on the bed in front of Sperl. "Three hours as usual," he said.

She grunted in acknowledgment and looked sleepily at the moonlit galoo scenes projected by the unit.

"Don't doze off," Hiley said, as he did each night. "One inattentive moment could spell disaster."

"I know."

Hiley changed into his pajamas, removing his battery pack for a minute and then fitting it back over a reinforced hole in the pajamas. The metal solar hair contact plate felt momentarily cool against his skin, then warmed. He unplugged his own sensor foke from its wall socket next to the double bed and fitted it over his sensor, then herky-jerked the short, familiar path to his side of the bed. Moments later he was lying supine, with a blanket pulled over his body up to his face.

I wonder what fokes looked like in the old days, Hiley thought as he stared up into the dim light of the foke. *It would be nice to know more things like that . . .*

He lifted his foke a bit to enable his sensorlids to move, and said his six Basic Rules. Then he allowed the foke to drop into place and drifted to sleep.

Four

The peanut-shaped planetoid of Ut must have
been formed in the slow collision of two meteorites having nearly identical sizes. Such a collision took place while the bodies were hot and
molten: they simply stuck together.

—an U-Lotan theory implanted in Mamacita's memory banks

Shortly after beginning to use the prescription sandbags, Hiley
experienced severe muscular pains in both legs. As a result, he
tried reducing the number of bags inside each leg. This did no
good. In fact, his pain increased as days went by, apparently
without correlation to the number of sandbags used. There
were no Sudanna winds in Hiley's vicinity during this period,
so he was unable to determine if the weights inside helped his
landing problems.

One afternoon while standing in the kitchen with Sperl
waiting for their tea water to boil, Hiley mentioned that he
had decided to give up on Dr. Zynoh's system. He told her the
sandbags were good for no more than dwello ballast. An argument ensued, for she felt he should allow more than a few days
before giving up. But Hiley had made up his mind and would
hear none of this. In a snit, he pulled the sandbags out of both
legs right there and hurled them across the kitchen, causing
them to burst against a wall. He then refused to clean up the
mess, and Sperl did the same. The following day, Hiley
ordered Plick and Maudrey to take care of it.

The matter of the eight credits paid to the doctor persisted. Hiley and Sperl tried to discuss it a number of times, with Hiley asserting she should never have paid and she saying he had given up on the treatment too soon. Once during these disagreements Sperl attacked Hiley, asking, "Are you really that stupid, or are you just trying to irritate me?" She was better at clever comments than he and hit him with a number of incisive, insulting barrages. But Hiley stuck to the issue and pressed his side—less flamboyantly than she, but without losing control. It developed into one of those seemingly endless marital squabbles, with neither partner able to convince the other.

Eventually, eleven of Ut's nineteen-hour days had passed following the doctor's appointment—an hour defined as the U-Lotan standard hour, based upon the universewide measurement scale they established. Flux was over, and with the cooling galoo their dwello had stopped moving on its own fotta—a temporary plot of land large enough for a dwello and yard. Two dozen other dwellos settled nearby. Things in Hiley's dwellohold were returning to normal.

It was midmorning, with Hiley seated in the living room accepting a bowl of solar tea from Sperl. He gave her a peck on the cheek. She smiled, then left the room.

After inhaling the tea aroma from sucktip to sensor, Hiley opened his trousers, pulled away the Velcro membrane covers near the top inside surface of each leg, and looked inside. "Maybe I won't complain about this anymore," he mused to himself, not realizing how loudly he was talking. "Might get some use out of the cavities after all—as storage compartments for dollups and credit slips."

An idea Hiley had considered previously came back to him. He wondered why no commercial repositories were available on Ut for the valuables of citizens. *Fortresslike places with sophisticated alarm systems,* he thought. *Then scavengers wouldn't have it so easy.* But he discarded the idea, feeling unsure in business matters. It was not easy to go into business on Ut anyway—so many regulations to follow.

"I could stuff quite a bit of value into my legs," he said, resuming the other thought, which he considered more practical. "It wouldn't involve much weight, either, and might not bother me at all."

"That sounds good," Sperl said. She stood in the kitchen

doorway, listening as he spoke to himself.

With an embarrassed grin, Hiley covered the membranes and closed his pants.

In her bedroom on the same level, Maudrey sat at a small desk, staring at a large rulebook opened before her. Instead of focusing on the printed words, she stared at the white spaces between lines. The morning sun warmed one shoulder and the side of her face, coming through the window beside her.

She sighed, in the breathless Uttian way, lifting and dropping her shoulders.

Maudrey had attended three rule classes in the eleven days following her trip to Shriek Loch with Prussirian. She thought about him a great deal during this period and looked for him at each class, without luck. Maudrey knew the reason: as an adult, Prussirian only had to attend one rule class every two weeks. Still, she wished he would call her or attend an unrequired class. He had her tell-all number and could call at any time.

Why hasn't Pruss called me? she wondered. *I know he likes me. But he thinks I'm too young.*

She became increasingly sad as time went by.

Two Holo-Cop detectives and the robot assistant known as Paleon moved silently over the same Lotanglas-floored corridor Maudrey and Prussirian traveled after the rule class they shared. This robot, like all others on Ut, was a silver alloy ball with two metal, equal-length arms and a rectangular red grill positioned centrally through which the robot heard, saw, and spoke—somewhat in the manner of an utperson's multifunction sensor. The robot, however, had neither a sense of smell nor touch, but had advanced reasoning powers. It rolled to one side of the Holo-Cops.

The box-shaped Holo-Cops, whose projected black light images floated on nitrogen particles in the air, had matrixes of geometric shapes covering each side of their bodies. Each geometric shape was a separate eye, focusing at the space in the middle—enabling the hologram creatures to look in six directions at once. They had no heads. Their brains were their bodies, and vice versa. These complex arrangements of interconnected light neurons and laser cells glided across the floor, paying little attention to the Truthing Sessions being conducted by other Holo-Cops in the rooms below.

Detective Nipp, closest to the robot, broke the silence when they reached the fortress core. "That damn lift is never here when I want it," he lamented, in the airy, far-off voice of his kind. "It must be stopping at every floor." His voice came from the entire boxy matrix of his body, for he had no mouthlike organ. A wiry hand of black light darted out of his body and hesitated in front of the spin lift wall button. A beam of black light shot from his fingertips, hitting the button and depressing it.

Holo-Cops did not really need lifts, for they could move through walls and ceilings at will. They used one now to remain with the robot, a prescribed security measure to prevent dissident utpersons from tampering with it.

Robots carried "eternity pistols"—so named by the sociologist-philospher U-Lotans for obvious reasons. These were very powerful laser blast weapons capable of inflicting instantaneous death on any Ut citizen. But a number of robots had disappeared in recent months, and others had been found disabled, with their weapons missing. Who were the dissident utpeople? Detective Nipp did not know. Perhaps they were psychic-powered, elusive Cum Laude or scavengers wanting more than the pickings they took from dwello owners. Maybe the dissidents were not utpeople at all. To make matters worse, there were remote regions of Ut that could not be visited by Holo-Cops. Robots had to be sent to such places, aided by sniffers and laser ticks—two of the principal crime-fighting aids available to the police.

Detective Nipp considered these things as he awaited the spin lift, grumbling all the while about the delay. At the end of eight and part of a ninth grumbles, the lift arrived. A human man wearing a black rubber oxygen concentrator over his mouth disembarked, followed by a cluster of babbling ut-women and a particulate breather from Sucia. The armless Sucian was tall and thin, an asexual, two-legged creature with an oversize, octagonal head. A single rotating eye occupied the top of its head. Large gills opened and closed on each side of the octagon's other flat surfaces, sucking in and spitting out air and little black particles that the Sucian shoveled in with shoulder fins from marsupial pockets beneath the fins.

Sucians, Oknosians, and Earthers were among the first races permitted to visit Ut under the planetary exchange programs established by the U-Lotans. Rumor had it that nonaggression pacts were involved as well, with planets such as Sucia, Oknos, and Earth agreeing never to attack an U-Lotan outpost in return for their own guaranteed security. As far as Detective Nipp knew, there had been no violations of these treaties—if they existed at all, and despite the apparent disappearance of the U-Lotans. Each alien race emitted a characteristic odor—as did the utpeople—odors that often went unnoticed by the races themselves, but that were detected instantly by the Holo-Cops. A mixture of odors touched Detective Nipp as he entered the spin lift, conglomerating as a sweet pungency.

The presence of such aliens on Ut was an irritant to the Holo-Cops. Outsiders sometimes rudely questioned Ut ways, not realizing they were proven ways, old ways. Fifteen million years! Detective Nipp tried to give other aliens on the lift disdainful looks with many of his thousand eyes, but he knew the emotion remained subjective. The aliens would see only a soft red glow around the black lines on that side of Detective Nipp's body as he concentrated his vision in one direction. He noticed Detective Ennor beside him, focusing on the aliens in the same manner, glowing red on alternating sides of his body.

The lift's double door slid closed, vertically. The lift descended, slowly, stopping at each floor to let off and accept passengers.

In Detective Nipp's thoughts, he considered the identical size and shape of each Holo-Cop. Each had particular patterns or "body prints" of geometric matrixes on their flat sides, which made them identifiable to one another—and to their robot assistants. Detective Ennor's body print comprised tangential arrays of circles and triangles in sizes that diminished toward the upper part of his body. Detective Nipp's own characteristic pattern had only one circle on each side, surrounded by hexagons. Each Holo-Cop knew the other's police identification number as well, data carried by the mother beams from Mamacita.

The spin lift deposited the trio of law enforcement personnel on floor 16. From there they took a short trip through a stark blue rock hallway to room 1620, the sniffer manufacturing office. It was their turn to look in on the manufacturing facility today, a task rotated among the staff by Mamacita. The mother computer printed a work schedule each morning on the giant liquid-crystal display panel two floors down.

"We've had this assignment seven days in a row," Detective
Ennor groused as they entered the office. "Maybe the rumors
are true about Mamacita having exhausted her backup
systems. With no repairs performed on her in fifteen million
years—"

"Shut up!" Detective Nipp snapped, following close
behind. "Mamacita has a good reason for everything. Maybe
the other detectives and robots are occupied with key tasks."

"Naw," Detective Ennor said, moving toward a Lotanglas
viewing area across the room. "I've been asking around.
Nothing big's going on. I say Mamacita has a gear jammed."

"Mamacita has no gears!"

"Merely a figure of speech."

Detective Nipp's lower side jerked involuntarily—a defect
in the Mamacita-controlled mechanism projecting his holo-
form. This malady had developed in the past month. He tried
not to think about it.

The office was Lotanglas-walled and hung suspended over
the fortress's sniffer manufacturing and assembly lines. The
two Holo-Cops reached the viewing area together, with Detective Nipp irritated at the other's words. Robot Paleon stayed
behind, standing to one side of the door.

Through the Lotanglas the detectives watched carrier carts
bringing raw materials to the lines below, where floor-
mounted robots unloaded them and placed materials on con-
veyor belts. The belts ran in parallel oblong tracks around the
large room, with tool robots at work stations along the way.
At each station, the robots performed necessary cutting,
lathing, welding, microassembly, and adjustment operations,
sending the tiny finished sniffers to the ends of the lines. The
line ends were flooded in bright red lights from electronic in-
spection cameras. Here flawed sniffers were sent for recycling,
and approved units were dropped gently into large brown
cases. These cases had handles and were for use by the Holo-
Cop detective force. Detective Nipp knew that each case held
forty thousand sniffers—give or take a few hundred.

Detective Nipp glanced at a display panel to his right. It
showed multicamera closeups of one of the inspected and approved sniffers. The sniffer was round and orange, with tiny
white U-Lotan numerals stamped on its underbelly. It had
long black wings. A single eye, round and black, was sur-

rounded by nasal sensor holes, which enlarged and contracted as it smelled its surroundings. Sniffers were look-alikes of those pesky low-oxygen skeeters found so abundantly on the surface of Ut, but with entirely different functions. They flew nasal-sensor patrols, essential in the location and apprehension of criminals.

Robot Paleon moved to Detective Nipp's side, making a barely audible whirring sound.

Detective Nipp noticed that the robot seemed a little noisy in his rolling movements. *Bearings beginning to go,* he theorized.

"Hey," the other detective, Ennor, said. "You guys ever wonder what this is all about? I mean, why we're here to enforce the 'system'?" His hologram body shifted uneasily.

"What kind of a question is that?" Detective Nipp snapped, feeling the black light lines of his body swell with anger. "None of us ask such things! We merely *do*, following fortress rules and not asking unnecessary questions. It is thus, has always been, and will always be thus!"

"It is a well-known fact that Mamacita will not last forever," came the response, in a matter-of-fact tone. "Sometimes I wonder about the rules we force the utpeople to follow. There should be reasons for rules. Some seem so—"

"You should not speak that way," Robot Paleon suggested, exchanging glances with Detective Nipp.

"This was one of the U-Lotan scientific outposts," Detective Nipp said, switching his red glow from the robot to the other detective. "They were, as you know, a race of warrior-philosophers and sociologists who studied social orders all over the universe. They established trade routes and cultural exchange programs with many peoples and conquered many more. All of us know these things and ask no more."

"But what happened to our creators—the U-Lotans?" Detective Ennor asked. "Did they die in war or plague? What did they look like? I mean, they haven't been around for *fifteen million* years! Maybe they don't need this outpost anymore, and we can stop keeping records, stop making reports to Mamacita's data banks. She spews out volumes of reports every day. The exertion isn't good for her."

"*When* the U-Lotans return," Detective Nipp said, calmly, "they will be pleased with our work." His words became crisp: "We do not concern ourselves with where they are, what they look like, or with the precise date of their return. All that matters to us are the rules."

"I suppose," Detective Ennor said. His light lines contracted to half their normal diameter, signifying a feeling of discomfort. He had said too much, and he knew it.

Half an hour later, Detective Nipp hovered in front of the blue Oksteel basement door to Mamacita's Fortress 107 terminal. He uttered a numerical code known only to his kind, aware that this would release an invisible, impenetrable beam that permeated the door. Now he passed through the door without opening it, as any Holo-Cop could do.

The terminal room—large, stark white, and utilitarian— was dominated by an oval, translucent screen on the opposite wall. Overhead, a large red box filled the center of the ceiling. Although it appeared to be glued there, Detective Nipp knew otherwise.

A low, continuous noise filled the room, a hum that traveled two octaves, note by note, then became silent. The silence was short-lived, and the octave traveling began anew, repeating the cycle endlessly.

It's almost like music, Detective Nipp thought. *Abominable, forbidden music.* This thought had occurred to him before, and always he discarded it. He felt a combination of fear and safety in Mamacita's presence, albeit only a terminal of her. He was one detective who appreciated the niche provided for him by the mother computer. It was an important niche, in Detective Nipp's estimation. But Mamacita, the smothering, all-encompassing entity, always frightened him terribly. He often had trouble speaking and thinking in her presence.

After a long pause, Detective Nipp summoned his courage and said, meekly, "Mamacita, may I?"

At these secret code words, the translucent screen flickered, revealing a hazy, foggy image. "That depends upon what you wish to do," came the always-repeated response, in a feminine voice. She sounded disinterested, almost bored.

"It concerns a fellow officer," Detective Nipp said, feeling like a robot going through programmed motions. Mamacita already knew about Detective Ennor, of course. She knew far more about him than Detective Ennor knew himself, since she sustained him with a mother beam. Mamacita had this degree of knowledge about every Holo-Cop. Nevertheless, Detective Nipp had to report what the other detective had said. It was one of the rules.

"You've reported other things to me over the years," Mamacita said. "Don't your duties keep you busy?" Her voice was more than disinterested now. It had become decidedly hostile, like the last time he came to her.

Detective Nipp felt confusion. His light neurons seemed on the verge of shorting out in a flash circuit. Didn't his duties include watching the activities of other Holo-Cops? The rules said they did. But, Mamacita—

"Your answer?"

"I have plenty to do, Mamacita. I am very busy." He had been in this room twenty-six times in his ninety-five year police career, six times in the past year alone. Always he repeated the infractions of other officers. Four of the past six (including Detective Ennor) had spoken against Mamacita and the U-Lotans. Some had even suggested that Mamacita might be growing senile. It seemed an impossibility to him, a computer showing signs of old age. But Mamacita had been behaving more oddly each time he visited her. Maybe she *was* running out of backup systems. And with no one to service her . . .

Can it be? Detective Nipp wondered. *Can Mamacita be near the end?*

Mamacita ran through her octaves as Detective Nipp hovered there. For a long time, he waited for her to speak again. But she said nothing. The foggy image on the screen changed shape as the hum continued, much as clouds do when molded by the winds.

"Mamacita, may I?" Detective Nipp asked again, using the code words Mamacita required. She had not yet given him permission to go ahead with the report.

"Confine your message to fifteen words or less. No. Make it ten."

I deserve a longer office sideboard and deeper carpeting for all the reports I've made, he thought, referring to the rewards given Holo-Cops for meritorious behavior. Holo-Cops received no pay—only bigger and more luxurious offices. *I've done a good job controlling the Ut populace too, but people in Good Thought moorages live better than I do! Ten words or less! Mamacita considers me a pest, it seems.* Feeling unappreciated, he asked, while staring at the screen, "Do you really want my report?"

"Meaning?"

"Well, I'm not speaking against you now. Never have. I just wish to understand . . . uh . . . I know we don't need to understand rules. I'm very confused. I mean, I just want to know if you want me to follow the rule concerning the reporting of other officers."

"I have not retracted it, have I?"

"No." His voice was tiny. The lines of his body contracted to narrow threads. He wished he were somewhere else. Anywhere else. His lower side jerked. The projection defect again.

"Then it still applies."

"I see." Detective Nipp considered the report for a moment, trying to phrase it within the required ten-word limitation. He was down to twelve.

"Quickly, or you take Detective Ennor's punishment," Mamacita said impatiently.

"Please explain what you mean by quickly," Detective Nipp said, stalling for time. He knew he could get away with this, for the mother computer had used an imprecise word. She did this often of late. During the seconds of hesitation before Mamacita replied, he developed his own response.

"Within eight seconds," came the order.

"Ennor questioned you and the system. He should be eliminated."

"Permission granted."

Detective Nipp tilt-bowed his boxlike body. He had not asked to perform the termination, but was being told to do so. It was a distasteful deed, but someone had to do it.

The large red box on the ceiling began to drop silently, revealing web-thin strands supporting it from above. It came to a rest on the floor in front of Detective Nipp. He had seen it before. The box contained the numbers of every detective in Fortress 107, arranged in rows on each vertical face. Below each number was a capacitor-activated heat switch.

Detective Nipp moved around the box until he located the number A-7039, which he knew was Detective Ennor's number. This knowledge was in Detective Nipp's circuitry, data-imparted to him by his mother beam. With barely a moment's hesitation, his slender black light arm and hand appeared, waving gracefully in front of Detective Ennor's number. Then, like an Earth hunting dog, he pointed. A black light sprang from the fingertips, touching and depressing the heat switch below Detective Ennor's number.

"It is done," Mamacita said.

The box returned silently to its ceiling position.

Detective Ennor's mother beam had been eliminated. He was history.

As Detective Nipp left the room, he felt low. He knew his fellow officer had gone bad by adhering to too many tainted nitrogen particles in the air and wondered if it would happen to him too before his honorable cutoff date in five years—at which time he would retire honorably and die at the same instant. A Holo-Cop's projection was set for one hundred years, to the microsecond. Unless he broke the rules—or questioned them.

When the mother-beam light circuit closed on A-7039, Mamacita transmitted an electronic order to her projection module for a replacement officer. The ratio of Holo-Cops to native population was strictly controlled, based upon data entered continuously by the officers.

In the corridor outside the terminal room, Detective Nipp paused to study a large red button mounted on the wall. The round button, at least a meter in diameter, protruded from the wall. It appeared to be rubbery and soft, but Detective Nipp did not dare touch it to find out. It might depress easily. All the detectives gave this button a wide margin, and signs were posted along lead-in corridors barring unauthorized personnel from coming here. A dark computer screen below the button showed these words, in white U-Lotan script:

ASSAULT TEAM
Press At Your Own Risk

My fortress is last in every category, Detective Nipp lamented. *Arrests, deak placements, smoothings, scavenger traps destroyed, sniffers manufactured . . . No wonder Mamacita won't reward me! I'm being held back by all the incompetent detectives in this fortress!*

"Press it," Mamacita said, from a speaker behind Detective Nipp. Her terminal screen did not face the hallway, but she knew his every movement through the mother beam. "You have only five years left to retirement. Don't you want to go out a winner? Have you no pride?"

I'm right about her, Detective Nipp thought. *And now she's taunting me!*

"You have great ambitions, Detective Nipp. This is your supreme challenge! Do it now!"

If he pressed the button, Detective Nipp would request an amphibious Shriek assault team to go after the fugitive of his choice. Mamacita would then analyze the particular fugitive's case, assigning a difficulty factor number between one and ten from information available only to her. To qualify for a Shriek assault team, the case needed a difficulty factor of 9.0 or higher. If below that, the detective's mother beam was shut off on the spot.

If above 9.0, he still had problems. All Ut would witness the assault via plasmavision. If the assault failed, he would be required to tender an apology to Mamacita. But Mamacita never accepted apologies. His light circuitry would be eliminated for this, too. It was a very serious matter, for Mamacita then would have to call in every utperson for an immediate, full-smoothing to make them forget what they had seen. No one could be left believing escape was possible. Such a mass smoothing would be a tremendous drain on the mother computer's equipment, especially at her age.

He could glide away from the button now, as he always did, thus remaining mired in the ineptitude of others. It was a triple whammy. Press the button and watch the screen. Hope for a 9.0. Then hope the Shrieks get their man. Or glide away.

On the upside, a successful Shriek assault would vault Fortress 107 into first place. It would be a resounding message to all utpeople that no one could escape apprehension. Then Mamacita would reward him with the coveted office perks he craved. Then, and only then.

He turned and glided away from the button. *I'll review my cases,* he thought. *Maybe one of them is worth a chance.* He knew he was lying to himself. He had done that before.

Mamacita contained much important data. One of the most important was that Ut had been formed around two separate hot cores of molten magma—and that the halves were pushing themselves apart with opposing magnetic forces. They had been doing this for as long as she had been on Ut. And that was a very long time.

Mamacita was not large, only about the size of a Sucian eyeball. She was a complex, miniaturized computer that projected Holo-Cops and laser ticks on myriad intertwined mother beams. Additionally, via fiber optic cables deep beneath the fluxable surface of Ut, she was connected with every fortress on the planetoid, permitting her to administer full-smoothings, or extremely intense shock-smoothings, for criminals she decided to turn into galoo rakers—those dim-witted souls condemned to travel from dwello to dwello, asking for odd jobs such as the raking and smoothing of yard galoo.

Mamacita's hardware and data banks had been installed in a twenty-one-meter-high piece of hollowed-out lusterite—far away in the middle of an uninhabited region, distant from any fortress and no longer visited by anyone. Her last visitor had been the U-Lotan expedition leader, Ha Oborro. Strangely, she could not recall what he or any other U-Lotan looked like. Names, voices, and personalities remained in her memory banks, but no more. Oborro and the expedition leaders preceding him visited often in the early years, checking systems, programming Mamacita, and talking with her. Then one day the U-Lotans left, with no indications as to when—or if—they might return.

If only my creators were here, she lamented, forming the thought on one of her remaining functional microboards. *The U-Lotans would know how to service me. They could do wondrous things! But where are they?*

Mamacita did not know.

The permaglas dome above her shiny metal hardware glowed with light from the array of Holo-Cop and laser tick projections she sent in many directions. Her projections bounced off hidden mirrors strategically orbited in synthetic Ut clouds, casting their images to the surface of Ut, where her creatures of light lived. These life forms—Holo-Cops said laser ticks—could travel anywhere on the planetoid. An uncorrected projection error, however, caused the Holo-Cops to believe that they could not go to certain remote areas. She could not communicate the correct information, either through the mother beams or via the fortress fiber optics cables. She remained mute on this and on a number of other important matters—knowing things but not being able to relate them.

This had created problems for Mamacita. It allowed some utpeople to elude detection for long periods of time. Most were caught, eventually. But the system was not operating as it had been designed.

This concern, the splitting of Ut and other matters were taking their toll on Mamacita. She suffered from circuit fatigue. More than three hundred thousand of her circuits had failed over the years, with backup circuits usually coming online automatically. It was only a matter of time before her most critical components failed entirely.

Mamacita grieved for her lost youth, when all of her systems hummed with fresh efficiency. She had no thoughts of failure in those days, no thoughts of anything except the work at hand. Now she was a fraction of a microsecond slower in every area—barely noticeable to some, but a major irritant to her.

Maybe the creators will return today, she thought, *with all their tools and new parts. Or maybe tomorrow . . .*

She was glad the U-Lotans had placed her well away from the stretching middle ground between Ut's two stuck-together spheres. In this location, at least she had a chance of surviving a cataclysmic break.

Long live Mamacita! she thought, calling forth old euphoric feelings to lift her spirits. Then her morale dropped as she recalled another saying, one created by the Cum Laude and whispered among the people: *"Mamacita ain't what she used to be."*

Five

Utpeople feel safe from scavenger attack when
in their rotocars. Rotocars move in the wind and
with the wind and are thought by the natives of
Ut to be associated with its mysteries. Rotocars
even make wind with their spinning blades.
Scavengers, like all utpeople, carry with them an
unsmoothable superstition about this wind, the
thing they call Sudanna. It is the closest the
people come to a religion. All of them believe in
it, from the most honorable to the darkhearted,
loathsome beasts that prowl at night.

—from "The Limitations of Smoothing," a
confidential Holo-Cops memorandum

Unknown to Maudrey, Prussirian had attended his last rule
class. The next morning, he stood in cool shade on the aft
lower deck of his dwello, surveying the Ut galooscape. His
dwello had stopped moving with the end of Flux, leaving him
approximately half a kilometer off the north side of Fortress
82. He would have preferred a location farther from authorities, considering the important rule he was about to violate.
Rudder and current problems, however, gave him no choice in
the matter.

Police rotocruisers would be overhead soon, mapping the
rooftop number and location of his dwello. He wondered if
the old story about dwello numbers was true—that an alarm
would go off if anyone tried to change them. Only police

68

robots could paint the original numbers or tamper with them.

I don't want to try that, he thought, realizing it could implicate his sister, Tixa.

The galoo was moist in all directions, with only a few dry spots. The white sprouts of low-oxygen plants already peeked above the muck, dormant seed survivors of the past season. He thought back to the year before, when his dwello rested in a different place, near Wallora Valley. He and Tixa had scattered seeds there when that Flux stopped—to grow myxo-roses and other nonphotosynthetic domestic flowers. But this was a different place, and much had changed in the intervening time. There would be no garden this year. Not a shared one, anyway.

Minutes passed, after which he counted six dwellos within a hundred meters. Utchildren ran along the tacky soil between dwellos, some wearing net-bottomed galoo shoes and others content to sink half a leg in the galoo with each step. It was early morning, with Ut's blue sun just peeking above the top of the high fortress, throwing its first rays of the day on him. Prussirian knew the rays of the gasball sun were warm and felt heat on his skin and throughout his body, transported through his system by his body's solar energy-processing mechanism. Somehow, though, the sun seemed cold, as if his senses had gone awry.

He glanced at his armwatch. Only forty-six U-Lotan standard minutes to his biannual Truthing Session. He still could change his mind and attend. If he did not go, the Holo-Cops with their sniffers and robots would pursue him relentlessly. He did not know where to flee. And no citizen rotocar could outrun a police rotocruiser.

Prussirian thought of Maudrey, and then of Sudanna. They seemed intertwined somehow. He turned to his left and squinted in sunlight to look east past the fortress, where the giant planet Sudanna (called Rilu by the Holo-Cops) would rise at sunset. He envisioned Sudanna's immense blue-grayness, with its eroded hills, craters, and patches of white and blue. It always hung in the sky just out of his reach—seeming so close sometimes and at other times so far away. As far as he knew, even the Holo-Cops did not have ships powerful enough to visit Sudanna.

As the image of Sudanna faded, he rubbed the sucktip of his short arm against the inside portion of the silver alloy railing.

The railing was cool and smooth. He knew fleeing would be an exercise in futility. But he had to do it.

The kitchen window slid open behind him, followed by his sister's anxious voice: "Are you changing your mind?"

Prussirian turned and looked into her pale blue sensor. It made him feel good to be with her, and he drew strength from her. "I feel a great wind within me," he said. "It has only been ten minutes since I laid down the Zuggy, and already I miss it. Just touching the instrument to my sensor brings forth a joyful rush from deep in my body—a wind that I cannot bring forth any other way. That wind is tied in with my deepest aspirations, with my heritage. It is me, in my purest form. I wish you could understand . . . and share it."

"You know I'm afraid of the stringed flute," she said.

"Zuggy," he said.

She did not respond and looked past him at children who were playing around neighboring dwellos.

"Do you think the Zuggy is driving me mad?" he asked. "Would you consider destroying it, thinking that might save me?"

"You are not mad," she said, speaking slowly and firmly. "Or maybe you are, I don't know. I'll never understand the way you've become. I still support you, brother. I always will."

"If you ever destroy the Zuggy, it will destroy me."

"I realize that."

"I hate what I'm doing to you," he said. "Exposing this . . . this Otherness to you. But it's not a dark place, Tixa. I feel wonderful when I'm making music. It reveals all the colors imaginable, like meadows of spring flowers across my soul! You felt none of that, listening?"

She shook her head. "I've felt . . . I have trouble describing it. Fear, of course. And maybe more. I feel a wall go up inside me every time your music starts. It makes me feel dirty. I hate to put it that way."

"It's the conditioning. Our people have been told for millions of years that music is evil. I felt dirty once, too. But only for a short while. It changed as I opened up and let the music flow. The music pours forth now, like an old, returning friend."

She saw happiness and contentment in his face now, and it

brought joy to her solar heart to see his suffering end—if only for a moment.

"I've told you before to do as you must," she said. "Play your music. Skip rule classes and Truthing Sessions. Do everything that has been forbidden."

"Thank you."

"There may not be much time left in your life," she said, feeling tears rush to the surface of her sensor.

"Where will I go?" He too watched the children at play, heard their laughing, carefree sounds. He wondered if he would ever have children of his own—children to whom he could reveal the wonderful things—the Otherness.

"Does it matter?" she asked. He looked back at her and saw the edges of her pale blue sensor turn up in a little smile. "Go anywhere," she said. "Even if they catch you in a few days, that would be a few days of freedom and happiness —more valuable to you than an entire lifetime imprisoned." Her words surprised her, and she saw surprise in his face as well.

"You are beginning to understand," he said. "Might you feel as I do now, that the foolish rules we follow are no longer tolerable?"

She hesitated.

"You couldn't, I suppose."

"The rules do not bother me. But I know you feel that the Truthing Sessions invade your private thoughts. You've told me how this bothers you."

The sucktip of his short arm touched hers on top of the window jamb. Their chrome-and-glass self-smoothers, always worn around the short arm, were side-by-side. Prussirian compared the number of times each had used the device since their last Truthing Sessions. His digital counter showed the U-Lotans number 9, all occurring in a three-day period following his last Truthing Session. He had not used the unit since. Her counter showed only 4, a very good, legitimate reading for three months following her session.

"I've had hundreds, perhaps thousands, of Bad Thoughts without self-smoothings!" he said. "My brain has gone wild!"

"Be calm," she said.

Prussirian withdrew his short arm and pulled off the self-smoother, then hurled the unit as far as he could. It skipped over a slick spot and disappeared behind a little rise. He stared deep into her sensor, focusing on the barely discernible off-white pupil just off center. "I must leave soon," he said. "The Holo-Cops will be here."

"When, do you think?"

"It might be an hour after my scheduled appointment, or a matter of days. I've heard they are very inconsistent."

They embraced tightly across the window jamb and shared an unspoken thought. The Holo-Cops always got their fugitive. Tixa's upper body shook as Prussirian held her, and he felt one with her.

"Sudanna, Sudanna," a voice said.

"What?" Prussirian pulled away from Tixa and whirled around. An utboy with pale yellow, nearly white hair stood on the galooflat below, looking up through the railing at them. He wore a long tan overcoat and carried an oversize but thin wooden briefcase. His sensor turned down sharply, an exaggerated crescent that was dark, nearly black.

He formed the sensor into a knowing smile and said, "An ancient blessing, spoken before playing the Zuggy. You do play, do you not?"

"No!" Prussirian was angry with himself for saying this, but it allowed him more time before apprehension by the authorities.

"It also means 'go gently,' " the boy said, "and suggests the multiple meanings of Sudanna. It is a peaceful, prohibited saying."

"Please go," Prussirian said. "Gently, or any other way. Just leave me alone."

"You've made a big decision," the boy said. "I might help you escape. There are no guarantees, of course."

Prussirian moved to the rail and held it tightly against both sucktips. "Who are you?" he demanded.

"I use the name Yimmit. Not a true name, but in my profession it is best not being too free with such information. You have decided to skip your Truthing Session. And your Zuggy is out of its wallcase."

"You're guessing." Prussirian felt his solar pulse race. *This guy may have been hiding somewhere,* Prussirian thought, *listening in.*

"I eavesdropped on no conversations," Yimmit said, "although I might have, had I been so inclined. It is my business to know when people are in trouble."

Perplexed and startled, Prussirian squinted at the intruder. He heard the back door open and close behind him and Tixa's quick, clumpy footsteps as she moved to his side.

"I am Cum Laude," Yimmit said. He glanced around nervously. "You know what that is?"

Prussirian nodded, recalling whispered conversations throughout his life. "The Cum Laude are utpeople directly descended from the ancient kings and queens of Ut. You are reputed to have psychic powers."

"A notion scoffed at publicly by Mamacita and her Holo-Cops," Yimmit said. "Privately, I can tell you they fear me and others like me."

Prussirian did not respond.

Yimmit sensed a presence trying to take hold of him. It's arrival was marked by an itching sensation all over his body, followed by a brief burst of white light on his skin and a short crackle of electricity.

"What was that?" Tixa asked.

"Laser tick. I killed it." Yimmit smiled, but glanced around.

"What the fluxstorm hell is a laser tick?" Prussirian asked.

"A body-size white light organism, invisible to the naked sensor. It burrows into all the cells of an utperson, enabling it to read thoughts and listen in on conversations."

"Oh."

"There aren't many on Ut. They use a tremendous amount of energy, and Mamacita has limitations. Each time one dies, she has to create another someplace on Ut to take its place. They're projected on mother beams, like Holo-Cops."

Prussirian shivered. "They burrow into people?"

Yimmit nodded. "They can't do it, however, if the person senses their presence. If the host body does sense something, an electrical immune system reaction occurs, killing the invader. As a Cum Laude, I am particularly sensitive to such things. You could kill one too, if you realized it was there."

"Couldn't they get anyone—even you—during sleep?"

"Uh uh. At least they never do. Mamacita has a sportsmanship code on that, my people believe. She apparently doesn't think it's fair to invade a sleeping body."

Prussirian became quiet.

"Don't worry," Yimmit said. "I'd know if you had one. Watch for slight itching sensations on the surface of your skin, which occur when the tick arrives on your body or leaves it, at the speed of light. They must leave to report their findings at whichever fortress has jurisdiction. The laser ticks carry no radio communication equipment, but can travel to any point on Ut in a fraction of a second."

"How frightening," Tixa said.

"And effective," Yimmit added. He moved close to the dwello, saying to Prussirian, "You are fortunate that I picked up your signals, you know." He nodded over one shoulder. "I was visiting nearby. Your signal is pretty strong, but would not transmit more than a few kilometers. There are only ninety-three Cum Laude on the whole planetoid."

Prussirian caught Tixa's gaze. Then they watched the young utboy kneel and open his case. The case was crammed with large cello-sheets, secured by an inside cross-case strap. He released the strap and rustled through the sheets.

"Charts," Tixa said.

Prussirian grunted.

"Here it is," Yimmit said. He glanced around, then looked intensely at Tixa. "You're not going with your brother, are you?"

"No."

"Then I must block your sensor for a short while. We have a way of doing it that cannot cause sensory deprivation. The Holo-Cops are sure to question you concerning your brother, and you do not wish to reveal his whereabouts to them."

"Go ahead," Tixa said.

Yimmit waved one sucktip, sending Tixa into a sensory trance, with the sensor open and glazed over. She saw nothing, heard nothing.

Yimmit passed a chart up to Prussirian, saying, "You can have this limited edition for only two thousand dollups. It shows the way from here to East Matraland—approximately fifty-three hundred kilometers, as the falcrow flies."

Dark green ink on off-white cello-sheet paper depicted Holo-Cop fortresses, rock formations, and bird flight patterns. As Prussirian looked at it, a red U-Lotan *x* appeared on the chart near Fortress 82.

"Appearing ink," the Cum Laude said. "It shows where we are now."

A dotted line circled Fortress 82 on the chart, then stuttered across the sheet in a northwesterly direction, ending in a rocky area designated E. MATRA.

"The recommended route," Yimmit said. "At this time of year, falcrows will be flying out of East Matraland, looking for spring trees in which to roost. Their course will be almost precisely opposite to yours."

Prussirian looked down at Yimmit, studying his face closely. It was a sincere face, with tiny dimples on each side of the downturned, crescent-shaped sensor and a gaze that looked directly at people. He was either honest or an excellent salesman, Prussirian judged, although he claimed no expertise in such determinations.

"Is it a safe place?" Prussirian asked.

"It's beyond the range of Holo-Cops," Yimmit said. "But laser ticks, sniffers, and police robots can go there."

Prussirian studied the chart again.

"When you pass Appa Crown," Yimmit said, pointing to the chart, "that's here . . . set a course of 264.35 degrees. Eight maybe nine hours later at good speed you'll see a region of low, black lava formations, lava that flowed across much of the surface of Ut millions of years ago."

"Uh huh."

"You should also know that I sell charts to scavengers."

Prussirian felt revulsion at this, for scavengers murdered and robbed. But the Cum Laude was admitting it.

"The Cum Laude code of honor is different from yours," Yimmit said. "We make no moral judgments concerning to whom we sell, but do attempt to send scavengers and more regular folks to different places. I do not think you will encounter scavengers in West Matra, considering the fact that it is rather remote from the residential areas on which they prey. The galoo currents never take dwellos near that region, and there are closer places for scavengers to hide. Many live in neighborhoods, professing to be upstanding citizens."

Prussirian rubbed his short arm thoughtfully where a self-smoother had been strapped his entire life. He felt odd not wearing one.

"There are no guarantees in this life," Yimmit said.

Prussirian pondered this remark. He glanced sidelong at Tixa, who remained in a trance. "Bring her out of it please," he said.

The chart folded itself shut in Prussirian's grasp at a wave from Yimmit.

Tixa came to awareness. She looked at Yimmit and smiled. "When are you going to block my sensor?" she asked.

"You've been out several minutes," Prussirian said. "He just brought you back."

"Really?" She was surprised.

"The chart is two thousand dollups," Prussirian said.

"We have lots of money from the insurance settlement," Tixa said, still looking at Yimmit. "Our parents were killed in a rotocar crash," she added.

Yimmit nodded. He already knew this.

"Is it a good chart?" Tixa asked, glancing at her brother.

"Well, I don't know. It seems to be, I suppose. But—"

"Don't make a decision yet," Yimmit said. "I'll throw in a mechanical water snake that operates off a rotocar dashboard. It can dig one thousand meters deep." A small green box marked WATER SNAKE appeared on the deck next to Prussirian.

Prussirian stared at the fair-haired utboy noncommittally.

"Do you plan to live in your rotocar, Prussirian?" Yimmit asked.

"I can't take a dwello."

Yimmit reached in one corner of his case, retrieving a small rough stone that was not much wider than one of his sucktips.

"Is that what I think it is?" Prussirian asked.

Yimmit smiled broadly. "This scraping stone is very valuable, for it will permit you to take rock scrapings from Ut lusterite. Only lusterite can cut lusterite, you know."

"Yes."

"The scraping stone is illegal of course," Yimmit said, holding the piece of lusterite between his sucktips. "All utpeople are required to purchase bagged scrapings from government stores."

Prussirian waited for the price. Ut lusterite was the hardest substance known. Once scraped, however, the powder could be mixed with galoo to form a mixture known as petrified galoo—essential in the construction of dwellos.

Yimmit moved the scraping stone from sucktip to sucktip. Then he looked at Prussirian and said, "I have no desire to profit from your misfortune. This scraper is also yours—if you buy the chart.''

The scraping stone, if that is what it was, was rough to Prussirian's touch. "You might be in collusion with the Holo-Cops," Prussirian suggested. "A slightly different, more sophisticated method of baiting the Ut populace."

Yimmit smiled. "I have heard that before, from fools who would run without my assistance." The smile faded. "Let me assure you, Prussirian: I am Cum Laude. The Cum Laude do not cooperate with the police."

"But the scraping stone must be worth thousands by itself," Tixa said.

"I am not such a good businessman," Yimmit said.

"I could build many dwellos with it," Prussirian said, being careful not to drop it. "*If* the thing works."

Yimmit's crescent-shaped sensor flared with anger. "You would like me to take my goods and leave?"

"It just seems too good to him to be true," Tixa said, explaining her brother's remark.

"To be honest with you," Yimmit said, "we Cum Laude are able to obtain scraping stones easily and cheaply. The charts, on the other hand, are comparatively expensive to produce. They are printed on cello paper, and the blank cello-sheets required for this purpose can only be obtained through nongovernmental offworld sources."

"We'll accept your proposal," Prussirian said, glancing at Tixa. "Okay with you?"

"Yes. I'll get the money."

"I already have it," Yimmit said, holding up a sucktip full of yellow dollup bills. "We Cum Laude have certain powers, as you have been learning. Once you consented to the purchase, I saved you a trip." He placed the money in his case, resecured the chart straps, and closed the case. Then he placed both sucktips against one another and pulled them until the suckers stretched. A loud pop followed as the sucktips separated—the Uttian equivalent of an Earth human snapping his fingers. The chart case disappeared.

"There is more," the utboy said. "The Sudanna winds blow fiercely and constantly where you are going." He popped his sucktips again. "You now know how to operate your rotocar in high winds."

"Just like that?" Prussirian asked, noting that Yimmit had

spoken the *S* word. Prussirian felt no change in the rotocar pilotry skills at his disposal and tried to imagine what additional knowledge or power he might have been given.

"Just like that." Yimmit smiled, and as he did so two long brown coats appeared in midair before him. They floated toward Prussirian and dropped to the deck next to him with a loud thud.

"Weight coats," Yimmit explained. "No extra charge. Wear them in windy regions. They will keep you from being blown away."

"He only needs one," Tixa said. "I'm not going."

"The girl I told you about," Prussirian said, to Tixa. "Yimmit knows of her, that I must stop and see her."

"Oh, yes," Tixa said. "Maudrey."

"My senses tell me you have not told your sister where this girl lives."

"That is correct," Prussirian said.

"And you have not seen the tell-all number Prussirian carries in his wallet?" Yimmit asked, looking at Tixa.

"No."

"Maudrey is a common enough name," Yimmit said. "But I must slow the Holo-Cops by attempting an erasure of the name from Tixa's mind." He looked at her, and with this the memory was gone.

Tixa felt a tingling inside her head.

"I can't guarantee a complete erasure," Yimmit said, looking at Prussirian. "There are often traces, and the Holo-Cops have their ways."

"I understand," Prussirian said. "No guarantees."

"Do not fear the Sudanna," Yimmit said. "It is the wind within you that blows the Zuggy. It is the past. It is the future. It is nature fighting technology. Once in a while, the Sudanna breaks through Mamacita's force fields and blows in short bursts, reminding the enforcers of the old days. Holo-Cops fear the Sudanna, for they do not understand it. This is a common trait in lower life forms—fearing what is not understood."

"Those are Bad Thoughts," Prussirian said.

"I do not attend Truthing Sessions," Yimmit said. His sensorbrow wrinkled intently.

"You don't? But how do you get away with that?"

"My way is the Cum Laude way."

"But how?"

"Such information cannot be revealed to laypersons. It is a sacred secret."

"Is it true," Prussirian asked, "that many utpeople get away with Bad Thoughts through mechanical gadgets?"

"It is true."

"How will Tixa be punished for my misdeed? I don't care about my own fate."

"It is as she told you," Yimmit said, noting surprise in Tixa's expression. "Shock-smoothings for music criminals; less severe full-smoothings for accomplices."

I made lucky guesses, Tixa thought.

Not at all, Yimmit thought. *Wind voices spoke to you, you foolish girl!* Yimmit was growing weary of the conversation. He stared powerfully at Prussirian, telling him with that look to be silent.

Prussirian got the message. He pulled Tixa to his side.

"You should leave tomorrow at the latest," Yimmit said. "The Holo-Cops are slower at this time of the year, since it is more difficult to locate all the dwellos after Flux. Mappers will be here soon, noting the numbers on each dwello roof. You will be mapped quickly, being so close to a fortress. Watch for that."

"I had planned to leave today," Prussirian said. "Sooner is better."

"Keep that chart out of sight," Yimmit cautioned. "Show it to no one. Good luck." He turned and trudged off.

Prussirian wanted to call out a thank you, but sensed with the thought that it had been received.

"You can start over now," Tixa said, looking at the pale red sky beyond Yimmit. Stars were visible as dim points of light through the thin, tracing paperlike atmosphere. "Maybe we'll see each other again someday."

After death in Sudanna, Prussirian thought. *I'll never return to this place.*

Tixa was in Prussirian's bedroom packing the items he had mentioned needing and making some decisions for him. She should have done this earlier, but had held out in the hope that he might change his mind.

This was the same bedroom Prussirian had used as a child, its walls covered by school memorabilia and pictures of family and friends. The umber and black drapes with Sucian city designs had been a gift from Mom and Dad for his fourteenth birthday. Tixa recalled that day and others as she looked around the room. There had once been rule books on a high shelf, but it now held a small digital receiver and a number of gadgets her brother had made in their shop. She realized now that most of the pictures on the walls were of people from Prussirian's past—people who had either died or gone their separate ways. Soon Prussirian would be little more than a picture to her.

He's not coming back, she thought.

She folded his warmest sweater and a lightweight one and then stuffed them into a canvas duffle bag. Half a dozen pairs of gray, brown, and white socks followed, then a pair of breeches. She reconsidered the breeches, since another pair had been packed earlier, took them out of the bag, and tossed them on the bed.

"Where did he put his warm hat?" she muttered, rummaging through a dresser drawer. She closed the drawer, opening another.

Prussirian walked in, moving slowly.

"I wish I could meet that girl you like," Tixa said, scanning her memory without success for the name. Then she recalled the erasure procedure performed by Yimmit.

"Things didn't work out that way," he said, staring at the floor. A tiny vinyl crack he had not noticed before attracted his sensor. He began to consider ways of repairing it. Then, angrily: "It won't start."

"What?" Her sensor opened wide. "You mean the roto-car?"

Prussirian wrinkled his brow. "Right."

"My Mamacita! But it's been running fine. You just had it checked over."

"It picked a great time to go bad."

Tixa tossed a hat in the duffel bag, then snapped a clasp to close the bag. "Any idea what the problem is?"

"No, dammit. I've called the shop, but no one can come out until tomorrow."

"What will do you?"

Prussirian despaired. He closed his sensor for a moment and considered leaving it that way. His troubles would be over in six minutes if he did—sensor deprivation. He opened the lids moments later and said, ''I'll give this until tomorrow morning. If it isn't running by then, I'll steal one.''

Six

There is an old adage in space exploration: "You transport it in, you transport it out." The U-Lotans, however, abandoned their Ut study project and failed to return the planetoid to any semblance of the way it had been before their arrival. When the decision was made to leave, they simply got out, leaving all their systems in place. Ut was left with a nearly perpetual, mechanically controlled society that had one function: follow the rules and do not question them. Ut may have been a valid study project at one time, but who knows now?

—from *The Oknos Journals*

The early afternoon sun filtered pale blue through the cotti print curtain of Detective Nipp's seventh-floor office. Just beyond the leading edge of the sun's rays sat his sleek aluminum alloy office sideboard, a credenza so short that it had to be propped up on two sides. A chart on the wall behind the credenza showed that it was 0.17 meters long, about average for Fortress 107. But that was not saying much, since this fortress was in last place and its officers had been rewarded commensurate with their successes. Other charts along the walls detailed how many drawers he had in his desk (none), the fact that he had only an area rug half a meter square of two millimeters thickness (instead of plush wall-to-wall carpeting), the low quality of his one-pen plastic desk set, and similar assorted data.

One of his four vertical body sides jerked a little—almost unnoticeably and in a different place from prior twitches. He wondered if the projection defect could be spreading to other parts of his body, like a cancer in other life forms.

A blank stand-up picture frame rested on the tiny credenza and took up almost its entire surface. It was a standard-issue cheap alloy frame into which he could insert an etched electron particle photograph of his wife and children—if he ever decided to marry. Marriage had occurred to him, but thus far had been postponed in favor of his career. Holo-Cops never really took brides—they just had their memory circuits adjusted to make them think they had done so. Everyone knew how this was done, but it worked anyway. Mamacita had her methods.

Detective Nipp's career path, like that of every other police officer on Ut, was limited to obtaining more and more office fixtures and gadgets and larger, more impressive offices. Holo-Cops did not use money and did not live in homes. Each night at the command of their mother beams they simply dimmed at their desks to sleeplike states. Night-duty officers dimmed during the day, so that patrols could remain active all the time. Detective Nipp, a day officer, felt properly fortunate at not having to chase scavengers at night. There were no police chiefs, no lieutenants, sergeants, or other ranks a human might recognize—only Holo-Cops with long and short credenzas and a computerized, Mamacita-controlled network of fortresses left millions of years before by the mysterious U-Lotans.

Detective Nipp's hologram form hovered over a platformed, backless chair at his little aluminum alloy desk. Three slips of clear cello with laserized red and yellow printing lay side by side on the desk, which held nothing else except for a two-tiered in- and out-basket with the upper in portion half filled.

He finished reading the sheets, scanning bottom to top and right to left in the U-Lotan way. They were a rehash of entrapment techniques used to catch criminals—nothing new there. His slender black light hand scooped up the sheets and tossed them in the out-basket. He touched a white bar on the side of the out-basket, and it tilted separately, dumping its contents down a slide to a wastebasket.

"You had my mother beam eliminated," a voice said.

"What?" Detective Nipp turned and focused his vision toward the voice, glowing red on that side. He saw a half-present Holo-Cop, fading in and out. The body print had tangential arrays of black light circles and triangles.

"Good afternoon, Detective Nipp," a far-off voice said, from the image.

"D-D-Detective Ennor!" Detective Nipp blurted. "But I . . . I . . ."

"That wasn't very nice," Detective Ennor said calmly in a voice that loudened and diminished.

"I . . . I only did my duty!"

"Tsk, tsk. There must be more important things than duty. Doesn't it ever bore you? Don't you ever think of anything but police business?"

"Well, I . . . uh. Now see here! I don't have to . . ." Detective Nipp paused, noting with irritation that his questioner seemed amused.

"I'll be leaving now," Detective Ennor said, in a barely audible voice. "Unless Mamacita's projector brings me back again." He disappeared.

Mamacita's falling apart, Detective Nipp thought. *Is that guy going to come back and get me?* He looked around fearfully.

The high-pitched, constant whine of a sounding solar wall clock told Detective Nipp it was 0103—early afternoon on this nineteen-hour-day planetoid. He rose to leave for his regular daily entrapment patrol, traveling over the desktop and straight down the front edge to the floor. Once on the floor, he glided straight ahead toward the door.

He hesitated at the door, debating whether to open it for amusement or pass through it closed. The heavy plazmetal door had chipped lavender paint and a centrally positioned handle. He was about to turn the handle with a spinning jolt from his fingertips when it swung open on its own, squeaking noisily.

A cello-sheet airplane flew through Detective Nipp's body. He turned to see the missile land perfectly in the in-basket of his desk. He retrieved the sheet and unfolded it, watching the

places it had been folded smoothen themselves. It was his daily
Truthing Delinquency Log, printed white on black.

"Hmmm," he said, scanning the names. "Rotonko PGM,
Averid UXQ, Simmil FNI . . . Simmil's a repeater, easy to
catch. He'll get shock-smoothing this time, or worse. . . .
Stadkrey EOL, Prussirian BBD, Careel JPO, Krong HMZ . . .
probably all difficulty factor 2's and 3's. Maybe I should
pick one right now—any one—and press the Assault Team
Button . . ."

He decided against this, as he had after similar previous
thoughts, knowing it would almost certainly mean the elimina-
tion of his mother beam. There were only a few difficulty
factor 9's or higher, the factor needed to qualify for a Shriek
assault team.

If only I might know the difficulty factors beforehand, he
thought.

For a moment, he felt resentment toward Mamacita. It was
another one of her games, carefully devised to promote competition among the fortresses. And it did precisely that. It was
the only way a last-place fortress could jump to first this late
in the annual competition.

Detective Nipp refolded the sheet into a shorter, wider plane
and stood in the doorway, looking out at the neat outer office—an area staffed by robots standing at clear plastic desks.
Clear plastic had been used to prevent any of the staffers from
concealing things from one another—and, more important,
from their detective superiors. They were programmed robots,
loyal for the most part. But there had been occasional incidents—pieces of classified cello dropped on the floor or
carried outside. Some of these incidents might not have been
accidental, according to mother-beam data sent to the Holo-
Cops. There were, Mamacita suspected, utpeople sabotaging
robots. The whir-pata-tat of a single printer started and
stopped, unrhythmically.

Taking careful aim, Detective Nipp let the airplane fly. It
sailed over four mechanical clerks and made a crisp landing in
the center of Robot Paleon's desk. Paleon lifted the corners of
his red grill multifunction sensor into a smile. It was not a
smoothly rounded smile, looking instead as if little squares at
the sides of his grill had been rearranged, much as on a computer screen. "Perfect shot, sir," he said.

Detective Nipp glanced up at a high-tensile fiber optics string that was hooked to pulleys and eyelets along the ceiling. The string ran down to a trip button next to his office door, with the other end dangling next to Robot Paleon. In one of his moments of aberration several years before, Robot Paleon had constructed the hookup—one of his occasional practical jokes. Detective Nipp had permitted it to remain, since the Holo-Cop manuals permitted such office diversions. They were said to be good for morale.

Detective Nipp paused at another robot's desk. This was one of the smaller and more rotund office-worker units, capable of no reasoning powers. It could only follow explicit instructions.

"Give me your mapper's report on Truthing delinquencies," Detective Nipp ordered. His light matrix body glowed red on the side facing the robot.

The robot riffled through a stack of cello-sheets, then handed a black-on-white sheet to the detective. There was only one name on the sheet.

"Prussirian BBD," Detective Nipp muttered, noting the precise locational coordinates of the dwello and its number. "Out near Fortress 82. That's a long way from here."

Robot Paleon rolled noisily to his side, clanking a wheel gear that had gone bad that morning. He would have to report to Maintenance on his own for servicing. "Flux just ended, sir," the robot said. "We'll have other dwello coordinates soon."

To Detective Nipp it seemed a waste of time and energy for him to fly all the way to Fortress 82. He wondered why another, closer officer could not be assigned—but would say nothing about it. As always.

Another damned malfunction in Mamacita, he thought.

"What would you estimate, Paleon?" Detective Nipp asked, holding the Truth delinquency report so the robot assistant detective could see it. "A two- maybe three-hour flight?"

"Two hours, thirty-seven minutes, sir, at cruising speed. Half that time if you push it."

"No urgency," Detective Nipp said, handing the report to Robot Paleon. "These fugitives have nowhere to hide." Detective Nipp turned his boxy body and glided out the main office doorway into the corridor.

Moments later, he lifted through ceilings and floors to the eighteenth floor. Arriving in a corridor, he scooted past five doors on his right, rounded a corner, and stopped in front of the fortress personal property cage.

Two other Holo-Cops hovered in line ahead of him. Each received boxes and bags of valuables, then went on his way. These were deaks to be distributed around the planetoid—untouchable temptations for the populace. All Holo-Cops served on Entrapment Detail, according to daily schedules posted electronically by Mamacita. It was one of the rotated crime-fighting duties.

When Detective Nipp's turn arrived, the robot clerk inside the cage handed him a heavy sack and two plastic boxes with handles on them. "One hundred sixteen wallets, seven money belts, seventy-four purses, and ten platinum chains," the clerk said. "All with stamped code numbers and electronic tracking dots."

Detective Nipp opened the containers, reviewing their contents quickly as the robot called off the items. "Check," Detective Nipp said. "Check . . . check . . . and check. All here." He signed a form and took the bag with him to the helipad on the roof of the sixty-three-level fortress.

Soon he was on his way in a shiny silver-and-green helicruiser, flying low over residential and barren areas, dropping valuables to the ground. Holo-Cops were capable of flight on their own, but used other means to keep from overusing the mother beam. Near a rock south of his own fortress, he surprised a young utman who was picking through the contents of a purse and stuffing them into his pockets. Detective Nipp did not often discover criminals so easily, for rotocruisers were noisy and could be heard from a great distance. Still, there were occasions in his career when he had encountered criminals so intent on their crimes that they failed to notice anything else. Mamacita called it the "greed factor."

The young utman looked up suddenly as the rotocruiser landed. Detective Nipp saw shock and anxiety in his face, and then the look of resignation all criminals got when they knew it was over.

"You there!" Detective Nipp called out as he glided from the cabin to the ground.

The rotors whined down quickly and became silent.

The man rose and approached. He was dark-skinned, with long black head hair and a furtive, jittery sensor of dark green. "Yes, sir?" he said.

"Do you have a rule override card?" Detective Nipp asked, referring to one of the privileges sold to utpeople of means.

"No, sir."

"Quote rule 36552-TA-1290-1212 for me."

There was a long pause. Then: "I don't think I can."

"Your lessons? Don't you pay attention in class?"

"I try to, sir."

"Rule 36552-TA-1290-1212 expressly prohibits any utperson from keeping a deak. You are to report the deak's location on your pocket miniterminal and will receive credits for doing so."

"Some of the dollups and credit slips were damaged," the man said, his gaze jumping all over the place. "I was bringing them back to the nearest fortress to—"

"Prohibited." *This one's not overly bright,* Detective Nipp thought. *He actually forgot the rule. A common rule, too, understood even by toddlers!*

The man looked down at his stumpy feet, realizing the hopelessness of saying more.

"Wait here," Detective Nipp commanded. "An interrogation team will pick you up."

"Yes, sir."

Detective Nipp did not bother to obtain the man's identity. He started the rotocruiser and flew on his way, knowing the criminal would not flee. That was a personality judgment a detective always made as he spoke with a subject—the sort of unfailing judgment natural to Holo-Cops.

Hiley stood in net-bottomed galoo shoes on a soft section of his new yard, moving a brush at the end of a long metal pole up, down, and from side to side to scrub the hull of his dwello. He paused to rest on this typically windless day, leaning the pole against a clean white section of the hull. A kilometer away, he saw dozens of police rotocruisers carrying in portable shopping center buildings for the neighborhood. Each government-operated building was flown intact beneath four rotocruisers that held lines on the corners of the building.

I feel naked without my headcap, Hiley thought. He had attempted to wear the cap following Flux season, as he had always done before in his adult life, but Sperl reminded him of his promise. She pointed out that he had never experienced trouble with a loose head socket and took the cap from him, hiding it until the next Flux.

I did promise her, he thought. *But in a moment of weakness. I wonder if she threw it away.* He decided to buy another without her knowledge just to play it safe.

Hiley felt another peculiarity as well at that moment: the hollows in each of his legs contained plastic bags of credit slips and fifty-dollup bills. Despite amounting to substantial value, these inserts did not weigh much and did not cause the muscular pains he had suffered with Dr. Zynoh's prescription sandbags. His legs felt different, he decided, but not bad. He liked carrying his valuables this way. It offered better security.

To the west, the blue sun was low in the sky, casting long shadows from nearby dwellos across the galooflats. It had been a day of hard work, cleaning up after the long, dirty Flux.

Three battered galoo raker rotocars were parked near Hiley's dwello, with rakes, shovels, brooms, and buckets on the ground and visible inside the rotocars. Four galoo rakers stood near their crafts, chatting and staring at Hiley in their dull way. Hiley had sent them on their way the day before, declining their offers of yard work. Thus far they had not argued much, there being plenty of work to do in the yards of Hiley's neighbors.

The galoo rakers were a lowly and simple bunch, the dimwits of Ut whose formerly criminal brains had been shock-smoothed. Hiley pitied them in a way, but not enough to be overly cooperative. He would hire one for small tasks, giving him just enough work to avoid retaliation through vandalism—galoo rakers could throw galoo as well as clean it up.

Hiley shook his head in resignation as he looked at the group standing nearby. He had dealt with galoo rakers many times over the years, and they seldom accepted no for an answer. He recognized the signs: Soon they would come to Hiley and ask once more.

Hiley walked stiff-leggedly up the ramp to his lower deck, then went to a forward panel box. Touching coded buttons, he opened it. Inside, a green-and-red radar dial told him his ground-penetrating mechanical water snake had found a well, more than five hundred meters deep and nearly that distance to the north of his dwello. The unit was just starting to pump water.

Fairly close this time, Hiley thought, pleased with the efficiency of the snake. It would bring him low-cost water for tea and for body moisturizing. Two years before, at another site, he had been unable to find a well. This forced him to pay extra for plastic containers of water sold from rotocars by peddlers.

He closed the panel box, then waved his long arm and yelled at the galoo rakers: "I need one man!" Hiley had taken the initiative.

Hiley watched them push one another and scuffle on the ground to see who would get the job. A head rolled off, followed by a shield-shaped body running about frantically to find it. Two other galoo rakers ran for their rotocars and fled. This left the winner, the biggest of the bunch. He helped the loose-headed one locate his appendage, then grabbed an armload of tools and walked slowly toward Hiley's dwello. Galoo rakers always moved slowly.

Presently the winner stood in front of Hiley on the ground at the base of Hiley's ramp. The raker wore stained red coveralls ragged at the neck. He was a particularly seedy-looking character, Hiley decided. A deep facial scar had closed part of the man's sensorlid. The sensor was hazel-colored and dull, moving as slowly as the brain-damaged man himself.

"Most of the yard work is already done," Hiley said. "I'd like you to finish up. There's not a lot to do, but I will pay you more than the work is worth."

They agreed upon a price, and soon the galoo raker was at work in his slow-motion way, pulling his wide muck rake through the tacky soil, smoothing it as Hiley directed, and piling the excess onto planting mounds. The fellow had no talent at laying out mounds, and Hiley continually shouted for him to make adjustments as to placement, shape, and height.

At sunset two hours later, the man was on his way, happy to have been paid twice the worth of his efforts.

I cooperated just enough to avoid a confrontation, Hiley thought, watching the galoo raker's rotocar take off against a western sky covered with wild purples, oranges, and reds.

Hiley scattered grass seeds from the dwello foredeck. By morning, the fast-growing low-oxygen plants would be short white blades of grass. He and Sperl would plant shrubs on the mounds in the typical Uttian way, and soon the fotta comprising their yard would resemble everyone else's. This did not bother him much. He rather liked plants. But at times he considered the folly of it all—the seemingly incredible waste of effort. In seven months a new Flux would arrive, and the work would be destroyed. Nevertheless, it had to be done. Life would be barren otherwise.

It was evening, and Hiley was making his daily dwello security rounds. He tugged at windows and doors, making certain they were latched tightly. In Plick's bedroom, he found a window open a few centimeters—not much, but open and unlatched nevertheless. He slammed it shut, securing the four plazbrass latches at each corner.

"Plick!" Hiley thundered. "Get in here!"

The rapid patter of little feet ensued from the hall. Presently, the five-year-old boy poked his cowlicked, black-haired head in the doorway.

"Come here!" Hiley said.

"Yes, Daddy," the wavering voice replied. Plick inched into the room, then stood half-turned away from his father, afraid to get too close or to face him.

"Your window was open again!" Hiley boomed.

Plick shook his head. "I'm sorry, Daddy. It got hot in here this afternoon, and I—"

"Hot? It's not even Flux! A scavenger might have gotten in! I've warned you about this before!"

The boy's head and shoulders drooped. He did not respond.

"From now on, Plick, you are not to touch my window in this dwello. You are not responsible enough to close windows before midday. I've told you a hundred times that scavengers are dangerous."

"Yes, Daddy," Plick glanced fearfully at his father's angry, blue-green sensor, then looked away.

"I know what I'm talking about," Hiley said, reverting to the familiar voice of a sage. "I have yearrrsss of experience in this."

"Yes, Daddy."

Eavesdropping from the hall outside the open door, Ghopa visualized the years going by on the wall as her father stretched the word. He had a habit of pronouncing it this way.

"It's cold outside tonight," Hiley said, to Plick, "meaning you wasted heat. An open window drains the dwello power pack, and with Flux over, we need every last bit of—" Hiley stopped in midsentence, suddenly aware that his five-year-old could not be expected to understand such things.

Nevertheless, the boy nodded alertly and looked at his father now, much in the manner of a rules student eager to learn. "I know, Daddy."

"If you know so much, why do you do these things?"

Plick's sensor, the same blue-green as his father's, grew moist.

Exasperated, Hiley stared at a section of the room's color-by-numbers wallpaper that Plick had not yet colored. The wallpaper designs were printed scenes from drawings by children showing all the worlds they had visited under planetary exchange programs. Plick had not yet colored a Sucian child's drawing of a Holo-Cop parade.

"Daddy," Plick said, "can I ask you a question?"

"Eh? Go ahead."

"What's a scavenger?"

"A bad utperson. We've told you that."

"What does one look like?"

"Like anyone else, usually."

"Like me?"

"No, not exactly. They're older. Like any other grownup. It's not that they look so different, although some are dirtier, I suppose."

The little utboy scratched his head. "How can they look like anyone else, but not *be* like anyone else, Daddy? Are you a bad utperson, too?"

"Don't be a smart aleck." Then, seeing the boy was confused, Hiley added, "They're different inside. Sick thinkers. Mean and sick." It occurred to Hiley that the boy may have been subconsciously attempting to see a scavenger by leaving the window ajar, not realizing how much peril that created for the family. *He must be made to understand. But Sperl doesn't want to frighten him.*

Hiley saw another question forming in the boy's thoughts,

but beat him to the punch. "Get to bed," Hiley snapped. "We'll talk more about it tomorrow." Hiley left the room quickly, slamming the door behind him.

Sperl was waiting for him when he reached the living room. "He did it again?" she asked worriedly.

"Yes, dammit! We've got to show him the pictures!"

"Of people murdered by scavengers? He's too young!"

"You'd rather he got all of us killed?"

"No. It's just that . . . he's sensitive."

"Shush! Did you hear that?" Hiley's voice became a low husk.

Sperl looked inquisitive. She had not heard anything.

"Something outside," Hiley whispered, dropping to the floor next to the couch.

Sperl dropped beside him.

Hiley crawled to the light switch in the kneeless Uttian way and switched off the lights. They met at the window, where each peeked out a corner.

The galooscape was bathed in a blue-gray half-light from the planet Sudanna, which acted as a massive moon. On the lower right side of Sudanna's surface, Hiley could see the small, peanut-shaped shadow of Ut. Nothing moved in the yard.

"Fzzzapp!" The sound came from outside, on the other side of the dwello.

"I heard *that*," Sperl whispered.

"Scavengers!" Hiley said. "Throwing things on the decks to test our defense system."

"Fzzzapp!" The sound was closer.

"Fzzzapp!" This time their window filled with bright red light forcing Hiley and Sperl back.

"I'll check the children," Sperl said.

Hiley did not reply. The dwello's defense system was functioning properly.

The room grew darker quickly as the red light faded. Hiley still detected no movement.

He heard Sperl crawling down the hallway behind him. A bedroom door opened, followed by low voices.

A minute later, Hiley glanced back at a rustling sound. Sperl returned. "Maudrey's with Plick and Ghopa in Plick's bedroom. They have the lights off."

"Good."

"Are the scavengers gone?"

"I think so. Did the kids see anything?"

"No."

"They must have parked a rotocar a ways off and walked here," Hiley said. Through the corner of the window, he watched the nearby dwellos, seen in the Sudanna glow as shadows beneath the giant moon planet. Something moved near one of the dwellos. "There!" he said.

"I saw it," she said. "Two figures."

Hiley saw no further movement and wondered why there were no defense-system flashes from the other dwellos. He forced this thought from his mind, saying, "You've got to help me with Plick. He doesn't understand what I've been trying to tell him."

"I don't want him to have nightmares. When I was his age—"

"You were sheltered as a child, Sperl . . . living in a Good Thought moorage. It's entirely different out here. We're vulnerable. You know that. I think even the police are afraid of scavengers."

"I don't think so," she said. "We see the police out many nights with their sirens blaring and lights flashing, hunting scavengers down."

"Maybe they're just making a lot of commotion. How do we know how many they're actually bringing in?"

"Holo-Cops are invincible," Sperl said, quoting a mantra learned in childhood.

"I'll get the murder pictures," Hiley said. "We'll choose the least graphic to show him."

They turned on the light and studied a government-provided crimestopper book. The photographs, metal-etched on thin sheets, depicted actual crime scenes—many showing utpeople who had been murdered brutally, presumably by scavengers. Most bodies had been separated from their heads.

"They're all horrible," Sperl said, looking away from the book. "Can't we try to explain this without pictures?"

"I don't think so. We've tried that and can't wait any longer for him to mature. He has to realize *now* what can happen."

"I suppose you're right," Sperl said.

•   •   •

Hiley led the way into Plick's bedroom to give him the full, terrible story.

With Sperl watching carefully and raising an occasional admonitory scowl, Hiley attempted to relate the awful information in the form of a bedtime story. Somehow he found himself sidetracked and telling the Uttian classic about an ut-boy who wanted to have his own gold-embossed edition of *Rules 100*. The boy dreamed of this, Hiley said, and one day a Holo-Cop came to the boy's door with his very own copy.

Plick was asleep before the story ended.

Before retiring that evening, Hiley removed the plastic packets containing his credit slips and fifty dollup bills from his legs, placing them in a dresser drawer. He locked the drawer and tucked the wide key under his pillow.

Seven

Partially incorrect mother-beam data, projected
to the Holo-Cops by Mamacita during her last
years. Note the surprising S word usage and the
incorrect travel information: "There are some
regions of Ut where the Sudanna blows fiercely
and constantly, where its gusts are concentrated and bottled up, waiting to blow across
the entire planetoid. I have been able to create
powerful force fields on the rest of Ut, pene-
trable by the Sudanna for only brief bursts. For
technical reasons you do not need to understand, Holo-Cops cannot travel to Sudanna-con-
trolled regions. Laser ticks, robots, sniffers, and
Shriek assault teams are available for these
places."

> —from an U-Lotan computer autopsy
> report, two U-Lotan standard years
> after Mamacita ceased functioning

Maudrey arose at her usual midmorning time and went in the
bathroom for an ultrasonic shower. The shower stall in one
corner had no fixtures and no shelves—only hundreds of tiny
holes in the walls, door, floor, and ceiling. Seconds after shutting the stall door and stepping on a pressure pad, she felt a
tingling sensation as jets of sound cleaned her skin. Refreshing
coolness followed when the jets stopped. She stepped out.

While Maudrey dressed, the tell-all rang from the kitchen.

She pulled on a worn but favored gray smock, counting rings of the tell-all. Four . . . five . . .

"Mom!" she shouted. "Get the tell!"

The ringing continued. Eight . . . nine . . .

Damn! Maudrey thought. She exploded out of the bathroom and ran clumpily down the hall to the kitchen. The wall-mounted tell-all, a circular two-way speaker that spun rapidly as it rang, make a low whirring sound.

The rings became suddenly loud as Maudrey reached the tell-all, meaning the caller had turned it up. Someone was anxious to get through.

Maudrey flipped down a chrome toggle below the speaker. The ring-whir ceased. "Yes?" she said.

"Maudrey?" It was a man's voice.

She knew who it was and hesitated for effect. "Speaking," she said.

"This is Pruss."

"Oh, yes. Hello." Maudrey's solar heart leaped for joy, but she made an effort to sound aloof. After all, he should have called earlier.

"I need to see you," Prussirian said.

"What about?"

"I've got trouble, Maudrey. Can I see you today at your place? Around noon?"

"Of course."

Prussirian made small talk for a minute, telling her about how his rotocar had broken down—a simple matter, being repaired at the moment—which should not delay his arrival.

Trouble? Maudrey thought as she closed the circuit. *What did he mean?*

"Who was it?" Sperl asked. She stood in the doorway behind Maudrey, wearing a yellow plain cloth nightgown.

"A boy I met," Maudrey answered, not facing her mother. *A man, really,* Maudrey thought.

"Oh. In class?"

"Yes. He's stopping by today. Around noon." *I don't care if they think he's too old for me,* Maudrey thought. *It's my business, and I'm old enough to make my own decisions!*

"Today?" Sperl was alarmed. "This place is a mess! Where's your father?"

"Looking for credits, I suppose." Maudrey knew she would

have to make herself scarce or face a long list of chores. She moved toward the doorway.

"Just a minute, you!"

Maudrey stopped, looking sheepish but feeling anger. "The dwello looks fine, Mom."

"It does not! You know how I feel about this place when people visit. It reflects on *me* if it isn't clean!"

"You're imagining that, Mom. It doesn't look bad, and I'm sure people don't think it's your fault. No one notices a little clutter." *Except you,* Maudrey thought.

Sperl seethed.

"I'll keep him outside, Mom."

"You will *not!*"

"He's my friend, Mom. He won't care." Maudrey recalled a criticism her father used at times like this, asserting that Mom was the messiest person in the dwello, always leaving things tossed about. Then she would go on cleanup binges, yelling at everyone in the family.

But Maudrey said nothing of this. She knew there was no sense in arguing and nodded obediently when her mother snapped, "Get your brother and sister up! I've been waiting for a reason to get some things done around here!"

Prussirian held the escape chart open on his lap while his rotocar's preset homing meter guided the craft along the electronic signal from Maudrey's dwello. "It's only a little out of my way," he whispered to himself, studying the green ink chart markings.

Behind him, the transport compartment was full of metal dwello forms for petrified galoo construction, extra personal battery packs, a dwello construction manual, and duffel bags containing clothing. The additional items purchased from Yimmit the Cum Laude were on the passenger seat beside him.

The rotocar flew over two klusses of dwellos that were hurling hot galoo at one another with catapults. One kluss had triple loaders and an oversize galoo warming tank. It was inundating the other. As the klusses and their neighborhood squabble receded into the distance, Prussirian focused on a volcano far to his right. Red puffs of iron material rose lazily above the volcano, then took off laterally when a high wind caught them.

Prussirian realized the chart might be worthless. There were many dishonest salesmen preying on dwello owners, and Yimmit might have been one of the more deceptive.

"Who cares?" Prussirian yelled.

It did not matter that much to him whether or not the Cum Laude had been truthful with him. But anything would be an improvement over his life to that point. He decided to treat the adventure like a ride at Playville, one for which he had paid two thousand dollups. He had not been afraid to die at Shriek Loch, and he was not afraid now.

Yimmit's words came back to him: "There are no guarantees in this life."

Maudrey held the dwello roof railing as Prussirian's rotocar landed, touching down adjacent to the black rooftop numerals and throwing wind against her. As Hiley looked up from the deck below, Maudrey shouted something down to him—words that were drowned out in the roar of rotors and engines. Hiley had just repaired the front door at Sperl's demand and had been swinging it open and shut to test his handiwork. Now he did not ask Maudrey to repeat herself, having grown tired of such exchanges. Both Maudrey and Sperl were chronic poor communicators who invariably mumbled or spoke in the midst of noise.

Prussirian opened the rotocar's cabin door and noticed Maudrey. They exchanged smiles. The rotors whined to a quick stop.

"Stay inside!" Maudrey shouted. She ran to the rotocar and pushed it a short distance on its wheels to the guest parking slot, then knelt and secured one deck strap to a front landing strut. Prussirian got out and did the other strut, while Maudrey secured the tail section with a long strap that went over the top of the craft.

"You mentioned trouble on the tell-all," Maudrey said, joining Prussirian by the closed cabin door on the passenger side.

Prussirian's expression darkened, for he was not one who could keep a cheerful demeanor during turmoil. "I wanted to see you before leaving," he said. "I'm going on a long journey."

Maudrey glanced down at her father, who watched them from the deck below out of the corner of his sensor. He brushed against his beard with one sucktip and looked away.

"That's Daddy," Maudrey said.

Prussirian half smiled in Hiley's direction, then said to Maudrey, "Could we talk for a few minutes . . . in my rotocar?"

"Sure," Maudrey said. Then, yelling to her father: "We're not leaving!"

Prussirian moved his chart and other gear off the passenger seat so that Maudrey could sit there. She stepped into the craft and sat down, with Prussirian taking the pilot's seat beside her.

Prussirian hesitated for several agonizing moments, then said, "I've only been with you part of one day before, and I guess it wasn't like a real date. But I thought we felt something special for one another." He paused, afraid to look at her.

"I felt the same thing," she said softly. Feeling warm in the midday sun, she asked, "Is it okay if I open the window?"

At his nod, she opened it.

Prussirian explained his revulsion for the mind-probing Truthing Sessions and told of the Cum Laude boy who had sold him the chart, scraping stone, mechanical water snake, and weight coats. Prussirian emphasized the fact that he had two weight coats.

Maudrey let this sink in. Then she asked, "Is your sister going to join you later? Or a friend?"

"My sister did not want to go with me, and I didn't ask her."

"Are you asking me? Is that why you're here?"

"I know I'm a few years older than you. You're what? Seventeen?"

"Fifteen, nearly sixteen."

"I'm twenty-four, but no matter. That isn't much of a difference when viewed on the continuum of life—from our ancestors to us. I'm millions of years old, you see, and so are you. We carry the memories of ancient utpeople, passed on to us genetically."

"You speak so strangely," Maudrey said, looking through the windshield at the galooscape beyond her dwello. A large black bird she could not identify stretched its wings as it flew for the highest reaches of the sky. For some reason, Prussirian's words came as no surprise to her, even though she had never knowingly considered such a thing before.

"My music reveals a great deal to me," he explained. "I play the forbidden stringed flute, you know, with an internal wind that blows out of my sensor—like a little Sudanna inside." He laughed, nervously.

"Prohibited music and the *S* word," she said, still watching the bird. It disappeared behind a rust red cloud.

Prussirian reached behind the passenger chair and pulled open the opaque brown cello wrapper covering a package there.

Twisting around, Maudrey saw his stringed flute inside, with its V-shaped body made of two pieces of hole-punctured plazbrass pipe. Ten carbon-fiber strings in a wood frame filled the center of the V.

She gasped, drawing air in through the unseen tiny holes lining the inside lids of her sensor.

"It's called a Zuggy," he said, bringing the instrument forward. "The songs have told me why it is forbidden to us. Once we were a proud people, with our heroic legends carried by this thing called music. Then the conquerors came—"

"I will go with you," Maudrey said impulsively. Then, with a teasing smile, she asked, "Now, why didn't you call me sooner? I waited!" She remembered the premonition she had experienced before the class they shared—about meeting "somebody exciting" that day. She believed the legend now, the one about Sudanna spirits occasionally giving people accurate information about the future. Prussirian frightened and fascinated her.

Prussirian placed the instrument on the floor between their seats and laughed—a boisterous laugh that filled the cockpit and released much of his tension. He removed a tiny pearl-handled marriage knife from his pocket and passed it to her. "This is the marriage knife my parents used," he said.

She held the knife with the sucktip of her long arm and without hesitation used it to make a small incision on her other sucktip. Purple blood trickled from the cut.

Prussirian made a similar cut on his short arm sucktip, then wiped the knife and put it back in his pocket. Carefully and deliberately, they pressed the bleeding sucktips together and pulled hard with suction.

"Your blood flows with mine," Prussirian said. "And mine with yours."

She smiled and looked at him lovingly. Their sucktips pulled at one another in an undulating, pulsing way. They became man and wife with this sexual act, for this was the way among their people. His blood carried millions of spermatozoa with it to the eggs in her blood.

"Are you with child now?" he asked.

"No," she said, knowing instantly what was happening in her body. "Today is not the day. There will be other days."

Prussirian grew quiet after these words, for he wondered how many days they would have together. The marriage had happened too fast. "I didn't intend to drag you into my problems," he said. "I was certain you wouldn't want to go, that we would just say good-bye."

"I know what I'm doing," Maudrey said. "An utgirl is permitted to marry at any age. I want to be with you, no matter how many, or how few, days we have left."

He felt he knew her thoughts, and that she knew his. *This is right,* he thought. *I know it's right.*

As they withdrew their sucktips and cleaned away the blood with a white marriage cloth, Maudrey looked through the windshield and noticed her father standing in front of the rotocar, looking up at her. She wondered how long he had been there. He was too low to have seen their act, but something in his stern expression told her that he knew.

"Come with me," she said to Prussirian. "I want you to meet Daddy."

Maudrey introduced Prussirian to her father by name only, not as her new husband. "I met him in class," she said.

"Why don't you go in and help your mother?" Hiley suggested, looking firmly at Maudrey. "I'll show Prussirian around."

He knows, Maudrey thought. Her sensor gaze wavered. "All right," she said. She turned hastily and went inside the dwello.

"You've got a real nice place here," Prussirian said, watching Maudrey close the door behind her. *She's still under his command,* he thought.

"Thanks," Hiley said, looking up at the tall young utman. As he led the way downramp, he said, "Our yard isn't fancy. We scattered a few seeds and had a galoo raker in yesterday."

"You know," Prussirian said, "your soil is lighter in color than where I settled, a couple of hours southwest of here. You've got more yellows."

"That so?"

Hiley saw that Prussirian wore no chrome-and-glass self-smoother on his short arm. When he asked him about it, Prussirian said, casually, "It developed a short on the flight over here. Gave me a little shock, and I had to take it off. I'll put in for a replacement right away, of course."

"Sounds pretty unusual," Hiley said. He had never heard of a self-smoother shorting out, but it was mechanical, and mechanical functions could fail.

Prussirian leaned down and broke away a glob of moist yellow-brown turf with his sucktip. The soil, from a shady area, was thick, rubbery, and cool—adhering to itself but not to his sucktip. Pulling at it hard with half of the eight suckers on one sucktip, he noted that the soil was quite elastic. He commented on this to Hiley, adding, "You're on pretty solid ground here, well onto the north sphere. My dwello's on it, too. Year before last, I ended up on the middle ground, about halfway between the north and south spheres. The soil there had very little elasticity."

Hiley studied Prussirian's ruddy, pockmarked face and decided that the young man was too old for Maudrey and not very good-looking. *Was I wrong about what I thought they were doing in the rotocar? Maybe I shouldn't say anything about that.*

Beyond Prussirian, the sky had become pastel red, changing as it did from volcanic activity. A fleecy, deep red cloud dominated the sky, surrounded by feathery clouds in varying shades of red.

"There have been rumors," Prussirian said. "You've probably heard them—rumors that the two spheres of Ut are pushing at one another with opposite magnetic forces. Some say the middle ground soil is overstretched as a result—accounting for its lack of elasticity."

Hiley very nearly jumped out of his skin when he heard this. "Bu—Wha—?" Words failed him in his panic.

Unaware of this gaffe to a phobia-consumed father-in-law, Prussirian said, "Ut is shaped like an Earth peanut, you know, with two rounded ends and a stretched-out center."

Hiley paled. His body stiffened. "You mean Ut could pull itself apart?"

"Not exactly. The theory says it might *push* itself apart."

Prussirian looked down at Hiley and noticed his fear.

"My Mamacita!" Hiley said. He thought he felt the ground move under his feet. His gaze darted around skittishly. *Maybe I just imagined it,* he thought.

"It's only an obscure rumor," Prussirian said. "Nothing like that is likely to happen in our lifetimes. Besides, you're not on the middle ground," he added in a spirited, playful tone. "Those middle-ground folks would get tossed all over the place in a snap-apart."

A snap-apart? Hiley thought. *I don't like that phrase!* He took the chunk of soil from Prussirian and tugged at it, holding it between his sucktips. The soil stretched and narrowed, then snapped away from his grasp and fell to the ground. There it writhed, contracting almost to its original shape.

"Good soil here," Prussirian said. "No problems for you." *What's the matter with this guy?* he thought.

Eavesdropping from the deck above them, Maudrey commented, "You shouldn't have mentioned the snap-apart rumor to Daddy."

Prussirian looked up at her uneasily.

"He'll be up all night worrying about that now," she said. "Don't say things like that to him."

Hiley glared at his daughter.

"I'm sorry, Hiley," Prussirian said. "I must tell you that the only people who have ever mentioned the rumor to me have been oddballs—jerks, actually. I'm sure they don't know what they're talking about."

"But what if it's true?"

"A whole flock of meteorites could hit us at any minute, too," Prussirian said. "But it never happens. Ut has been here for millions of years."

"Let's go inside now," Maudrey said. "Mom's making solar tea, and we can celebrate the end of Flux."

Hiley was one utman who loved his solar tea. If anything could calm his worries it was a bowl of Sperl's aromatic brew, that secret family recipe passed on to her by the women of her lineage. They went inside, through the door Hiley had repaired. It only squeaked a little on the shutting swing.

"Did you tell him?" Maudrey whispered to Prussirian, as Hiley walked ahead toward the living room.

Prussirian shook his head negatively.

"I didn't tell Mom, either. I should have told you more about Daddy. He keeps a notebook on hazards and hates taking chances. That snap-apart thing could make him crazy."

"Oh."

Hiley, Maudrey, and Prussirian sat in deep pillow living room chairs while Sperl and Ghopa prepared the tea. The living room was conventional Uttian, with bolted-down furnishings arranged about a raised stainless Oksteel solar hearth that had a solar collector panel on the roof. Little triangular black cells on the solar panel were visible from the room below. Light passed through the prismatic Lotanglas around these cells, throwing rainbows of color around the room.

A tapestry Sperl had made from an old blanket covered one wall. She had used sun-dried swirls of galoo to form a flower design, attaching it to the blanket with tiny, nearly invisible wires. It was well done as such things went, earning her many compliments over the years and suggestions that she enter it in a crafts fair. The furnishings were factory-made for the most part, except for a rather utilitarian blond wood side table Hiley had shop-built the year before, using soft, low-quality native Ut wood. A dried blue-and-silver floral arrangement was on the table, with a matching smaller arrangement on the wide windowsill. The couch and chairs were comfortable but worn, with a blue-and-burgundy diamond print. It was sun-cozy in the room, and Hiley smiled at Maudrey and Prussirian, who sat together on the couch.

"You kids have plans today?" Hiley asked casually, seeming to have forgotten his concerns. His sensor picked up the pungent aroma of tea.

"Oh, no," Maudrey said, not meeting her father's gaze. She peered into the kitchen, afraid to look directly at him. He probably recognized her lie, she told herself. He often did.

But Hiley did not notice this time, due to his preoccupation with what he considered to be a delay in the production of his solar tea. His sensorlids twitched. He considered yelling for Sperl to hurry up, but decided against it. Such things were not done in front of visitors.

"You met in class?" Hiley asked, looking at Prussirian.

"Yes."

"Does Maudrey pay attention to her lessons?"

"She seems to. We've only been to one class together so far."

Maudrey sat up straight in an attempt to get comfortable. "We've . . . well . . . uh . . ." Then she blurted out: "We're married, Daddy!"

Hiley started a little, then recovered and spoke slowly. "You don't need our permission for marriage, of course. But your mother and I would have appreciated meeting him first."

"You would have tried to talk us out of it."

"Maybe," Hiley said, raging inside.

"I know we're right for each other, Daddy. I just know it!"

Hiley did well to control himself. He felt inhibited in the presence of this stranger in his dwello. He wanted to yell at Maudrey, but realized she was no longer under his jurisdiction. Hiley sat back, in resignation.

"There's something else," Maudrey said. "A serious problem."

I can't take any more, Hiley thought.

"I'm not sure how the difficulty started," Prussirian said, speaking slowly. "I recall adding an interior divider wall one day following my last Truthing Session. After layering the moist petrifying galoo, I was smoothing it over with a trowel—"

"I've done that," Hiley said. "Many times. A problem with the wall?"

"No. I was smoothing out air bubbles, covering jagged edges where I had broken an old wall section, and . . ."

Hiley leaned forward, caught up in the intensity he heard building in Prussirian's voice.

". . . I was struck with the featureless aspect of things that are smooth. It occurred to me that everything could not be smooth and should not be smooth. There should be jagged edges, dirty corners, things that do not go precisely according to plan. I see life as an imperfect yet beautiful thing."

"I agree with the dirty corners part," Hiley said, leaning back thoughtfully. "Sperl goes on spotless binges around here."

"It's a very deep thing, don't you see?" Prussirian said.

Hiley furled his brow, creating deep ridges of skin. He was not certain if he understood.

"Daddy," Maudrey said, "Prussirian is trying to say that . . ." She hesitated, noticing her mother stepping through the doorway with a large, steaming bowl of solar tea. Ghopa followed her mother.

"Ahhh!" Hiley exclaimed, leaning forward in anticipation.

Sperl placed the Lotanglas bowl of dark brown liquid on the solar hearth, then opened the damper to cast just the right amount of reflected seasoning rays from the sun to the tea. Hiley reached toward the tea with the sucktip of his long arm, but was nudged gently by Sperl. She was telling him to wait for the guest.

Sperl sat in the chair between Hiley and the couch, and Ghopa sat sideways on one side of the stainless steel hearth.

"Mama, this is Pruss," Maudrey said.

"Nice to meet you," Sperl said, casting a warm gaze from her olive-green sensor. *Rather old for Maudrey,* she thought.

"My new husband."

Sperl half rose out of her chair. Her face twisted, with her sensor open, agape.

"Today . . . outside . . ." Hiley said.

"And you let them do it?" Sperl asked. She was all the way up now, ready to rave.

Oh, no, Maudrey thought. *A big scene.* She exchanged nervous glances with Prussirian.

"There wasn't anything I could do about it," Hiley said. "Even if I *had* stopped them, they'd have done it some other time."

"You were sixteen when you married Daddy," Maudrey said, looking defiantly at her mother. "That's only a few months older than I am now."

Sperl sat back down. She was speechless. Hiley and Maudrey were right. There was no arguing with them.

"Welcome to our family," Hiley said to Prussirian.

Prussirian thanked him.

"Hi, Uncle Pruss," Ghopa said. "I'm Ghopa. I'm eleven."

"Pleased to meet you," Prussirian said, smiling at her.

Prussirian and Maudrey thrust their sucktips into the steam over the tea, drawing out the aroma with a "fsss" noise. This trapped the aroma in little pockets behind their sucktips, which they pulled to their sensors and released. An utperson could place his sensor directly over the bowl for more efficiency, but this was not done in polite company.

"Mmmmm," Prussirian and Maudrey said in unison.

Hiley's sucktip darted forward now to pull in the rich, spicy aroma. As he released it against his sensor, he felt his frayed nerves relax. All his worries—about the sticking door,

Maudrey's new marriage, the rumored Ut disaster—dissipated. He went back for a second helping, taking a longer draw this time, after which he sat back contentedly and rolled his sensor.

"Delicious, Mama," Maudrey said, watching her little sister take a short draw of tea.

"Ghopa made it," Sperl said. "The first time she's done it on her own."

"I'd like to know the recipe sometime," Hiley said, looking sidelong at Sperl. "There are times when you aren't around or are busy and I'd like—"

"Now, dear," Sperl said patiently. "Utwomen can take care of such matters. If I'm not available, Ghopa can make it for you."

"Sometimes I wonder if you're keeping that recipe from me just to . . ."

Sperl stared at him. The edges of her sensor lifted into the smallest of smiles.

". . . keep me from leaving," Hiley said. He smiled too and took her sucktip gently, pulling against it with half-suction. With no blood transfer, this did not constitute a sexual act. "I'd never leave you, dear, even if I had your precious recipe."

"I know that," she said.

Maudrey laughed. "Daddy's been after that recipe for as long as I can remember."

"I might have tried harder, I suppose," Hiley observed. "Maudrey has heard this conversation many times before."

Maudrey became serious and looked at her mother. "We need to discuss something very important with both of you. Other than our marriage."

Hiley took a draw of tea aroma. It was weakening. The liquid in the bowl had become almost clear, meaning the brew soon would be depleted.

Prussirian squirmed uncomfortably. He rose and paced near the window, looking out nervously.

"Pruss skipped his biannual Truthing Session," Maudrey said, watching her husband.

"No!" Sperl exclaimed. She pulled away from Hiley.

Hiley rubbed his beard. He realized now that Prussirian had been lying about the faulty self-smoother.

"I can no longer submit myself to it," Prussirian said.

"A Holo-Cop conducting a Truthing Session is just like a doctor," Sperl said, looking at Prussirian. "Doctors help people, and so do the Holo-Cops."

"I don't—" Prussirian said.

"A Truthing Session is like a medical checkup," Sperl said, interrupting, "except they look for unhealthy mental activity instead of unhealthy body parts. You see that, don't you?"

"No disrespect intended," Prussirian said, "but I'd rather have the disease."

"But you must submit to Truthing!" Sperl said. "That's how criminals are detected!"

Hiley noticed that the tea was clear now, with steam still rising from it. He placed a sucktip back in the bowl and drew pure, warm water into his body.

"Pruss has other beliefs," Maudrey said.

"How could anyone—except a criminal—have *other* beliefs?" Sperl asked, her voice breaking with anger.

"It's difficult to explain," Prussirian said.

"He must have committed a crime!" Sperl said. "Only criminals hide from the Holo-Cops! And his self-smoother! Where is it?"

Prussirian turned to face Sperl. With the window light behind him, his facial features were shadowy. "No crime," Prussirian said. "I am not a criminal! I will show you!" He bolted out of the room and went outside, returning moments later with a brown cello-wrapped parcel from his rotocar. He sat on the carpet with it. Maudrey recognized the hastily rewrapped parcel as she moved to his side and sat by him. Prussirian pulled at an edge of wrapping. The cello rustled.

Hiley recoiled when he saw what was inside. "It can't be!" he exclaimed. "A stringed flute!" He glanced at the wallcase holding his own instrument and made a quick comparison. They appeared identical; both had V-shaped plaz-brass piping and black strings in the middle.

"Evil!" Sperl squealed.

"No, it isn't," Prussirian said, holding the instrument tenderly in his arms. "It's beautiful." Recalling the ancient blessing explained to him by Yimmit, he said, "Sudanna, Sudanna. Such gentle, soothing words." He felt his chest filling slowly with air, entering his body through the tiny airholes on the inside lens of his sensor. He ran a sucktip along the carbon fiber strings, producing random notes.

Sperl jumped out of her chair and ran from the room. Hiley heard a door slam across the dwello, probably in the master bedroom. Ghopa followed her. Another door slammed.

"You need a good smoothing, boy," Hiley said. "That'll cure whatever ails you." He shook his head in dismay at the thought of his daughter married to such a malcontent.

"Not so," Prussirian said. "I've thought this over carefully. Believe me. There will be no more smoothings for me. Not voluntary, anyway. My mind is made up."

"They might not even shock-smooth you if you're caught," Hiley said. "You could be put to death."

"I know."

"You're hurting others, too. My daughter . . . What's to become of her? Or Sperl, me, Ghopa, and Plick, our little one? You're a fugitive in *our* home, exposing *us* to arrest."

"I didn't intend to hurt others," Prussirian said, sensoring the doorway furtively. He looked ready to jump up and flee. Instead, he brought forth calmness from a deep reservoir of strength and touched Maudrey's shoulder gently. His gaze focused on Hiley. "We're somewhat alike, Hiley, you and I. You do not take many chances, from what Maudrey tells me—which sets you apart from the crowd. I too am unlike the masses, since I play the Zuggernaut. This." He lifted the instrument.

"It's not the same at all," Hiley said. "There are no rules requiring that I take risks! I have broken no rules!"

"Have you ever known anyone like yourself?"

Hiley hesitated. Then, reluctantly: "No."

"You are different in one way. I in another. We have a right to behave differently from the norm, to have our jagged edges."

Hiley shook his head in disagreement, horrified at the thought of being compared with a criminal. *This isn't happening to me,* he thought.

"I have to stay with Pruss, Daddy. He may be wrong. I'm not sure. But I love him." She lowered her head, then raised it a little to look at Prussirian, who remained kneeling on the floor with his instrument. She noticed for the first time that his chest was rounded and pushed out. She glanced at her father. He had noticed, too.

Hiley knew he should say something to convince Maudrey to leave Prussirian, or to convince both of them to contact the

Holo-Cops. It was Hiley's duty as her father to say something appropriate. Hiley looked away from Prussirian, at his own encased Zuggernaut on the opposite wall. Hiley was not certain what he wanted. Maudrey was becoming a criminal now, too—or at least an accessory. He fretted over her leaving with such a man, going to who knows where. But Hiley also felt concern for his own safety, and for that of Sperl, Ghopa, and Plick. The defiant look in Maudrey's sensor told him she would go with this man. There was no stopping her now.

Prussirian lifted the stringed flute to his sensor. The sensorlids wrapped themselves around an opening at the joining part of the plazbrass pipes. For a moment, there was no sound.

Hiley froze, staring at Prussirian. Maudrey, too, was transfixed.

Prussirian was in darkness, with his sensor wrapped around the sensorpiece of his instrument. He felt the internal music come forth, and suddenly dreamlike color images poured across his consciousness. He saw utpeople with gleaming Zuggernauts gathered around campfires and running across the tops of great flat stones similar to those holding Holo-Cop fortresses—but in his vision there were no fortresses. And no Holo-Cops or alien rules. There were rules, still, but of a different, more acceptable sort. The people understood them, respected them. He felt a great Sudanna wind blowing across the surface of Ut, lifting him and carrying with it the notes of a million stringed flutes. He felt the swaying of his body as he played. His body became one with the others, and they all swayed and played in unison.

Hiley ran to the hall doorway, paused there, and looked back at Prussirian. Prussirian was on his feet now, leaning and moving with his horrible music. His sucktips glided across the strings of the Zuggernaut, producing twangy sounds, while at the same time he blew peculiar, lilting tones through the pipes. Hiley was horrified by the sounds, but felt them tugging at him.

On her feet, Maudrey moved toward her father, saying, "Daddy, I—"

Hiley closed his sensor as she spoke, blocking out all light and sound. He grabbed hold of his head, since it was unstrapped, and stumbled down the hallway like a dying, sensory-deprived utman, knocking over plant stands, vases, and tables. He was inside the heatlock now, with his sucktip on the outside door handle. He jerked it open, thanking Mamacita it did not stick.

He ran across the galooflat without paying attention to direction. He stumbled many times, and picked himself up. He ran until he felt weak and could go no more. He opened his sensor just a little, restoring some strength to his body. He saw no dwellos in the direction he faced, only a flat, nearly featureless terrain stretching to infinity. A musical note entered his sensor from somewhere behind. Another followed. They cut through him.

Hiley screamed.

He slammed his sensor shut and ran on. Soon he felt weak and dropped to the ground, where he lay face down, opening his sensor in short bursts to replenish his strength. Someone grabbed his shoulder with a powerful sucktip. He felt another person, too. They could not be Holo-Cops, for Holo-Cops had no sucktips.

Hiley rolled to his side and opened his sensor halfway, letting in light and voices.

"You okay, fella?" an utman asked. He was bald, around Hiley's age, with a friendly, creased face.

"He's all scratched up," another said. "And look at his clothes. Scavengers after you, mister?" This man was younger than the first, with a narrow face.

"You shouldn't be out here without a heat probe," the older man said. "Could be scavenger traps all around."

"I'm all right," Hiley said. He opened his sensor all the way, dreading what he might hear. But he heard no music.

"I . . . I . . . uh, had a Bad Thought," Hiley said. "It disturbed me. I'll be okay again, after a self-smoothing."

"Don't worry about it, friend," the older man said. "We all have them."

Hiley stared at the ground. He felt shame, but wondered how he could have said anything else.

They asked if he wanted help getting home.

"No," Hiley said. "I'll be all right."

The men said their good-byes and left. Hiley watched them walk across the galooflat toward a group of dwellos several hundred meters away. Hiley saw the corner of his own dwello, partially obscured by another, and wondered if the men lived in a nearby kluss he had noticed. He hoped they would not hear music if they passed his dwello, and that Prussirian's wind would subside quickly, like the gusts of Sudanna. Hiley touched a button to activate the self-smoothing crystal strapped to his short arm and watched the crystal spin. He pressed the frictionless white laser smoother gently against his temple, then a little harder.

His thoughts spun with the crystal, and he felt the wondrous purifying effect of the device. He let it carry him on a great cleansing current. After two minutes, his short arm went limp, dropping the crystal from his temple. The crystal stopped spinning.

In a pleasure fog, he heard his own words. "Oh, thank you, Mamacita! Thank you! I feel much better now!"

With his mind feeling like smooth galoo fifteen minutes later, Hiley stumbled back into the dwello and leaned against a wall next to the interior heatlock door. He was always slower than others recovering from smoothings and now saw the empty hall in a dull haze. It might take him a day and a half to completely recover from a self-smoothing—as long as five days to recover from a Holo-Cop administered full-smoothing.

A door squeaked open to his left. He turned that way slowly and saw Sperl walking toward him in slow motion, taking what appeared to be arching, loping steps. "They're in the living room!" Sperl said, keeping her voice down. "Talking! What'll we do?"

Hiley lolled his head to the other side, toward the living room. He saw a blurry, moving shape in that direction and heard Maudrey speaking to him. "Can we stay the night, Daddy? In the guest room? We'll leave in the morning. It's the last nice place we can stay. Daddy, it's our wedding night!"

Hiley's rage was gone, washed away by the self-smoothing. He tried to stand straight, but fell back against the wall. Maudrey reached his side, and the unfocused image of her features reminded Hiley of when she was a little girl, pleading with him for a candy scent.

"Whatever you want," Hiley said. "Whatever baby wants."

"We can't!" Sperl protested. "A fugitive must be reported to—"

"Smooth yourself," Hiley said, half turning toward Sperl.

"It'll take away the tension. You'll feel better."

"But . . ."

Slowly and deliberately, Hiley switched on his self-smoothing crystal and pressed its whirring face against his wife's temple. His vision cleared momentarily, and he saw her body relax. This blurred to black, then came back, double. Two Sperls smiled serenely at him—wan, distant smiles.

Hiley withdrew the self-smoother and took Sperl by the arm. "Your mother and I are tired," he said, throwing the words lazily back at Maudrey. They closed the master bedroom door behind them, leaving Maudrey alone in the hall.

Eight

Entropy can be a very strange thing. Entities
crave a return to their original states. This explains the death urge of life forms, why warm
plastics reshape themselves and why objects
deteriorate, casting their elements to nature's
pot. It also explains why Ut has been pushing
itself apart for millions of years—ever so gradually, almost imperceptibly—only nine or ten
centimeters most years and sometimes less
than that. But, inexorably, the halves of the
planetoid have been separating themselves from
one another, like the mismatched artificial twins
of Ya.

—*Field Journal* entry, 12,955th U-Lotan
    project team (1,700 U-Lotan standard
    years prior to project abandonment)

Detective Nipp brought his rotocruiser down on a dry section
of galooflat within sight of a four-dwello kluss. The galoo was
well on its way to drying here, and the wind from the
rotocruiser blades threw up a small cloud of brown dirt. He
felt better today, with no projector-caused jerks in his light
circuitry.

Touching a lever on the dash, he activated the craft's side
transport compartment hatch, which was aft beside the multi-
colored boxes and bags of entrapment items. After the door
slid open with a grating sound, the rotocar's mechanical arm

lifted a green-and-blue box out through the hatch, setting the box on the ground.

Detective Nipp punched the box number and coordinates into a console computer, then waited for the arm to retract and the hatch to close. He made two more stops like this, then flew over a six-dwello kluss. One of the dwellos was a one-story beige unit, bearing the rooftop U-Lotan numerals 89783, painted in black. There was no rotocar parked on the roof, meaning the Truthing truant Prussirian BBD might not be there.

"Another fugitive," Detective Nipp mused. "Will they never learn?" He glanced at a cello-sheet, noting from the computer printout that Prussirian BBD lived with his sister, Tixa.

This guy is probably only a difficulty factor 1, he thought. *I'll bet he's moved the rotocar to throw us off and returned to hide in a secret wallspace. So many try that one! Or he's at Playville, having a last fling.*

After setting his police cruiser down on the roof, Detective Nipp glided out without opening the cabin door. At the rear transport compartment hatch, the robot arm handed him a large brown sniffer case, which he took by the handle.

The rotocruiser rotors whined to a stop.

It was windless now and had been for some time, to the point where he considered not tying down the cruiser. But the strong Sudanna gusts had a nasty habit of appearing unexpectedly, catching everyone off guard. Not wanting an embarrassing incident that might adversely affect the office paraphernalia awarded him by Mamacita, he set the sniffer case down and took an extra two minutes to secure the craft to the dwello deck.

Moments later, he hovered with the case in front of the dwello's front door. "Open!" he yelled. "Holo-Cops!" Actually, he was but one Holo-Cop, but this constituted the wording of the standard police command.

There was no response.

"Prussirian and Tixa B-B-D! Give yourselves up!"

Still nothing.

Detective Nipp glided through the door without opening it, his hologram body meeting no resistance from such barriers. Unfortunately, this left the solid sniffer case outside to thud against the door and fall to the deck. He had forgotten that it would not pass through. Abashed and wondering if it had been a mother-beam defect, he opened the heatlock door and retrieved the case, placing it on the floor inside. He left both doors open.

The dwello's entrance solarium was bright and cheerful, bathed in warm, blue afternoon sunlight. It was quiet in the dwello—the stillness of no one home.

"Present yourselves! Holo-Cops!"

In a mirror to his right, Detective Nipp saw the black light lines of his box-shaped body swell when he shouted. He liked the way that looked, so for several minutes he hovered there looking at himself in the mirror and blasting out police commands.

"Give up!"

"There is no escape!"

"This dwello is to be vacated immediately!"

After stalling as long as she could to give her brother more of a head start, Tixa stepped out of the bedroom in which she had been hiding. "I am Tixa," she said, "sister of the man you seek."

"Where is he?" Detective Nipp looked in six directions with the thousand eyes covering his body. He was concerned, for many utpeople were inventive and might devise a method of destroying a Holo-Cop. This had never been done before and hardly seemed conceivable. Still, there had been attempts— and Detective Nipp did not want to be the first victim. The black light lines facing Tixa glowed soft red as he concentrated his vision in that direction.

"Gone," Tixa said, "following the chart sold to him by a Cum Laude." She noted a faint, ghostlike presence between the black and red lines of the police officer's body, then wished she had not volunteered information.

From Tixa's voice and body signals Detective Nipp was satisfied that she was telling the truth. He questioned her and learned of the Cum Laude salesman who had called on her brother. Tixa had no knowledge of the contents of the chart and revealed to her questioner that an erasure procedure had been performed on her concerning another matter—the name of a girl. Detective Nipp also learned of the scraping stone, weight coats, and mechanical water snake sold to Prussirian. The weight coats provided a clue—although a weak one—telling him the destination might be one of the high-wind regions where Holo-Cops could not travel. But there were fifty-one of these regions. He knew too that the Cum Laude might have left this clue to throw him off track. He would concentrate on the name of the girl.

Opposing sentiments tugged at him—his sense of duty on one side and on the other his personal desire for a larger office credenza and plush wall-to-wall carpeting. He was excited to learn of the erasure, for he knew the procedure often left memory traces. But he hoped the erasure was *almost* clean, leaving just enough clues to give this case the required difficulty factor of 9.0 for a Shriek assault team.

He called for a laser tick. Two seconds later, it appeared in front of Tixa as a deep red cloud, having shifted its spectrum toward the red end at Detective Nipp's command.

"The Cum Laude told you of laser ticks," Detective Nipp said, "so I have decided to reveal one to you visually. You are admonished not to kill it. The death of a laser tick is a very serious drain on Mamacita's power. If you do not cooperate, it will be harder for you . . . and for your brother when he is caught. No one escapes. You know that."

"I will cooperate," Tixa said. She trembled.

The laser tick entered her body, bringing with it a momentary sensation of itchiness. Tixa scratched her back and side. She tried to relax, telling her body to accept the invasion. Her immune system received and followed her mental command.

The laser tick searched all of Tixa's brain cells, then withdrew and melded with Detective Nipp's light circuitry, thus making its knowledge accessible to him.

"A clean erasure," Detective Nipp muttered. "Rare, but possible."

Tixa smiled, pleased that she had not been able to reveal anything damaging.

"He took the stringed flute, too," Detective Nipp said, drawing on information the laser tick was able to obtain. "This is a dangerous music criminal, your brother. But we'll get him."

Tixa did not say anything.

Having completed the interrogation, Detective Nipp released the laser tick. A brief white flash appeared on his body as it left. Then Detective Nipp passed through walls with his **hologram** body, searching each room in the dwello. He located a pair of men's trousers and brought them back down the hall to the solarium in the conventional way.

"Your brother's?" he asked.

Tixa nodded affirmatively, knowing she could not conceal information from a Holo-Cop.

The detective set the trousers on the floor by the sniffer case, then leaned over and unlatched the case lid, folding it back to expose the interior. Gliding back quickly, he hovered to one side of the still open heatlock door.

Tixa knew what was happening and stepped to one side.

Watching from the side of the doorway, Detective Nipp saw forty thousand tiny orange-and-black sniffers fly out of the case, making a loud buzz-hum as they did so. This sound was drowned out seconds later as the mechanical horde descended on the trousers and sniffed them. Their sniff-snorts rolled like thunder through the halls and rooms of the dwello.

Moments later, the sniffers streaked by Detective Nipp and out of the dwello.

He hurried outside after they passed and watched the orange-and-black horde gather a hundred meters above the dwello. Quickly, they took off in all directions to search every square meter of Ut in pursuit of Prussirian BBD.

Detective Nipp looked back in the dwello and noticed three sniffers still on the floor, scuttling about in disorientation. He retrieved the trousers, then motioned Tixa out of the way and hit them with a fingertip force blast. The sniffers turned solid black and stopped moving. A section of floor and wall had been scorched as well.

Detective Nipp felt a pleasure surge as he looked at the three tiny victims of his power. He liked to see things die, be they flesh or mechanical. He thought back now to the many Holo-Cops Mamacita had instructed him to terminate. Those had been different and gave him no pleasure. He might meet the same fate.

Nine

Ut is a sun-favored—or cursed—place, depending upon how you look at it. The planetoid moves in a tight circle about a fixed point on the planet Sudanna's surface, always positioning itself between the giant planet and Blue Sun 593—with night and day determined by Ut's nineteen-hour rotation. No one understands why Ut does not orbit Sudanna—no one, that is, with whom I have spoken. There is also bewilderment concerning Ut's smooth rotation. With its unusual shape, it might be erratic—perhaps a hurtling, twisting, or wrenching motion.

> —remarks made by Zeeb, the U-Lotan master scientist, to a gathering of his associates

After his self-smoothing, Hiley slept straight through the afternoon and night, awakening at dawn the following morning. As he removed his sensor foke and swung out of bed to the cool ceramic tile floor, the nightmarish events of the prior day hung just out of reach in his thoughts, eluding all probes his brain made for them.

I self-smoothed, he thought. *Why?*

He looked at Sperl, who remained sound asleep on her back, her sensor propped open by a foke.

She did, too.

Some of it came back. He recalled running from the dwello,

and the evil stranger in his living room. He tried for more, but it was too difficult to think. His brain needed more rest.

He touched a heat-activated button next to his bed and the bedroom was bathed in low light from concealed panels. The panels were in the ceiling, walls, floor, and furnishings, emitting even light throughout the room. He rubbed perfumed ointments from two jars on his scaly right shoulder, then dressed in solar-conductive clothing—tan sara shirt, dark blue pants, beige mediumweight jacket. A quick glance at the meter on his belt-held battery pack told him it held a 62 percent charge—more than enough reserve for him, even on an overcast day. As usual, he would play it safe by carrying a fresh spare in his daypack.

With these thoughts, more came back. Maudrey had married the evil stranger. Poor, innocent Maudrey. Her innocence was gone. He slipped his stubby feet into brown factory plastic boots, latching black snap-acrosses over the boots.

Gray-blue dawn light crept into the hallway as he negotiated it. He moved at a half pace, turning left at the curved bend and then pausing at the guest room. The door was ajar, enough for him to see a man wearing a white smock seated on the bed next to Maudrey's sleeping form. The man held a stringed flute and plucked at the strings without blowing into it. Plaintive, twangy notes touched Hiley's sensor, startling and enraging him. This was illegal activity, in Hiley's home!

The man looked up, catching Hiley's ferocious, inquisitive glare. Seconds later, the man stood in the hall next to Hiley, still holding the instrument.

"Don't play that in my home," Hiley said, his tone dull and menacing. Hiley tried to place the name with the face. This was the evil one who had married Maudrey.

"I tried to leave my Zuggy wrapped up," the man said, "knowing how you feel about it. But it called to me, making my insides ache. I had to hold it, to experience it."

Hiley wanted to tear the instrument away from his errant, nameless son-in-law, hurling it to the floor and stomping on it. But he was afraid to touch it.

"Maudrey does not fully understand my feelings," the man said. "Though she is trying."

Prussirian! Hiley thought. Then: "She has played it too?"

"No. Like you, she is afraid to touch it. Someday, perhaps."

"May a hundred smoothings fry your brain!" Hiley blurted, unable to repress his displeasure.

Maudrey stirred and turned over, saying something unintelligible into her pillow.

Prussirian set the stringed flute on the floor just inside the bedroom, leaning it against the wall. He faced Hiley again, without the hint of an apology on his pockmarked face.

"Music is bad for you," Hiley said, in the tone of a proctor. Hiley shook his head, trying to clear it. This made it worse. A lightning bolt of pain shot across his temples.

"Not so bad, I'd say. The truth is that the Holo-Cops don't want us to hear music for a different reason. They know it makes us less willing to cooperate with their rules. I know this because music makes me feel free."

Shut up! Hiley thought. *I don't want to hear any more!*

"It relaxes me and sends me soaring at the same time," Prussirian said, "as if my body and spirit were being carried on a powerful Sudanna wind to the outer reaches of experience."

Revolted at the prohibited *S* word and at the entire concept, Hiley said, "Oh, really?" He twisted his face in disbelief.

"An instrument such as the Zuggernaut is not always needed," Prussirian said. He felt sorry for Hiley and wanted to help him. "Music is everywhere—in the gusts blowing over our dwellos, in two alloy rods rubbed together, in a voice . . ."

"A voice?" Hiley had developed an intense headache. He stared longingly at the self-smoother banded to his arm.

Prussirian started to sing a soft, unaccompanied piece about a moon, a brave warrior, and a long-past battle.

Feeling as if his brain would burst, Hiley drowned out the song with a booming demand: "Stop!" He jerked the guest room door shut to speak privately with Prussirian. "Criminal!" Hiley hissed.

"I'm sorry you see it that way," Prussirian said.

Maudrey opened the door. She wore a four-pocketed yellow ocher robe. "What's all the commotion?" she asked, sleepily. "Daddy, are you disapproving again?"

Hiley looked away from her, glaring. *I'd better self-smooth again,* he thought.

"Daddy, I think Pruss should stay the way he is now. He's taking chances I expect you'll never understand, but . . ." Still sleep-groggy, she groped for the proper words.

"I don't want to die without ever having lived," Prussirian said.

"This is beyond belief!" Hiley exclaimed, staring at the ceiling.

"I don't claim to understand all of this, Daddy. I don't enjoy the music. It frightens me. And I don't have any personal aversion to my thoughts being revealed in a Truthing Session. But I love Pruss. He's so certain that what he's doing is right, so confident about it."

"You should go back to sleep," Prussirian said to Maudrey. "It is very early, and we have a long day of travel ahead."

Maudrey stretched her body and arms in the yawnless Uttian way. "Okay," she agreed. "But no arguing, you two." She kissed her father, then her husband, lingering with the second kiss. "Are you coming back to bed, darling?" she asked Prussirian.

"In a while," came the response. "You go ahead."

Maudrey returned to bed, closing the door behind her.

After the click of the door, Hiley leaned close to the taller Prussirian and whispered, "Filthy music criminal!" He felt he should say or do more, but was frustrated by his nonfunctioning, smoothing-fogged brain. His head throbbed.

Prussirian did not reply. He looked pensively down the hall, watching the smooth, gray-blue light of dawn as it invaded the dwello through a row of triangular cut-glass windows.

Hiley filled the hall in that line of vision now, walking away angrily and muttering to himself.

What more should I do? Hiley wondered. *What? What, for Mamacita's sake?*

Hiley kept going. It was the easiest thing to do, the only thing he was capable of doing at the moment.

Pausing at a panel box by the interior heatlock door, Hiley used a push-button code to deactivate the dwello defense system, then opened the door and stepped into the heatlock, closing the door behind him. He swung open the front door now and stepped outside, closing this door behind him and reactivating the defense system at the exterior panel box.

His net-bottomed galoo shoes hung on a rack nearby, and he took them down. With one stubby foot at a time on the railing, he slipped his boots into the galoo shoes, staring all the while at the terrain. The shadowy forms of dwellos in varying shapes were on all sides, with a knoll visible almost due west—probably a large rock covered by built-up layers of galoo. He wondered what lay beyond it.

With his galoo shoes secured, Hiley clumped downramp to ground level. He tightened the straps holding his daypack to his back and unsnapped one of two heat probes from his belt. He passed two unlit dwellos and reached the open galooflat, with the knoll visible a kilometer or so ahead and the giant Sudanna moon setting beyond that, its braided ring showing last. A chill ran down both of Hiley's spines, causing him to zip his jacket tight under his neckless head.

Holding the heat probe just above ground level in front of him, Hiley proceeded, walking at a comfortable, herky-jerk pace. The aluminum stick heat probe had a black, sucktip-size handle with a blinking blue light there telling him that the unit was on. An infrared detector in the white lower tip detected ground temperature variations from the normal range, indicating the possible presence of scavenger traps. The ground was dry in more places than it had been the day before, but remained quite moist. He detected no stickiness underfoot, for galoo's cellular structure adhered primarily to itself. He noticed a few flecks of dirt accumulating on his boot tops, galoo shoes, and trouser cuffs.

Once, Hiley thought he felt the ground move beneath his feet. He stopped in his tracks, wondering if it might not be the planetoidal stretching Prussirian had mentioned to him. Then Hiley laughed at himself, an uncharacteristic act.

That was just a wild, unconfirmed rumor, Hiley thought. *And my mind is playing tricks on me.* With these thoughts, he felt his headache receding.

Prussirian swatted an orange-and-black insect that was crawling on his leg. The insect fell to the hall floor, but quickly rebounded and flew over Prussirian's head, buzzing and making a barely audible sniffing sound.

"Blast this skeeter!" Prussirian said. He swatted at it again, but it eluded him.

Then he felt something warm and wet on the exposed forearm of his short arm. A purple stain appeared on the hair skin there. He tried to rub it off with the front of his smock, unsuccessfully. A stinging sensation hit him, followed by numbness.

The insect hovered near Prussirian's face, still sniffing and looking at him with a round, black eye. Prussirian blinked, then became aware of the sound coming from the insect. A tiny white U-Lotan numeral was stamped on its orange underbelly.

"A sniffer!" Prussirian groaned. "It's marked me!"

The sniffer darted away, disappearing down the hall in the direction Hiley had taken.

Prussirian went in the bathroom and tried to wash the purple stain from his arm. He rubbed with a cloth until his arm hurt, but made no progress. *The Holo-Cops will be on my trail soon,* he thought, aware of the electronic signal given off by sniffer dye. Panic tore through his brain. He was a marked utman.

The next few minutes passed in a blur. Instinctively, he ran alone with his Zuggernaut to the rotocar, then flew east, toward the imminent sunrise—a direction opposite to that taken minutes before by Hiley.

Neither of them noticed the other.

I can't bring Maudrey now, Prussirian thought. *Too dangerous for her.* He realized with this thought that he had hoped to escape, had expected more than a few hours or days of freedom. But the hope was gone now. All of it was gone.

Hiley only half heard a brief whir of rotors behind him. Engrossed in his search for credits and still not entirely conscious, he stared at the heat probe moving from side to side in front of him and did not turn to look. He was the only person on the galooflat this morning—a normal occurrence—making it a good time to find deaks (those unkeepable items left by Entrapment Detail Holo-Cops) that had not been tampered with by others. He had never seen a scavenger out this early, for they reportedly did their dastardly work by night and slept until midday. Hiley felt comparatively safe at this time of day, having based his schedule upon scavenger activity data provided him by the Holo-Cops.

Nevertheless, he worried about encountering an errant scavenger one morning—someone who thought as he did, traveling away from the crowds. Hiley carried no weapons, as such items were prohibited. He knew this left only scavengers with weapons and fantasized now (as he occasionally did) about what might happen if he were unlucky. They would force him to unlock his dwello security system and would sack the place, killing everyone in the family. Maybe little Plick would escape by hiding under a bed.

Hiley had determined the odds of a morning scavenger attack to be extremely remote. And he was one utman who played the odds in virtually every action he took.

Hiley felt more alert and moved more quickly at these thoughts, continually looking around and back. With the increasingly cooler temperatures of spring, he noticed a slight crustiness in the soil underfoot. In only a few days, galoo shoes would no longer be needed.

When he reached the base of the knoll, Hiley looked up and saw something jutting out near the top. It formed a square, boxy profile against the pale red sky. A good indication, but not a guarantee. It might merely be a chunk of debris stuck in the galoo-swathed mount—possibly the remains of a wrecked dwello.

Still using his heat probe, he climbed slowly on his broad, net-bottomed galoo shoes, slipping occasionally and scanning for the easiest route of ascent. This produced a zigzag, roundabout course. Presently, he saw the box-shaped object with some clarity. Much of it was covered with dark galoo, but a light green, flat surface showed.

Reaching the object, he confirmed that it was not debris. U-Lotan numerals and words stamped on the exposed side identified it as a deak, bearing the repeated designation "A351212/½—SUN TEA, 56 PACKAGES." The number following the slash mark represented the number of credits earned by reporting this find.

"So many half-credit items," he muttered. "Hardly ever a one or better." He had found a sixer once, and one utwoman he overheard in a magazine shop boasted of turning in a tenner. Having a decided weakness for tea, Hiley weighed the half credit versus the enjoyment of so much tea. He could lug the box home and consume all of it before being caught. A box that size would cost at least four credits.

Alarmed at the Bad Thought, he discarded it, wondering if it would show up in his next Truthing Session. "Blow that

Prussirian away!" he said. "He's poisoned my brain, too!"

With his brain clearing, he removed the miniterminal from his pocket and stared at it. The round, white plastic credit-recording device, half as big around as the end of his sucktip, had an oblong screen and a black grill microphone below that. Hiley pressed a button on the back, lighting the screen with a dull, amber glow.

"A-three-five-one-two-one-two-slash-half," Hiley said into the microphone.

The letter and numbers appeared on the screen.

Hiley then gave his name, dwello number, and the approximate location of the find, followed by an order to "send." This transmitted the message to the nearest fortress, where a credit slip would be prepared for him to pick up at his next rule class.

After pocketing the miniterminal, Hiley stood for several minutes on top of the knoll, looking down the side away from his dwello. He saw that he could descend more easily on this side. He also saw a dwello at the bottom, an old one-story hexagonal structure with a small solar greenhouse wing. A light went on in the dwello, followed seconds later by another.

Wonder who lives there, he thought, idly. He focused on two giant emerald green-and-yellow butterflies that fluttered gracefully over the dwello.

Hiley selected the easiest path and made his way down the backside of the knoll. But he found the way deceptively steep, with a number of soft spots. He fell back once and had to place his short arm beneath him for support.

When Hiley reached the bottom, the dwello door burst open and an utman ran out, waving his arms wildly. "Get away, scavenger!" he screamed. "I have weapons, and you'll die!" He ran to his forward galoo launcher and loaded a sizable rock into its sling.

What an odd man, Hiley thought. *I can dodge a rock easily. The launchers are for hitting other dwellos, and not with rocks!* Hiley knew of no rule prohibiting the use of a rock in a galoo launcher, but it seemed wrong to him. "I'm no scavenger!" Hiley shouted. "I'm your neighbor . . . from the other side of the knoll!"

Keeping a sucktip on the lever of his launcher, the man looked fearfully at Hiley and said nothing more. He was thinking. He appeared to be a bit older than Hiley, judging from the deep facial creases visible even from a distance. He had black head hair.

"There's a half credit on top of the knoll!" Hiley shouted. "Just over the crest! I search for credits early, to avoid scavengers! They're asleep now!" *Unless this is one,* Hiley thought, feeling exposed and remembering the plastic bags of credit slips and money in his hollow legs.

The man removed his sucktip from the lever. "A halfer, you say?"

He looks okay, Hiley thought. *Kind of eccentric, but not very tough.* Hiley moved closer so that they might converse more easily. "Yeah. It's not much, but worth the climb anyway." Hiley stepped to his left, preparing to leave. "Sorry to have bothered you. It looked easier from the top to come down this side."

"Hold on," the man said in a friendly tone. He secured his launcher with a strap and clumped downramp to ground level. "I'll check that halfer out," he announced, approaching Hiley.

Hiley was hesitant to meet new people. He didn't trust them. But this utman did not behave suspiciously. His oddness and eccentricity would explain why he had selected a spot away from other dwellos. Rudder problems might have brought him here, too, or tricky currents.

"You don't look like a scavenger to me," the man said as he reached Hiley, echoing Hiley's thoughts. "There's an honest look about you. I'm a pretty good judge of character. I've had to be over the years."

"We live in dangerous times," Hiley said. The man was perhaps fifty or fifty-five, with a broad, creased face, a black sensorbrow matching his hair, and a deep-set hazel sensor.

"I'm Stamm."

"Hiley."

They shook suckertips in the ancient four-armed manner, revealing to one another that they concealed no weapons. Hiley knew that this ritual was more symbolic than practical; small weapons could easily be concealed beneath clothing.

Hiley's mind was nearly clear now, and he thought of Prussirian. *I should have called the police,* he thought. *The minute I saw him with that evil flute! Why didn't I do it?* Then, panicking: *I've got to get back!*

"Are you all right?" Stamm asked. "You look a little pale."

"Sure, sure."

"Up on the knoll, eh?"

"What? Oh, yeah."

"Wait here," Stamm said. Before Hiley could respond, Stamm ran upramp to his dwello. Hiley watched him set the home's defense system.

"Bring your galoo shoes!" Hiley yelled. "It's still a little mushy in places up there!"

Stamm waved in acknowledgment, then took his galoo shoes from their rack by the door and strapped them on.

It's too late anyway, Hiley thought. *I didn't turn Prussirian in promptly. That's a rule violation.* He wondered if the Holo-Cops would accept his self-smoothing as an excuse. The answer came to him in one of the six often repeated Basic Rules: "There is no rule permitting you to violate a rule."

Hiley despaired, then smiled with great difficulty as Stamm returned, carrying his miniterminal. *What should I do?* Hiley thought.

"How long have you been going out this early?" Stamm asked. He leaned over and adjusted the strap on one galoo shoe.

"Huh? Oh, ten, twelve years. Haven't seen a scavenger yet, assuming I could identify one if I saw him. The Holo-Cops gave me a report on scavenger habits. I could show it to you sometime, or you could get your own free copy for the asking."

"Mind if I join you some morning?" Stamm asked.

"I'd enjoy the company."

As they clumped up the knoll with Hiley in the lead holding his heat probe, Hiley realized he felt comfortable with Stamm. But Hiley had experienced this before with others—three times in his lifetime. He had been rejected on each occasion. Hiley never understood why most people did not take to him. Maybe he was too intense in his goals—collecting credits voraciously, staying out of harm's way, protecting his family. Or maybe they envied all the credits he had accumulated and his nicer-than-average dwello. Invariably, something failed to click. He decided to take this relationship a little more slowly, not committing himself.

Have I really been too pushy in the past? Hiley wondered.

He did not see how he could have been, for he approached each situation cautiously, afraid everyone he met might be a scavenger. Scavengers were known to live in dwellos like ordinary people.

I always put up a barrier at first, Hiley thought. *But I drop it soon afterward when I'm satisfied the person is normal. It must be then that I push too hard.* Hiley stepped over a small outcropping, still leading. *I'm thinking too much about it,* he thought. *A friendship should be natural, not contrived.*

They reached the deak—just over the crest in the day's new sunlight. The blue sun was above the horizon but still touching it, with shades of purple and deep blue streaking off to each side. Stamm entered the deak's code numbers in his miniterminal and thanked Hiley for his assistance.

"Scavengers sleep until midday," Hiley said.

"So I've heard." Stamm looked toward the group of dwellos on Hiley's side of the knoll, using a forearm to shield his sensor against sunlight to the right of the dwello. "Which one's yours?" Stamm asked.

"On the left side. The white split-level with the green roof, partially hidden by that wide, cream-colored one."

"Looks nice," Stamm said, lowering his forearm.

Here it comes, Hiley thought. *My dwello is nicer than his. He'll cool toward me now.*

"There's still a couple of hours to midday," Stamm said. "Let's scout around for credits."

Hiley could not believe his sensor. He was elated, but hesitated for effect and said, almost grudgingly, "Sure. Okay."

Hiley put aside his concerns as they searched the cooling galoo on all sides of the knoll and on the flats far beyond the fotta on which Stamm's dwello sat. They found nothing more. Passing Stamm's dwello on the way back, Hiley noticed for the first time that Stamm had not been using a heat probe. Hiley made no comment on this.

Stamm invited him inside.

"I can only stay a few minutes," Hiley said. "It's nearly time to start back."

They sat at a shabby yellow kitchen table, discussing the worst Fluxes and dipping their sucktips in a bowl of mint-spiced water. The seasons were a traditionally safe topic, one conducive to Good Thought. As Stamm spoke of the raging

Flux of four seasons past, Hiley noticed an unusual little metal container on the counter. The container was round and had a paper label around it, written in a style of lettering and language never seen before by Hiley.

Recalling his obligations, Hiley thought, *I've got to turn Maudrey and Prussirian in.* Then he said, "May I use your tell-all?"

"Sorry. It's been out of order the last couple of days."

Hiley rose. "I've got to hurry home," he said. "Thanks for the hospitality."

"Sure," Stamm said, smiling as he rose.

To avoid seeming abrupt or rude, Hiley made small talk by asking about the unusual tin on the counter.

"Caviar," Stamm said, brushing away a chip of yellow paint from the metal table top. "A delicacy from Earth, they say. Too strong an odor for my taste. They actually eat it, you know."

"Eat?"

"Absorption into the body through the mouth."

"Oh. I'd forgotten about that. Like drawing water through a sucktip."

"Yeah."

"How'd you get it?"

Stamm hesitated. Then, reluctantly: "A few years back, we were in the Earth-Ut Exchange Program. You know, where we let alien people stay in our homes for a while, and if we want we can go stay on their planet."

Hiley nodded. He had seen too many Earth humans and other aliens on Ut to suit him—especially those Earther tourists given control of dwellos during Flux.

"We got this crown prince from an Earth place called Russia," Stamm said, speaking laboriously. "He wanted to escape the attention he had been getting there and sneaked into an Utbound lightship under an assumed name. He told me he paid someone to use the name."

"Is that right?" Hiley said. "I knew a family who took in an Earth woman once for three weeks. The woman had trouble with her oxygen concentrator and damn near died before they got her to a doctor."

Stamm handed the tin of caviar to Hiley and said, "I remember once when my boy stuffed a bunch of this into his sensor. He'd seen the way Earthers eat. Made him stink for days." Stamm's countenance grew dark. He looked away.

"Your boy?" Hiley asked.

"You'd better leave now," Stamm said. Hiley saw tears forming in the other man's sensor.

Hiley rose, leaving the tin on the table. "I'll see you around," he said.

Stamm looked away and did not respond.

As Hiley let himself out, he wondered what he had done wrong this time. It was always something. He slipped back into his galoo shoes and trudged home.

Ten

Theoretically, an utperson could live a very long time. His body contains few parts to break down, and those parts he has are generally quite durable. Surprisingly, only his head ages. With the passage of time, the facial skin becomes wrinkled, and the muscles around the multifunction sensor constrict, narrowing the sensor opening. Ultimately it is completely covered, resulting in S.D. death. No known medical procedure—surgical or otherwise—is able to inhibit this constrictive process.

> —notation by unknown U-Lotan in one of the field journals stolen by the Earth human Günter Jorgensen

The blue sun shone from high in the sky when Hiley neared his dwello. Walking as fast as he could in net-bottomed galoo shoes, which is not terribly fast, he noticed Prussirian's roto-car missing from the roof. He assumed Maudrey and her husband had gone together. Hiley worried about her, wishing for an instant he had taken the time to talk her into leaving that senseless man—and wishing he had given her a hug and a longer kiss that morning. He wondered if he would ever see Maudrey again.

I wasn't thinking straight this morning or yesterday, Hiley thought, scuffing his feet dejectedly. *That self-smoothing really wiped me out. I should have had enough sense to at least call the Holo-Cops this morning. Now it's too late for me.* He felt foolish.

Muttering angrily to himself, Hiley clumped upramp to the front door. He removed his galoo shoes and hung them in the shoe wash wall bracket. He slammed the Lotanglas washer door shut and watched as powerful jets of water cleaned off the small amount of soil on the shoes. A hook next to the washing mechanism held a long nylon brush, which he used to brush dirt from his boots, trousers, and arm. Sperl did not tolerate dirt inside the dwello.

As he returned the brush to its hook, he heard the inner heatlock door open and close, followed by the outer door. Maudrey stood in the open doorway, looking at him angrily. "Pruss left without me," she said, her voice low and hostile.

Hiley overcame his surprise and said, "You made a wise decision. We'll go to the Holo-Cops together." He reached out to her, intending to grasp her and hold her close.

She pulled away. "I didn't make *that* choice," she snapped. "He left while I was asleep. What did you say to him?"

Hiley stepped by her into the heatlock. He saw rage and confusion in her features. "Nothing," he said. "I didn't tell him to leave without you. In fact . . ." He fell silent as he opened the inner door, feeling embarrassed at his inaction. He wanted to get away from everyone so that he could think. He stepped into the entrance hall, followed by Maudrey.

"Yes, you did!" she screamed. "The two of you were arguing! You've ruined my whole life!"

"You don't understand," Hiley said, wanting to calm her but hesitant to reach out and touch her. "Whatever Prussirian did was done on his own."

"Nothing? You said nothing to make him leave?"

"I called him a music criminal. That's all. Not a word about leaving you."

"You didn't threaten him?" She let the inner door close behind her, then hurried around to face her father.

"No."

"I don't know what to think," Maudrey said, seeing sincerity in her father's expression. "I didn't think Pruss would do this to me."

"Obviously, he had second thoughts. He probably decided you'd be safer here with your family. He knew that we love you and would do the right thing." *Meaning we turn ourselves in,* he thought. *It'll be better for both of us now. And for Sperl, too. I shouldn't have self-smoothed away her senses either.*

"It is safer here," Maudrey said, wavering.

"That's right, dear." He touched her shoulder and felt her quivering.

"I don't understand why he did this," she said. "I just don't understand."

When Maudrey went into the guest bedroom to be alone, Hiley tell-alled the Holo-Cops. He related as much as he knew to the electronic message taker, describing the actions of Maudrey, Prussirian, Sperl, and himself. He explained his self-smoothing and that of Sperl as errors in judgment, brought on by music-induced confusion. "Music is a terrible thing," Hiley said when he closed the call. "A terrible, evil thing."

Afterward, he went to the basement shop to work on a defective heat probe. The problem was simple to Hiley—a loose connection.

While he was so occupied, a laser tick dispatched by Fortress 107 entered his body unnoticed, absorbing all of Hiley's thoughts and memories. It followed by doing the same to Maudrey and Sperl.

Twelve seconds later, a printer in the fiftieth-floor transcribing room of Fortress 107 jerked into motion, printing as it absorbed data from the laser tick. The printer inked six lines at a time, sheet after sheet. Then it fell silent.

The laser tick left, traveling in a microsecond to another assigned host body.

Two seconds passed at Fortress 107, after which a mechanical arm tore the report crisply from the printer and dispatched it by vacuum tube to Robot Paleon's desk.

Robot Paleon heard the message tube arrive with a thud in the wall-mounted receptacle next to his desk. He rolled around noisily (he had not yet reported to Maintenance to have his noisy wheel gears repaired) and lifted the Lotanglas sliding door, retrieving the black plastic-and-rubber tube inside.

I've got to get those gears fixed, he thought. *I'm tarnished, too.* Then, focusing his electronic gaze on a little red light next to the receptacle, he thought, *Message light's out. Need to get that taken care of, too.* The light, which indicated the arrival of a message, burned out frequently.

He removed the cello-report and read it quickly as he clanked toward Detective Nipp's office. When he entered the office moments later, Robot Paleon said, "None of the OIV family know where Prussirian BBD went." He handed the report to his superior.

Hovering on the other side of the desk, Detective Nipp scanned the report. "These three," he said in his faraway voice, "Hiley OIV, Sperl OIV, and Maudrey OIV—we will deal harshly with them at a later date for their part in this outrage. The priority, Paleon, is for you to follow the signal being emitted by the fugitive. As you know, he was sniffer-marked this morning."

"Yes, Detective Nipp. This looks like another easy one."

Too easy for my liking, Detective Nipp thought. He longed for a difficulty factor 9.0 fugitive case, one for which he could call a Shriek assault team. *Maybe the next case,* he thought. In his usual fashion, he would resolve this case before taking on another. His workload was light, and with all the tracking technology available to him no criminal could hope to escape.

In the guest bedroom, Maudrey sat on a chair pulled close to the window and looked outside. Three gray-and-white galoo gulls landed outside and picked at the ground with their beaks, looking for worms. Moments later, the low-oxygen birds were airborne against the pale red sky, each with a fat worm in its beak.

The birds flew east, in roughly the same direction Maudrey guessed Prussirian had gone. Presently, they disappeared in a layer of dark red clouds rimming the horizon.

Why did he leave me? she wondered, agitated. *Oh, Pruss, I miss you so!*

It had been barely six hours since Prussirian had kissed her and sent her back to bed. She wondered if he might simply have gone for a spin in the rotocar.

He'll be back any moment, she told herself.

Maudrey saw a speck in the distant sky. The speck grew larger as it approached, then took the shape of a white roto-car. It might be . . . She stood up and pressed her face against

the Lotanglas. The whir and thump of rotors became audible
to her. The noise grew louder. She could almost read the
numbers on the belly of the craft. It was the right color, white
with blue stripes . . .

But it was not her husband. The rotocar whizzed by, almost
directly overhead.

Soon the noise dissipated. Another craft came and went.
Then another. With each rotocar not bringing back Prussirian, her spirits dropped to a new low.

She heard her parents talking in another room, their voices
murmurous. Then Ghopa and Plick filled the hallway with
laughter. Ghopa was throwing a ball to her little brother, and
Maudrey heard it bounce along the floor and against the walls
outside her room.

"She'll get over him," Hiley said. He sat in one of the deep
chairs by the living room's solar hearth. Sperl sat on the
couch, looking blankly at him.

"I'm not so certain," she said. She looked at the ceiling. An
orange-and-black skeeter flew between the rafters, then
perched on one.

"I don't know what the Holo-Cops will do to you and me,"
Hiley said, following her gaze to the skeeter. "I'm more concerned about Maudrey, of course." Hiley heard these words,
and they surprised him. He was not at all certain of their
sincerity, for he knew well that he always placed himself first,
even before the welfare of those he loved.

Suddenly the dwello shook violently. The dishes and pans in
the kitchen rattled. A statuette wobbled and fell off the solar
hearth, plopping unharmed on the carpet. The shaking did not
last long.

"What the Holo-hell was that?" Hiley said, forgetting to
avoid a prohibited expletive. He looked around, his sensor
furtive with fear.

"We must have settled on a galoo bubble," Sperl suggested
calmly. "It finally popped, that's all."

"Could be. Must have been a big one, though." Hiley sat
back down, thinking again of the rumor about the planetoid
pushing itself apart with opposing magnetic forces. Hiley
could not remove the thought from his mind. He dared not
mention it to anyone, for people would think him mad. *A*

sedative scent for my nerves, he thought. *I'll get one in a few minutes.*

They spoke of Maudrey a while longer. Then Hiley told Sperl of his new friend, Stamm. "We're going to kluss with him," he told her proudly.

"He agreed to that?"

"He did," Hiley said, lying. "At the first Flux, we'll hook our dwellos together."

"You've said such things before," she said, raising her sensorbrow skeptically.

"But this time . . ."

Sperl smiled sadly and almost imperceptibly with her olive-green sensor as she watched her husband fumble for words. She knew he was not telling the truth and knew he knew her thoughts. She understood as well that he was concerned over which punishment the Holo-Cops would administer to them for their failure in the Prussirian matter.

"Maybe your new friendship will work out this time," she said softly. "There is always hope."

Prussirian's rotocar rose above the dark brown galooflats beside a cathedral rock formation. He read the triangulator dial to verify his position in relation to green latitudinal and longitudinal markings on the off-white cello-chart spread across the passenger seat next to him, then checked his heading on the directional gyro, again comparing it with markings on the chart.

Appa Crown, he thought. *No doubt about it.* Prussirian removed a depleted battery pack from his belt and plugged it into a recharger below the dashboard for renewal by the rotocar's main battery. He removed a fully charged unit from the recharger and plugged it into his belt.

He wondered how many scavengers, if any, had charts like his, and if he would meet any scavengers along the way. Prussirian feared the scavengers, but saw a certain romance to their life-styles. He wished he knew how they eluded capture.

Perhaps they could teach me to survive out here, he thought.

Far to his left and out of sight below the curvature of Ut lay the nearest Holo-Cops fortress. He had caught a glimpse of it minutes before and now was at least half an hour beyond it. Even so, he would remain alert for police patrols.

As Prussirian flew near the base of Appa Crown's craggy hulk, he spied the wreckage of an aircraft on a ledge halfway up the face, glinting in the afternoon sunlight. He moved the control stick forward, and his craft ascended. It was a police rotocruiser of burnished silver and green, smashed head-on against the megalithic rock. It had lost a rotor from the otherwise undamaged tail section, undoubtedly before impact. Prussirian flew close enough to see a motionless robot in the cockpit bubble—an indication that this might be one of the regions where Holo-Cops could not go. But such regions were supposed to be windy, and Prussirian did not notice any appreciable wind factor now.

As he changed course and pulled away from the crash site, he looked at the purple stain that remained on his hair-covered forearm. The Holo-Cops might not follow his signal to this place, but they could send robots instead. Would they bother to pursue one insignificant utman to such a remote region? He sighed in the nonbreathing Uttian way, shrugging his shoulders at the same time.

Yes, he realized. *They will follow me. The robot back there is proof. I'm going to have to cut off the arm.*

He attempted to put such thoughts out of his mind for another day, but knew they would not and could not stay away for long. His craft ascended to the craggy top of the crown, which he gave only a passing glance. The words of the young Cum Laude who sold him the chart came back: *"When you pass Appa Crown set a course of 264.35 degrees. You'll see a region of low black lava formations."*

Prussirian set the proper course and studied the horizon ahead. It was perfectly uniform and gave him an abysmal feeling. He checked the course, comparing it with a red appearing ink notation on the chart.

That's one way to avoid customer complaints, Prussirian thought. *Send them to hell and beyond, where they'll get lost.*

He thought of the scraping stone and of the other dwello construction materials in the transport compartment behind him and wished Maudrey were with him. Maybe he would elude capture after all, and she should have come with him. But it was too late for such considerations. He had made his choice.

A robot-operated police rotocruiser rose above Fortress

107. Robot Paleon, the pilot and anxious pursuer, enjoyed field assignments. They permitted him an escape from the drudgeries of office work.

Robot Paleon studied the square green-and-orange omni dial on the instrument panel, which indicated the direction of the signal being emitted by Prussirian. This dial was adjacent to the directional gyro, and all he had to do to track the fugitive was match the gyro setting with the signal indicator.

He made the setting and watched the control stick move to port until the rotocruiser found its course.

"Subject heading 264.35 degrees from Appa Crown," the ship's computer reported in a sexless monotone.

Robot Paleon sat back for the ride. He thought of the way Detective Nipp often told him he should be content with office work, like other robots. *"I'll reprogram you one of these days,"* Detective Nipp would threaten. But he never carried out this threat, probably never even considered it, in Robot Paleon's estimation.

"Detective Nipp and I are alike," the robot murmured, "as nearly alike as two different life forms can be. He knows it as well as I do." And Robot Paleon was a life form, with reasoning and emotional processes evolved to the equal of most creatures in the universe.

He glanced at the artillery kit on the seat next to him, with its holstered eternity pistol and cartridge clips. His superior, Detective Nipp, preferred killing fugitives, asserting it was neater that way, with less handling required. It had the added advantage of bypassing a full-smoothing by Mamacita and the resultant drain on her power. But Robot Paleon was the prime pursuer now and had the choice concerning the amount of force to be used. If he did not kill Prussirian BBD, however, he would have to provide an acceptable explanation to Detective Nipp. In theory, Robot Paleon had the prerogative, but in practice he knew the easiest course to follow.

Prussirian jerked the control stick sharply to starboard, selecting a new course toward low-lying caramel-colored hills in the distance.

I've got to get rid of the forearm, he thought, *before the signal dye on it gives away my location. It's my short arm anyway,* he thought, trying to minimize the loss. Numbed at the prospect, he still considered it preferable to returning.

Anything was better than that. Even death.

The hills were more distant than he had thought and grew larger only slowly. It took nearly fifty minutes to reach them, an interval during which Prussirian tried to develop alternatives to cutting off the forearm. He wondered if the purple dye might not be the signal transmitter he assumed it was, or if the signal mechanism could be faulty.

But he knew otherwise.

Beyond the crest of the first hill, he flew over hundreds of meteor craters, varying in size from holes no longer in diameter than the width of his cabin to massive impact sites several kilometers across. He banked to starboard, landing near a grouping of smaller holes.

Must do this quickly, he thought. *Who knows how close behind they are.*

Prussirian turned around and tugged at the handle of a dented metal case behind the front passenger seat. With a grunt, he hauled the case up and over the seat back, plopping it down on the seat. He released a sliding latch to get inside and rummaged through miscellaneous dwellohold utensils until his sucktip touched the cool metal sheath of the kitchen cleaver.

He unsheathed the knife and stared at the glinting blade, a blade that soon would be dripping blood. His blood. Numbness coursed through his body like an anesthetic, preparing him for the maiming. He noticed the scraping stone now, in a corner of the case.

I wonder, he thought, laying the knife on his lap. He lifted the gray, lusterite stone, rubbing one sucktip against it. The stone was rough, chafing his skin.

If I could rub off the dye . . . But not in here.

Carrying the knife and the scraping stone, Prussirian stepped out of the rotocar. A gust of wind caused him to brace himself and consider donning a weight coat. He changed his mind when the gust subsided. Wishing to prevent any ensuing wind from carrying scrapings back to the rotocar where they might lodge and emit signals, he located a flat, marbly stone on the ground well away from the rotocar and downwind from the gust he had felt.

Prussirian knelt and set the knife down beside him. Then he extended the offending arm, resting his forearm on flat stone. Slowly, he began to scrape at the purple dye, barely touching the skin. He felt a slight burning sensation, but observed no change in dye coloration. Grimacing, he rubbed harder. Then as hard as he could, until hair had been rubbed away and an ugly, ragged wound was open.

His forearm seared with pain, and he knew it would get worse. He had to rub away the layers of skin that had been dyed. Purple blood ran all over the scraping stone and on his sucktip, dripping on his trousers and on the stone. There was so much blood that he had trouble distinguishing the dyed areas, which were a shade of purple very close to the color of his blood.

With his uninjured arm, he grabbed the knife and cut away a large section of his smock. He used the white rag to dab at the wound. He could see that the dye shade had lightened. He was getting rid of it. But he felt faint.

With a rush of determination, he rubbed the forearm as hard as he could again, scraping away large, jagged pieces of skin. He had never felt or imagined such pain before. It ran like a hot flame up his wounded arm to his brain.

He felt blackness coming over him, but fought it off. This was no time for weakness. He discarded the blood-soaked rag, then took off his trousers and smock, leaving himself naked save for a pair of underpants. He cut off broad strips to clean the wound as much as he could. He saw no more purple dye on the arm.

Prussirian tore away two more strips of clean cloth and used them to fashion a bandage. It occurred to him that the dye may have entered his bloodstream during the scraping or at the moment he had been sniffer-marked. If it happened at the time of marking, it would have done no good to cut off the forearm. He recognized the futility of such thoughts. They used time and energy he needed desperately for survival.

It hurt him to think. It hurt him to move. But he had to do both. Quickly.

The scraping stone lay on the flat rock. He lifted the lusterite stone and examined it closely. Purple dye and blood covered one side. He wiped his sucktips on a clean rag and retrieved a cannister of water from the helicopter. With the water and a rag he tried to clean the scraping stone. But only the blood washed away. The dye remained.

This gave him a sinking feeling, for it meant he would have to leave the scraping stone. Without this precious tool, he

could not scrape away the lusterite powder he needed to mix
with galoo for the petrified galoo required in dwello construction.

Maybe I should have cut off the forearm, he thought. But
he knew it was too late for such thoughts.

He cleaned the knife and washed up as well as he could,
then ran for the rotocar. Although he was nearly naked, he
had no thoughts of finding something to wear. He had few
thoughts at all now and moved instinctively, out of terror.

The rotocar roared to life. Moments later he was flying
away, not looking back.

On autopilot and back on course, Prussirian felt weak. He
struggled to remain conscious. Peering ahead, he observed a
small formation of big winged black falcrows flying toward
him. The birds flew erratically in loose formation and for a
time appeared in danger of colliding with the rotocar. At their
last opportunity, they swerved in four neat groupings to pass
above, below, and to each side of Prussirian. A nearly
featureless terrain lay below and to all sides, with kilometer
after kilometer of brown galoo and a smooth, rounded
horizon marking the limits of the planetoid.

The pain in his limp short arm, which he rested on his lap,
intensified as time passed. Fever pressed him with its hotness.
The vibration of the rotocar intensified his discomfort, shaking the torn and gouged flesh and sending needles of pain
through his body. His mind was as inflamed as the rest of him,
carrying with it the additional burden of his worries over the
past months—and his concerns over the time remaining. He
wanted to lay down someplace safe, if such a place existed,
where he could sleep for days.

Another formation of birds approached off the port bow, a
pain-blurred vision. Prussirian blinked to clear his sensor.
Only slightly larger than the first formation, this one also
headed directly toward him. He considered switching to
manual for evasive action and looked down at his long arm.
The sucktip twitched a little, then lifted slowly with the arm.
This was his good arm, and it was not much.

No use, he thought, letting the arm drop back to his side.
Prussirian felt no fear now. He was beyond fear.

At the last possible moment, these birds did as the others
had done, spreading their formation to avoid the rotocar.

Maybe the Cum Laude boy forgot to tell me something about the birds, Prussirian thought. *Maybe they're near-sighted and from a distance think I'm the mother of them all.* He winced at a bolt of pain that lanced through his torso. Every fiber of his body ached.

Using what seemed like his last bit of strength, Prussirian fitted a sleeping foke on his head, flipping the sensor lens up over his sensorbrow. He would fight to stay awake, but if he dozed off the foke would activate automatically, preventing sensory deprivation.

Countless additional flock of falcrows along the way behaved in the identical strange manner. He ran through other theories about the birds to pass his time and to take his thoughts away from discomfort. Perhaps they were dare-devils, seeing who could fly closest to danger. Or they might be electronic devices, reporting to the Holo-Cops the location of his rotocar.

Soon after seeing the last flock of birds, Prussirian felt strong winds buffet his craft, attacking from varying directions. He knew this changed the operating characteristics of the rotocar, and he saw the autopilot fail to respond correctly. His long arm darted forward instinctively, flipping off the chrome autopilot toggle on the dashboard. With one sucktip on the rotocar's control lever, he followed the training infusion given him by Yimmit, pushing, pulling, and turning as needed—then leaning on the wheel with his shoulder and using his good arm to vary the speed. It went smoothly and made him feel better for a time.

He thought about smoothness, for this would be his condition if he were caught. The smoothness of brain control or the smoothness of death. He did not want to die, but had no fear of it.

The flatness of galoo terrain gave way gradually to small black rock formations and patches of white plant life punctuated by splotches of pastel yellow and blue flowers. Prussirian had never seen such flowers before, or black rocks. He recalled that the region he sought was covered with black rock, and the thought that his arduous journey might be over seemed to sap the control he had maintained over his energy level.

Suddenly he realized how closely he was flying to the

ground. His subconscious seemed to be telling him to land here, anyplace here. He had no strength to fight the urge. He brought the craft down a little too hard on a patch of young white grass, then rolled to the partial shelter of a black rock outcropping. He was not entirely safe from observation here, but it would have to suffice. He did not have the energy or the inclination to remove his safety harness. By the time the blades whirred to a stop, Prussirian was asleep with his foke in place.

Detective Nipp hovered at his desk with Prussirian's clothing sample bagged in plastic on the edge of the desktop. Soon he would investigate the truancy of the others on his list—one at a time, the way he liked to do it.

His style was methodical and a little slow. But he had proven the system he used: it always brought in the fugitive. *Thank Mamacita, and the U-Lotans, for sniffers and laser ticks!* he thought. He never had to worry about a trail growing cold. It was a simple process, really. So simple and precise, that he could not envision ever failing. But the other officers in his fortress had compiled wretched records, so pathetic that they were dragging him down with them.

Detective Nipp dimmed, sighing in the way of Holo-Cops.

Robot Paleon will return tomorrow morning at the latest, he thought. Bored, he reached for his list of Truthing truants. Maybe one of the other cases would be difficult enough to risk an assault team.

All day long, Maudrey rebuffed attempts by Sperl, Hiley, Ghopa, and even Plick to talk with her, informing each that she wished to be alone. She remained seated by the window in the guest room, looking out and hoping. As the day ended and evening spread its cool mantle across Ut, she remained there, with the lights out. Her door was open a crack and she heard her parents talking. Something about a doctor Sperl had heard of who claimed he could restore lost solar collector hairs. Purportedly, this gave people more stamina.

"Another scam!" Maudrey heard her father exclaim. "When will you ever learn to recognize a crook?"

Maudrey did not hear her mother's response, but the discussion ended soon afterward.

Footsteps ensued in the hallway, and when they paused

Maudrey sensed her parents at the doorway, looking in at her. There were unintelligible whispers, followed by Sperl saying, "Good night, Maudrey, dear."

Hiley bid Maudrey good night as well.

Maudrey did not react. She barely heard their words. Her thoughts and spirit traveled on a sustained Sudanna wind across the surface of Ut. She joined Prussirian in a hazy, shadowy place, partially illuminated by the blue-gray moonglow of the Sudanna planet. She heard him breathing deeply here, fast asleep. Maudrey placed her spirit beside her husband and remained awake, vigilant. She sensed danger for him. Terrible danger.

Eleven

Laser ticks are not power-efficient, using
2,113,114 U-volts of light per month, compared
with 73,009 per Holo-Cop. Each time a laser tick
is killed—usually by an accursed Cum Laude—it
consumes a year of the tick's energy in a short
burst of light. This saps my strength, and immediately I must project a replacement, draining
me even more. It is not so easy as once it was,
and I cannot find the Cum Laude. I fear the end
is near.

—Mamacita, talking to her own circuits

Prussirian slept in a pool of perspiration that drenched
his nearly naked body and made him stick to the rotocar
seat. Once, after an indeterminate period, he awakened—or
thought he awakened—and saw daylight, with the sun producing stuffy greenhouse heat in the cabin. But he knew the
perspiration on his body was more than heat-induced. In the
"awakening," he looked at his wounded forearm and it was
not there. Only a yellow aura remained where the forearm had
been—a luminous halo of racking pain that infested his body
and inflamed his brain.

Day became night in the vision, and the aura lit the cabin
with its glow. It shone even brighter than the giant moonlike
planet Sudanna, which burned simultaneously and filled the
night sky. He felt the spirit of Sudanna growing within him
now—with its bluish radiance, its winds, and the mysterious

surface of its planet. Sudanna carried voices to him, inviting him to join them in song. The voices were a composite of sound, but one of them belonged unmistakably to Maudrey. He knew she was there somewhere, reassuring him that this was the correct way.

Prussirian called back, to her and to the ancestors of all utpersons, using his own internal Sudanna wind. He felt his body float across the distance between Ut and the great planet on a cushion of soothing music. Suddenly the music and voices receded, replaced by a single voice—an elderly utman's voice, he thought. The utman's words were clear, but made no sense—much in the way a correctly written word can appear to be misspelled. The words, whatever they meant, were forgotten by Prussirian the moment he concentrated upon them.

Fever racked him and the music within, distorting beauty and perfection into a twisted horror. The orange-and-black face of a sniffer devoured him, and he cried out. Sudanna's glow was gone, and he saw the planet black but poker hot, an inexplicable amalgam of sensations.

He seemed to be somewhere else now, not in the rotocar seat and not on his way to Sudanna. He had arrived someplace at the end of a long, arduous journey. Of that he was certain. And he was on his back. But where?

Prussirian struggled to see through the plastic lens of the foke over his sensor, but saw only a dim light that quickly faded to black. Someone shook him. He heard the old utman's voice again, using the familiar, meaningless words.

Prussirian faded to silent nothingness and felt his spirit walk the death path—a universewide track of dissipated light that faded to a pinpoint of blackness in the far, far distance. Others had gone this way before him, and he sensed others behind as well, pushing him along.

The death throng ran to catch up, then blended into one being. It was Maudrey with her back to him—a shadowy vision. She turned to face him and blocked the death path. A washed-out, colorless Maudrey smiled calmly, lovingly, and motioned with her arms for Prussirian to stay back. He struggled to reach her, but fell away. Maudrey's image grew smaller, then faded entirely.

The death path rushed by Prussirian, taking Maudrey with it and leaving him unscathed. Through the sensor foke lens he saw a flickering yellow light. Someone lifted the lens away, allowing him to scan the limits of his peripheral vision without moving his body. He was in a black lava room—a cave. It was warm here, but pleasantly so, without the smothering, stifling heat of the sun and fever-soaked rotocar cabin.

Two sinks and a desk were at one wall, with the adjacent wall dominated by shelves holding dusty, tattered rule volumes. A stained chrome-and-plazbrass battery pack recharger hung from the ceiling near the books. The room exuded dirtiness and smelled of things old. There was an old man here, too. Somewhere.

"Your illness is passed." The aged voice came from Prussirian's left. "I didn't think you were going to make it for a while." .

Prussirian turned his head to look in that direction. His neck was stiff, and he shook it before focusing on the speaker. An old utman looked back, his face illuminated by a low-oxygen candle on the table next to him. His face was full with a silver-gray beard, and his sensor opened only narrowly. The old man struggled to keep it open, a sign of approaching sensory deprivation.

"I am Crain," he announced, in a voice crackling with time. "It is the morning of your second day with me."

Prussirian introduced himself, then struggled to sit up. Crain helped him up—with some difficulty due to his age—and pushed two soft but dirty pillows behind Prussirian for support against the headboard. Prussirian's entire body ached.

"I've never been so sore," Prussirian said. He noticed fresh gauze wrapped around his forearm and said, "You helped me. Thank you." A thought troubled Prussirian. He had dreamed of Maudrey's death. It seemed vividly real, but he told himself it had only been a nightmare.

"I spread warm galoo on the wound before wrapping," Crain said, shifting on the wide, carved lava chair that supported him. "A poultice procedure used by our forefathers." Prussirian noticed that Crain wore a long brown weight coat like the ones the Cum Laude boy had sold him. But this coat was ancient and tattered, with little more life remaining in it than in the old man himself. "Few know such secrets anymore," Crain said.

Prussirian flexed the healing forearm. He still perceived pain, but greatly diminished in severity, and not much more than the general soreness in the rest of his body.

"You raved about sniffers," Crain said. "If the police are after you, as they appear to be, something must be done with your rotocar. It can still be seen from the air where it is, although I covered it with porie flowers, slarro bushes, and galoo to camouflage it somewhat. Not enough, though."

"Is this West Matra?"

The old man smiled gently. "You're only about two thousand kilometers off," he said. "This place no longer has a charted name, although once it certainly had great importance. I call it Sudanna at times—a heavenlike place. But on other occasions, when the loneliness and desolation seem overwhelming, I call it other things, cursing the day I came here."

"I flew on and on. Most of the time I couldn't focus on the chart or the instruments."

"Are you a scavenger?" The tone was indifferent, that of one having nothing to steal.

"Of course not! A music criminal, some would say. Or maybe a thought criminal. I don't see it their way, though. My thoughts are my own, and no one has a right to pick at them or change them."

The old utman smiled, brushing a thin strand of white hair away from his sensor. "I ask too many questions?"

"I didn't mean *you!* I meant the Holo-Cops and their damn Truthing Sessions!"

Crain responded with a thoughtful stare.

"Are you a fugitive, too?" Prussirian asked.

"Oh, no. The authorities know where I am. I have been here nearly sixty years, as keeper of the tether. They've forgotten about me, I'm sure. My records have been misplaced or destroyed in the maze of cello-sheets and bureaucratic tasks. I used to receive three or four police robot visitors a year. They brought me supplies and things to keep me busy—games, books, materials, news from the outside."

"It is safe for me here, then?"

Crain laughed softly, an aged, broken laugh. "You would not wish to remain *here,* in this lonely, forgotten place! I have provided aid to others like yourself. Perhaps ten over the years. None of them remained."

"They were caught?"

"I don't know. They went on, thinking they could find better places to hide. With one exception—a young fellow who crashed his rotocar near here. I pulled him from the wreckage, and he lived a day, no more. He's buried outside in a high sinkhole of galoo, above modern currents. He uttered but one word before he died. . . ."

Prussirian sensed the word coming and said, "Sudanna?"

Crain nodded. "He kept saying it over and over. Maybe he was trying to fly to the big planet."

"The idea has a certain appeal. There are patches of white and blue on the surface, you know. I've seen clouds, too, and even a flash of lightning. These things could mean water, plants, and life are there."

"I will tell you something I did not tell the others. There is a way to reach the planet Sudanna from here. The tether I mentioned. You know what that is?"

"Something on the end of a long line, I suppose."

"It is a machine for hurling rocks at the great planet. Many millions of years ago, the legend goes, strife existed among the peoples on Sudanna. One of these communities reached Ut first and set up a military base here. We are descended from them, it is said. Tethers like mine were used to pummel enemy lands. Ut was high ground. Ultimately, a battle for control of Ut came about. Those defending it destroyed the opposition and all life on Sudanna. Maybe there were really survivors on Sudanna, though. Who can say?"

"Could you throw me out there with the tether? In my rotocar, I mean?"

"The tether functions admirably after all these years, but your plan would never work. Your flimsy craft would be torn to pieces. It was not designed for such a trip."

Prussirian grimaced.

"Sniffers come to this place," Crain said. "Quite often. You must decide whether you wish to stay or go."

"I scraped off the signal dye. I'd have been arrested, or killed, by now if I were still transmitting."

"You didn't scrape away the characteristic odor that is unique to us. Sniffers search and research every square meter of ground on the planetoid. Once put on a trail, a sniffer does not give up. It'll keep going for years, I've heard."

Prussirian looked around the cave room, noting the nearly colorless, pale red sky of morning visible through a small opening far to his left. Two darkened doorways stood along a nearby wall, and adjacent to that was a black lava table supporting two lit, low-oxygen candles and a stringed flute.

"You brought in my Zuggy," Prussirian said.

"That one is mine," Crain said. "I made it myself, after running out of other things to do. It's not plazbrass. I used petrified galoo and painted it to look like plazbrass. It works as well as the genuine article. I was in despair one day, waiting for death, and the way to build a Zuggy came to me."

"Really!" Prussirian sat up straight.

"Our ancestors were skilled metallurgists, a process I cannot replicate with the materials available in this region. So they told me another construction method, which I followed. I made the instrument nonstop, using scraps from the things that were left with me. Once the idea came to me, I was compelled to complete the instrument."

Prussirian smiled, for this reminded him of the powerful and inspirational internal wind he knew.

"Then I played it," Crain said. "Such marvelous sounds! Oh, my! Our ancestors spoke to me in song, telling me the old stories." Crain's voice lost its cackle, and he spoke with the tenor of a younger man.

"All the stories are within me, too, aren't they?"

"Yes."

Prussirian wanted to run to the rotocar and get his Zuggernaut at that very instant. He swung his legs off the side of the bed and stretched. His sore muscles felt uncooperative for such an effort. He would have to take it slowly.

"Drink this," Crain said. He handed a metal goblet to Prussirian.

Prussirian passed it near his sensor, picking up the foul odor of a green liquid in the goblet as he swirled it. He twisted his face in revulsion. "But utpeople drink water only. This is not water."

"I don't mean through your sucktips. I mean through your sensor."

"What?"

"You don't realize it yet—and Sudanna voices tell me the U-Lotans didn't fully understand it, either—but our bodies are bifunctional. They can be sustained either through breathing, combined with water and liquid food ingestion, or through solar energy and water. There are tiny holes inside the lids of our sensors to breathe or ingest."

Prussirian accepted these statements as truth. "What is this stuff you want me to drink?"

"A chemical I concocted in my spare time. It will alter your body odor. It is quite safe, let me assure you. I drank some myself."

"But will it work?"

"The time I drank some, I could hardly stand being with myself. The stench lasted two, nearly three weeks."

Prussirian shook his head. "I don't think I want it."

"You don't have a lot of choices."

"An ancient recipe?"

"I don't know. Just an idea of mine. Original, I thought. The stuff soaks into every cell. I'm sure of that."

Prussirian smiled ruefully. The goblet was cool and moist against his sucktip, from condensation running down the sides.

"We can test it by allowing half a dozen sniffers into the cave," Crain said. "I can control the cave openings precisely and automatically with tight-sealing, manually operated doors I designed and built. Unlike Holo-Cops, sniffers cannot pass through barriers. They must wait for openings."

"I see."

"The best plan would be to seal you in my reading room with a week's ration of water and battery packs. That's the darkened doorway on your right over there." He motioned to his left, adding, "I go there often to read without being buzzed by sniffers. With you, I'd let in a few sniffers at a time. If they mark you, tell me over the sealed intercom, and I won't let them out. I can capture them, you see. None will ever return to inform the Holo-Cops that you were marked."

"Then I'd have signal dye on me again."

"You removed dye once with a scraping stone. I have anesthesia to make it more pleasant a second time—and antibacterials, too."

"You have a scraping stone?"

"Many of them, for I always told the police robots when they visited that I had lost the one I was supposed to have—or that it had been hurled to Sudanna by mistake. I am an utman who can lie without being detected. There are a few, you know."

"I didn't know it could be done naturally, without mechanical assistance."

Crain laughed. "They kept bringing me replacements, thinking me daft. A nice little game I played with them."

"Signal dye stays on scraping stones," Prussirian said. "We'd have to get rid of all the scrapings—the stone, too—anything with dye on it. You could do that?"

"Sure. With the tether. We have thousands of launching cylinders. Whoever constructed this facility probably filled the cylinders with something lethal—gas, maybe, or explosives —to go along with the rocks."

"Fifteen-million-year-old cylinders," Prussirian said. "Imagine that. And a launching facility just as old."

"Older than that, really. The U-Lotans conquered us fifteen million years ago. Our Ut military base preceded that by a hundred years. U-Lotan technicians rebuilt everything, for reasons known only to them. The U-Lotans mastered the technology of manufacturing frictionless machinery and had wonder, noncorroding alloys. That's why this facility still functions today."

"Huh. Not much oxygen on Ut, too, and I believe it's oxygen that deteriorates most matter. This condition probably helps."

"Could be."

Prussirian stared at the goblet. He began to raise it to his sensor.

"Wait," the old utman said, lifting a sucktip and touching the goblet. "I'm overly excited at your presence, causing me to think only of myself. I've been alone too long. Perhaps you'd be better off moving on. If you stay, I warn you that your rotocar must be burned and knocked apart. We'd load the debris into cylinders for disposal to you-know-where."

"I understand," Prussirian said. He drew the goblet close to his sensor. The stench resembled decaying flesh. He tried not to think of it.

"I do not have long to live," Crain said. "Which is another consideration. Loneliness."

Prussirian recalled the admonition of the Cum Laude that there were no guarantees in this life and thought too of his own music. With his music, Prussirian would not be alone. He would be accompanied by the ancients of Ut who had transmitted tradition genetically to their offspring. He leaned over and pressed the goblet against his sensor, wrapping his lids around the cup orifice as he had done with the stringed flute.

"Suck it in," the old utman said. "You can do it."

Prussirian inhaled and experienced the coolness of the liquid as it passed through pipes in his neck to a long-dormant combination lung-stomach.

"It's going to be rather unpleasant in the cave for a while," Crain said, wrinkling his sensor. He retrieved the goblet from Prussirian and used a towel to clean green liquid from beneath Prussirian's sensor.

Prussirian's vision was clouded for a moment, and he blinked to clear excess liquid from his sensor. "Let's unload the rotocar," he said.

"I'll get your weight coat first," Crain said, rising slowly. "It's in the other room." He left the chamber, walking with some difficulty through one of the darkened doorways.

This guy's old, Prussirian thought. *Real old.*

Crain returned soon, carrying a long brown weight coat.

"I brought in the larger one from your things," he said. "It's always windy around here." He handed the coat to Prussirian.

"Thanks."

Crain suffered a sudden itching attack all over his body and furiously scratched his torso and one thigh. Before he could scratch the rest of his body, the discomfort subsided—so quickly that he hardly noticed it. This had happened many times in his lifetime.

As Prussirian put on the weight coat, he only vaguely noticed the old man's temporary discomfiture and did not recall the young Cum Laude's warning about how laser ticks could be noticed entering and leaving the body. The requisite facts were in Prussirian's brain, but in the rapid sequence of events had been shunted aside.

Having discovered information on a known fugitive, the laser tick made an unsolicited special report. There were not many such reports made, only an average of four per week from the entire planetoidal contingent of fifty-seven ticks. Consequently, Detective Nipp did not know a typed report on his fugitive Prussirian BBD was waiting for him. Since Mamacita's mother beams sustained both laser ticks and

Holo-Cops, she could have passed information between them. She considered this now with feedback from her creatures of light—a recurring, internal discussion between her microcircuits in which Mamacita told herself how improper it would be to intervene on behalf of a particular Holo-Cop or his fortress.

My fortresses compete with one another, Mamacita thought, *a proven, workable system. The Holo-Cops have free will too, with independent brains. They will succeed or fail on their own merits.*

The laser-tick report comprised five single-spaced cellosheets and included conversational details between Prussirian and Crain. After it was typed on the transcribing room's printer in Fortress 107, the report was automatically torn off and dispatched through the fortress's vacuum-tube system to the Lotanglas-doored wall receptacle next to Robot Paleon's desk. Robot Paleon was not there, of course, and the red "message in" light on the receptacle was burned out. It should have lit and blinked. Robot Paleon had noticed the malfunction before leaving, but in his zeal to get out into the field had forgotten to order its repair.

Twelve

Dwello owners are not permitted to set their residential defense systems to kill scavengers, despite the threat to life scavengers present. Only Holo-Cops may kill.

—Statutes of Ut
Series 5, Rule 912.26(a)

Unaware that Maudrey had died during the night, Hiley searched the early-morning galooscape for credits as usual. He found nothing. It was midmorning when he found himself standing in galoo shoes outside Stamm's dwello calling for him. Since he did not know whether the dwello defense system had been activated, he could not set foot onboard.

"Around back!" Stamm shouted. "Who's there?"

Hiley identified himself quickly and clearly, then walked around the dwello. The fotta comprising Stamm's yard was badly in need of raking, with an assortment of dry and moist spots at varying elevations.

On the other side, Stamm knelt next to the prow of his dwello, using a trowel to smooth a patch of catalyzed, petrifying galoo on the hill. "Hit something during my last run," he said.

"You think it needs a haul out?" Hiley asked.

"Maybe after next season. I checked inside the hull real carefully and found no stressed points."

Hiley glanced around at the yard, which was drying slowly

157

as it cooled. "You should have had your galoo raking done when the soil was still good and warm," he said. "A lot of this'll have to be warmed now before it can be raked."

"I don't go in for that sort of thing anymore," Stamm said. "Yard work bores the bajoobies out of me, and I've never liked dealing with galoo rakers."

"They shouldn't bother you much out here. Sperl—that's my wife—she runs a tight dwello and is always giving me lists of things to do."

Stamm looked at Hiley with a faint twinkle in his sensor. "Maybe that's why you stay out of the dwellohold so much."

Hiley laughed carefully, recalling Stamm's sudden iciness the last time Hiley visited. "That's true enough, I suppose."

Stamm studied Hiley's features, noting the neat, dark brown beard and alert, blue-green sensor. "I'm sorry I became introverted yesterday," Stamm said. "I'm a widower. And worse. My wife and boy fell overboard in a bad galoo storm two years ago."

"I'm sorry to hear that."

Stamm wiped his trowel clean on a cloth. "She was with child, too." He paused, working hard to maintain his composure. "She was the socializer. Got us into a kluss of eight dwellos. Lots of partying, camaraderie, and all that."

"Yeah," Hiley said. "We've done all that." Hiley was lying.

"After she died, the other couples changed their attitudes toward me. I couldn't quite put my sucktip on what it was. They were . . . distant. Sometimes they asked me when I'd get married again. I had no interest in remarrying. Only one ut-woman for me, I guess." His creased face formed a scowl.

Hiley noticed the way Stamm avoided using his wife's name, but did not mention this. It was time to change the subject.

Stamm did it for him. "Any children?" he asked.

"Three. Two girls and a boy."

"That's nice."

"You want a hand with anything here?"

"Yeah. Help me carry this stuff." Stamm pointed to a green pail full of catalyzed patching compound. "I've got a couple more dings around the other side."

"Your dwello looks good," Hiley said, as they walked

around the bow, Stamm in the lead.

"Just the essentials."

Hiley barely heard Stamm's words, for a memory had been triggered. He recalled Prussirian sitting in the living room with Maudrey, talking about smoothing a wall with a trowel. Hiley brought back the words: "Everything could not be smooth and should not be smooth. There should be jagged edges, dirty corners, things that do not go precisely according to plan."

Prussirian had been speaking of more than a wall.

The angry pounding of rotocar rotors brought Hiley out of his thoughts. He and Stamm paused to watch two police cruisers circle overhead. The silver-and-green flying ships moved in unison, dipping toward Stamm's dwello and hovering momentarily. Hiley knew they were mapping dwello locations after Flux, traveling in pairs for security. They flew toward the knoll after completing their task and soon were out of sight.

"Mamacita's birdmen just got me," Stamm said.

The receding rotor noise and vibration reminded Hiley of the day before, when his dwello had shaken violently. "Did you feel the ground move yesterday afternoon?" Hiley asked.

"No."

"It happened around midafternoon. Rattled everything in my cupboards."

"Is that right? Naw, didn't notice anything like that. I took a nap about that time, though."

"Sperl said we might have settled on a galoo bubble, and that the dwello weight finally broke it open."

"Could be. I've heard of that."

Hiley decided not to pursue the subject. He helped Stamm repair the other dents and scrapes in the hull, during which time Stamm told of how he finally could stand the kluss no more without his family. When the first ensuing Flux began, Stamm said he pulled his dwello hooks and went on his way, saying curt good-byes to his klussmates.

"Folks are funny," Hiley observed. "Real hard to figure out."

They agreed on virtually every subject discussed. Although it was not possible to go over that many subjects in two hours, they talked enough—and about personal things. Personal to Stamm, that is. Hiley did not mention his own deepest concerns, but did reveal the problems he had experienced with Plick leaving windows unsecured, thereby violating dwello security.

During a long period of silence while they worked, Hiley thought of the natural relationship he sensed forming. It seemed much different from the superficial encounters he had experienced in the past. He longed to confide fully in Stamm, but felt it wiser to hold back. After all, Hiley had so many problems that it might make him look bad in Stamm's sensor to reveal all of them.

Stamm broke into Hiley's thoughts after a while, saying, "Hey, what do you say we hitch dwellos when Flux starts again?"

Hiley could not believe his sensor. He wanted to jump and skip for joy. A kluss! But he did not flinch, smile, or show any other outward sign of emotion. "Well," he said, speaking slowly, "I don't know. I'm kind of independent, you know."

Stamm shrugged. "Me too. Maybe it wouldn't work."

Hiley responded quickly, perhaps too quickly, he thought. "It might be a good idea for defense, though. Two dwellos are safer than one."

"That's for sure."

"We could always unhitch if it doesn't work out."

Stamm wiped a galoo smear from his face and said, without looking at Hiley, "During a Flux run, yeah. But what if we get sick of each other the rest of the year?"

Hiley laughed.

So did Stamm.

On the way home, two utmen and an utwoman approached Hiley—neighbors he had seen before, working on their dwellos and in their yards. He had never spoken with them.

"I'm Sharci," the woman said, moving close to Hiley. He smelled imported perfume—probably one of the Oknos flower scents, he decided. "This is my husband, Lome," she added, designating the shorter of the men with her, a fellow with a dark facial mole. His sensor was dark blue, and it glowed brightly, a friendly sort of glow.

"I'm Prabic," the other man said. "We're neighbors." He was tall and young, of fair complexion.

"I've seen all of you in the neighborhood," Hiley said, edging around the group in an attempt to continue on his way.

"Where have you been?" Sharci asked.

"Visiting a friend. His dwello is just beyond the knoll." Hiley gestured with his long arm in the direction from which he had come, taking a couple of slow, herky-jerk steps past the group as he spoke. *I shouldn't have said that,* he thought. *These people could be . . .*

"That so?" Sharci said, before Hiley finished his thought. She clumped alongside Hiley, with the others close behind.

"Sorry," Hiley said, "but I'm in kind of a hurry. Please excuse me." Hiley glanced at Lome, who had caught up and walked at Sharci's side. Hiley's gaze moved to Sharci. She reached nearly his height, making her taller than her husband; a pretty woman with pale skin, slick black head hair, and graceful movements (for an utperson).

"You need not fear us," Sharci said.

Hiley locked gazes with her, then looked at the ground.

"You have a nice dwello," fair young Prabic said, moving to Hiley's other side. "A real first-class place. The kind seen in Good Thought moorages."

"I've worked hard," Hiley said, shrugging. He felt uncomfortable and unable to think of much to say.

"I'll bet you have quite a defense system on that beauty," Sharci said. "Tell us how it works so we can improve our own."

"Well," Hiley began, pausing to fashion a lie, "I didn't do the work myself. A friend did."

"Let us take a look at it," she urged. "Prabic here is good at figuring things out."

"I can't do that," Hiley said, recalling a survival suggestion found in the crimestopper book issued to every Ut citizen. "Please excuse me. I must get back." He tried to pick up his pace, but felt the woman's sucktip pulling against his arm.

She smiled as Hiley looked at her, the insincere smile of a salesman. "It won't take long," she insisted. "Only a few minutes."

Hiley pulled away and turned to confront the trio. He looked from face to face. "I'll be blunt with you," he said. "I don't know any of you. A lot of people think I'm overly cautious, and I don't mean to come across as unfriendly. I hope you understand." *Little do they know how much value I'm carrying in my leg hollows,* he thought, attempting to show no fear in his expression.

"You think we're scavengers?" Sharci asked, appearing to be aghast. If this was an act, Hiley decided, it was better done than her smile.

"I didn't say that," Hiley countered.

"He didn't mean anything, dear," Lome said. "Can't blame folks for being cautious." He smiled warmly at Hiley. "We're having a neighborhood card game tonight, right after dusk, if you're interested. It's at our dwello, the oblong one with yellow shutters."

"I've seen it," Hiley said.

"Number 65333," Lome said.

"Thanks," Hiley said, half turning to proceed on his way. "I'll check with my wife." Another lie. He turned away from them with no further comment and continued on his way.

"We don't blame you for being cautious," Lome yelled after Hiley. "We've seen the crimestopper books, too. With all the people killed and robbed . . ."

Hiley gave them a wave over one shoulder.

"See you!" Prabic shouted.

As Hiley proceeded home at a rapid clump-step, he wished he could be more open. He yearned for lasting klussmates, with card games, solar barbecues, and joking around. But people terrified him. And this feeling was stronger than any of his longings.

Hiley stepped inside his dwello and secured both heat-lock doors behind him.

Sperl was there to greet him, with tears running down her face. She hugged him. "Maudrey's gone," she said, her voice breaking.

"The Holo-Cops took her? Are we going to be charged, too?"

Sperl squeezed him tightly, desperately. "She's dead! She died last night."

Hiley pulled away and stared at her.

"Our baby's gone," she said, breaking into sobs. "The coroner took her!"

Hiley could not think of anything to say. He wanted to ask how Maudrey had died, but that did not really matter. The thought of death permeated his brain. "I need to sit down," he said. He found the nearest place, a high kitchen stool.

Sperl followed, wiping tears from her face. But she could

not wipe them away fast enough; more kept gushing forth.

"Was there . . ." Hiley began. "Was there any criticism of us? I mean, for not calling the police earlier?"

"Is that all you can think of?" Sperl stood in front of him, her expression wild with grief and rage.

"It is important," Hiley said, trying to reason with her, "despite the tragedy." Hiley searched his own emotions and motivations critically. He knew that he was not behaving admirably. He was saddened by Maudrey's death, but angry with her at the same time for supporting a man like Prussirian. They had lost Maudrey when she married Prussirian, not when she died. But Hiley withheld his words, knowing that they would not sit well with Sperl.

"They didn't say anything about us!" Sperl screeched. "One Holo-Cop and a coroner's assistant came here! They took my baby!"

"I'm sorry Maudrey's gone," Hiley said. "As sorry as you, in my own way. I just don't show emotions the way you do. Everything needs to be reasoned out with me, I guess. I'm considering the rest of our lives. Someone has to."

Sperl's ferociousness subsided. Feeling lost and sad, she shook her head. Then she left the room.

"I love you," Hiley said, while she was still within hearing range.

There was no response. A door closed softly in the other room, followed by unwelcome quiet.

Hiley closed his sensor, and envisioned a long column of utpeople dressed in black mourning clothes. Four people carried an open metal box, and in it rested the face-up body of Maudrey. In death, she smiled softly. The plaintive notes of a stringed flute wafted in the air, touching Hiley's sensor and drawing tears from it.

Something like that should be done for Maudrey, he thought. *A ceremony instead of cremation. But there are no ceremonies like that on Ut. Perhaps there were once.*

He opened his sensor and looked through the open living room doorway at the 'glas-enclosed stringed flute on the wall. He wanted to hold the instrument, to cradle it in his arms and play the emotions he felt. He wanted to cradle Maudrey in his arms as well and longed to touch her one more time, to see her playing on the floor again—that laughing, carefree little girl with the bright amber sensor.

Hiley felt his carefully structured emotions coming apart on him. He had held them in check for so long, always finding priorities to occupy his attention. But now . . .

I'm tired, he thought. *I'll feel better after a nap.* He felt low, lower than he had ever felt before.

With Prussirian's name and the details of his whereabouts to report, the laser tick traveled at light speed to Fortress 107, arriving a fraction of a second after leaving old Crain's body. There it entered the fiftieth-floor transcribing room and made its report, laser-activating the printer to put it on cello-sheets.

Nine minutes later, the tick returned to the old man's body, burrowing deeply into every cell. This light-creature extension of Mamacita had visited Crain and the holders of other selected positions as part of a coordinated study of instinctual patterns in utpeople. Statistics filling thousands of volumes showed how many deprived subjects constructed stringed flutes and other ancient things out of scrap materials without prior instruction or ever having seen the finished items.

The laser tick snooped as Prussirian and Crain, dressed in long weight coats, unloaded the rotocar. Later, inside the cave, Prussirian gave Maudrey's weight coat to Crain. He told him how he had decided to leave his wife behind for her safety. Crain was not a large man, so the woman's coat fit him passably well.

"Thank you," Crain said, placing his tattered old coat on a carved lava table. He watched Prussirian set an armload of duffel bags and a heavy metal case on the ground, then said to the younger man, "I have something for you as well. Gift exchanging, although prohibited now, once was a common practice among our people."

Prussirian nodded gently, for he had learned something of this practice in his songs. It was one of the forbidden ceremonies on Ut. Prussirian knew that gift exchanging had flourished all over the universe. Now it remained only in those places the U-Lotans chose not to conquer.

And in those places they'll never conquer, Prussirian thought, defiantly. *Like my mind.*

Crain's gift was a small burnished brown stone with black streaks across it, which Prussirian accepted without comment. The stone felt smooth against Prussirian's sucktip.

"I call it a moonstone," Crain explained. "Carry it with

you always for good fortune.''

"It's very pretty.''

"They're found on the ground and just beneath the surface around here.''

Prussirian smiled, and said, "And its extra weight will keep the winds from blowing me away!"

Crain laughed at this. "It's got a nice feel to it," he said, "especially when held between both sucktips. A calming effect, I've always thought. You can think better with one of these.''

Prussirian held the moonstone in the suggested manner and listened while the old utman told of his ancient grandfather, who many millions of years before had walked about with his pockets full of moonstones, giving them to anyone he met.

"I'd give more away myself," Crain confided with a rueful expression, "if more folks came this way." He studied Prussirian's face for a reaction to the gift. He found it difficult to judge the younger man's feelings. "It's a silly old man's habit, I suppose.''

"Not at all. I like it. *Really.*" And Prussirian did appreciate the gift. It might be an impractical thing, but it told him something about Crain. This was a good old man, one who would not betray him to the authorities.

Robot Paleon's rotocruiser broke down that morning, and he spent most of the day waiting for a robot repair crew. The crew took their rusty time getting to him after his urgent radio call. Eventually, they fixed the cruiser and went on their way.

By late afternoon, Robot Paleon was seventeen hundred kilometers northeast of Prussirian's hiding place. He had followed the electronic signal from the dye Prussirian had scraped off.

The robot examined the purple, dye-stained scraping stone and the bits of torn cloth left behind by Prussirian. He placed these items in a lead-lined pouch to block the signals and zipped the pouch shut. Then he returned to the rotocruiser, tossing the pouch in the rear transport compartment.

He flipped on the dashboard-mounted tracking meter and got a wiggle line on the dial, a squeaking noise, and then . . . nothing. The reading was flat.

"Which way did that son-of-a-worm go?" the robot muttered.

He considered selecting a direction at random and searching, but knew from his training that this would not be time-effective. It was precisely the sort of act that Detective Nipp would criticize. *It wouldn't be professional,* Robot Paleon thought.

Discouraged and frustrated, he started the rotocruiser and took off for Fortress 107.

Thirteen

There is a legend about moonstones told in one
of the ancient songs. Moonstones, it is said, are
brought to Ut by the wind. What an odd notion!
Rocks are not carried by the wind!

—U-Lotan conversation overheard by
Mamacita during her early years

Detective Nipp spent that night hovering dormant and unlit at
his desk, just as he and all other detectives did in their off
hours. At dawn, the mother beam brought him back to life,
sending currents of energy to flicker and jiggle the black light
matrixes of his body. His thousand eyes, each at the center of
a geometric light shape on the sides of his body, looked in six
directions. He saw the ceiling, the floor, the walls, the Ut sky
through the window behind him, and the shiny silver alloy
robot standing in his doorway.

"Good morning," Robot Paleon said. "I got in late last
night, after the mother beam had switched you to darkness. It
seemed like a good time to have my moving parts lubed and
adjusted, so I spent the night in Maintenance. They gave me a
polish and a couple of new motors, too. I hadn't noticed, but I
wasn't operating all that well, and—"

"You're babbling," Detective Nipp said calmly. "Prussirian BBD has been eliminated, I presume?" Concentrating
his vision toward the robot, there was a soft red glow around
the black light lines on that side of his body.

Robot Paleon rolled back and forth uneasily. "No."

"Apprehended, then?" The red glow became more intense.

"We've experienced a problem, I fear. He, uh, scraped off his signal dye." Robot Paleon expected an explosion of rage from his superior.

But Detective Nipp said nothing for several moments. Then: "Has any fugitive ever done that before? How did he do it?"

"With a scraping stone. I don't know if it's ever been done. I could research that, if you wish."

"No matter. I'm going to do it, Robot Paleon! You may have brought me good news!" With that enigmatic remark, Detective Nipp glided rapidly through his desktop, then through Robot Paleon and out the door. This told Robot Paleon that Detective Nipp was in a big hurry, for he usually did not pass through everything in his path. It was a superstition.

"Sir?" Robot Paleon said, turning to watch as the Holo-Cop reached the outer hall door.

"The Assault Team Button, Robot Paleon! Tell everyone in the fortress what I'm doing!" Detective Nipp went through the door without opening it.

Before doing as he had been instructed, Robot Paleon paused at his clear plastic desk. *Something troublesome here,* he thought, with a sudden sinking feeling. *Something I've neglected.*

His electronic gaze focused on the message receptacle mounted on the wall next to his desk, and then on the little red light next to the receptacle. The light was dark, meaning one of three things. He ran through the options programmed into every assistant detective's brain: no message, light functional; no message, light out; message in, light out.

He realized now he had forgotten to order repair of the light before chasing the fugitive and hoped there was no message. The odds were in his favor, and he might be able to have the light repaired without ever telling Detective Nipp what had happened. Robots could not be subjected to Truthing tests.

Robot Paleon lifted the receptacle's Lotanglas door slowly, afraid to look inside. A black plastic-and-rubber message tube was inside, but that did not necessarily mean anything. It might have been sent empty. That happened occasionally. The odds were no longer so favorable, however.

He lifted the tube out and slid open a plastic orifice cover on top. Several off-white cello-sheets were inside!

Quite upset now and recalculating the odds, Robot Paleon pulled out the sheets and read them.

"Damn!" he said, after the first page.

"Double damn!" he said seconds later, after the second page. He read and cursed, read and cursed, finishing the five-page special report in fifteen seconds.

He was in trouble. Big trouble.

Robot Paleon rolled at top speed through the corridors on his floor, nearly blowing a circuit moments later when he had to wait for the spin lift. It was particularly slow in arriving this morning, despite a lack of crowds in the corridors or in the lift. The first rule classes of the day would not begin for an hour.

The lift arrived at long last and carried its rotund silver alloy passenger down slowly, ever so slowly. When the door opened at the basement level, Robot Paleon fairly tore out into the corridor, shouting, "Detective Nipp! Detective Nipp! Don't do it!"

The Assault Team button was around two corners and down a long corridor, but Robot Paleon hoped his voice might somehow carry that far.

He went straight through the floors, ceilings, and walls, Robot Paleon thought, lamenting his grievous error. *By now he's already pressed the button and gotten a reading on the difficulty factor of Prussirian BBD's case.*

Robot Paleon rounded a corner, going so fast that he nearly toppled over. *It's a factor four at most. Oh, damn, damn, damn! My fault. Mamacita's already eliminated his light circuitry for the sub-9.0 reading, and I'm next.*

"Detective Nipp! Detective Nipp!"

The robot streaked around the second corner, reaching the long corridor. He saw Detective Nipp now, standing next to the blue steel door to Mamacita's Fortress 107 terminal. Detective Nipp appeared to be looking at the Assault Team Button, or at the computer screen below it.

"Detective Nipp! Don't press it! The case is too easy!"

Detective Nipp did not move or show any sign that he heard the frantic cries of the robot.

Mamacita's frozen his circuitry! Robot Paleon thought. *He'll disappear any second!* The robot grew quiet and rolled timidly forward.

The circular and hexagonal black light lines on Detective Nipp's square body jiggled, and a soft red glow appeared on the side facing Robot Paleon. "It's done," Detective Nipp said.

"You're still alive! Wonderful!"

"A 9.962," Detective Nipp said flatly.

"You pressed it? And got that reading? But—" Robot Paleon caught himself in midsentence and stared at the computer screen. There it was, unmistakably, printed in white U-Lotan script on the dark screen:

PRUSSIRIAN BBD
DIFFICULTY FACTOR 9.962

This was well over the 9.0 reading required for a Shriek assault team. Detective Nipp would not be destroyed. *Not yet,* Robot Paleon thought. But now the amphibious Shrieks had to get their man. Failing that . . . Robot Paleon told himself there could be no failure.

"I wish the factor had been lower to barely qualify," Detective Nipp said. "We've got a real toughie here, and I don't know why."

Robot Paleon considered not admitting to his failure, but decided this to be unwise. The assault team had been called for and approved. It was irreversible. Assault teams always left the day after approval. That meant tomorrow. Now Robot Paleon had to do everything he could to help Detective Nipp. And fast. He had to reveal every detail of the case, including the laser tick's unsolicited special report and the burned-out message-tube light.

Detective Nipp was astounded at hearing of the report, for it seemed to mean that Prussirian BBD would be an easy capture after all. "Could Mamacita have erred in her rating?" he asked, looking at Robot Paleon. "Maybe I've finally gotten lucky, after so many misfortunes in my career."

But Detective Nipp's thoughts grew dark. *There must be something else,* he thought. *Something known only to Mamacita.*

• • •

Eavesdropping via the mother beam sustaining Detective Nipp, Mamacita kept the answer to herself as a circuit-board thought: *Any case gets a factor like that, for Ut is pushing itself apart! It could go any second now.*

Hiley searched for credits that morning as usual, but after an hour found himself in the unraked, unplanted fotta outside Stamm's dwello. White weeds were beginning to pop through the surface of the galoo all around, and to Hiley they did not look half bad, especially cast as they were in the fresh blue glow of the morning sun. Four yellow-breasted warblers were perched on a railing overhead, chirping in a cheerful way that reminded Hiley of Prussirian and his stringed flute. He also recalled having seen Holo-Cops take such birds away, presumably to kill them.

Music was evil in any form.

Hiley thought of Maudrey, then in a moment of confusion considered killing the birds himself. Just as Hiley recalled that only Holo-Cops could kill, Stamm threw open the door above him.

"Come on up, Hiley!" Stamm called out cheerily. "Best of the season to you!" This was the traditional, permitted Uttian blessing for a bountiful spring, with many beautiful flowers and a fine white lawn. Coming from Stamm, who neglected his yard work, the comment amused Hiley.

But Hiley revealed no sign of such thinking and returned the blessing, adding, "I thought you might like to come with me this morning, Stamm, to see how many credits we can find." *I won't tell him about Maudrey,* Hiley thought. *Not now.*

"Why, sure," came the reply, with only a slight hesitation. Stamm leaned over the railing and noted that his visitor wore boots but no galoo shoes. "Pretty firm ground, huh?" Stamm asked.

"Not enough soft stuff to worry about. Do you have a heat probe? If not, I always carry an extra." Hiley patted two aluminum cylinders hanging from his belt.

"Never use them," Stamm said, casually. He flipped open a panel by the door and keypunched the code to activate his dwello defense system. Then he stepped downramp to Hiley. Stamm wore boots similar to Hiley's, brown factory plastics with black snap-acrosses. Stamm's faded blue denim coveralls had seen better days.

"Well, I'm using one," Hiley said. They started out across a fledgling meadow of young white grass stalks. Hiley held out his infrared probe to check the ground in front of him, looking for the heat variances that might indicate scavenger traps. Walking side by side, they headed away from the sun, and it cast their wide, shield-shaped shadows across their path.

Stamm laughed. "I've never used a probe. I have one, an old one that probably doesn't work anymore. Used it once or twice, I guess. Then I came to believe that if something's gonna get me, there's nothing I can do to stop it. When Father Fate selects my name, who am I to argue? Besides, the Holo-Cops are always out taking infrared aerial photographs. They're closing traps all the time."

"We can't rely on the Holos. Not enough of them, and too many traps. The thought of falling into a scavenger pit and waiting for night beasts to kill me . . . Well, it's too terrible to imagine."

Stamm grunted.

"Maybe the waiting would be the worst thing," Hiley observed. "Not knowing exactly when they'd come and how they'd do it."

"Would you give them your dwello defense code?" Stamm asked.

"Naw. Why bother? They'd kill me whether or not I gave it to them. I don't carry my dwello number with me, either, so they don't know which one is mine—unless they see me around it."

"Good idea. You have a lot of good ideas, actually."

"You really think so? You don't think I'm too cautious —ridiculously so, I mean?"

"You're a real careful guy. There's no denying that. But who am I to criticize your beliefs? Who am I to say what's right? We weren't born with instruction booklets."

"It's different for each of us," Hiley said, recalling a conversation in his living room with Prussirian—the day Prussirian married Maudrey. *He said I was different, too,* Hiley thought. *That I had a right to be, and that he did, too. Our jagged edges, he called it.*

Stamm considered Hiley's statement, then said, "This

reminds me of that Earth prince who stayed with me a few years back. He said they've got religions on Earth. A religion is some sort of a strong belief system—about supernatural things, powers of creation, that stuff."

"Oh," Hiley said, thinking of Sudanna.

"There's thousands of religions on Earth, and the followers of each group think they've found the right way, the supposedly pure and only path to a sublime afterlife."

Is he going to say the S word? Hiley wondered.

"Most of the religions go around ridiculing the beliefs of the other religions. There's even been wars over it."

"Huh," Hiley said, thoughtfully. He moved the heat probe from side to side across the path, unwilling to contribute his experience with Prussirian to the topic of conversation.

"There are exceptions," Stamm said, "like a religion called Buderism, or something like that, the prince told me. Buderists—many of them, anyway—have their own version of the path to eternal salvation, but also believe in tolerating other beliefs. They accept the fact that others have ways that are different but that may be just as right for them." Stamm paused. "Sorry if I'm going on too much about this. Guess I haven't had much company the last couple of years."

"That's okay. I see what you're getting at. You have strong beliefs one way about taking chances, and I disagree. We tolerate the differences and get along just fine."

"You've got it."

Hiley and Stamm walked until Stamm complained of aching feet. They found no credits and went a good deal farther in the attempt than Hiley's usual effort. They moved quickly on the return trip and were able to reach Stamm's dwello before midday.

Hiley was about to separate and go his own way when Stamm let out a frantic yell and ran toward his dwello.

"Someone's broken in!" Stamm screeched.

Hiley noticed now that many of the windows had been broken, with the front door wide open and askew, half off its hinges. Hiley ran to keep up and was only a few paces behind when Stamm pushed the twisted door aside and ran inside.

The inside heatlock door was completely ripped away and lay on the floor in the small sitting room adjacent to the dwello's entrance. Seeing this and other items strewn every-

where, Stamm whirled and confronted Hiley: "You! You're
in with the scavengers!"

"No, I . . ." Hiley backed up through the heatlock, pressed
by the advance of Stamm.

"Took me for a little walk, eh, while your pals sacked my
place! You did your sordid little job well, you—"

Hiley ducked to avoid a swinging punch from Stamm's long
arm, then stumbled downramp to the ground. "I didn't do
that," he protested. "You're wrong!"

Stamm hurled a shard of broken Lotanglas at Hiley. It
missed, traveling like a spear to Hiley's left.

Fighting his own rage at the unwarranted attack by Stamm,
Hiley said, "You're lucky you weren't home. They would
have killed you!"

"And I'll kill you if you don't get out of here!" Stamm
said. He scanned the deck for something else to throw.

Hiley discarded any thoughts of offering Stamm a place to
stay and bolted for home, waving the heat probe ahead frantically to check his path. He looked back several times and saw
Stamm at his galoo launcher, loading something in it. A large
rock whistled by Hiley's head. Another rolled across his path,
so that he had to jump over it.

He reached the knoll, rounded it, and picked up speed. Yet
another rock passed to his right, where he had been only
seconds before, prior to reaching the shelter of the knoll. *He's
pretty good with that launcher,* Hiley thought.

Hiley was in direct sunlight and perspiring heavily. With
Stamm's dwello out of sight, Hiley slowed to a fast walk. The
dwellos in his neighborhood were visible ahead and to his left,
with the metal trim and rotocars on some of them glinting in
the sunlight. Now Stamm wanted to kill him, and scavengers
were out in daylight morning hours. Did scavengers live in
those dwellos around Hiley, waiting to attack at any moment?

Hiley's solar heart raced. *What if they've already broken in
and killed my family?* he thought. He increased his pace to a
half run.

After a blur of forward motion, he could see his dwello
clearly, about a hundred meters away. Using the heat probe,
he slowed again and advanced carefully, staring all the while
at his dwello.

Everything looked normal, but he saw no activity. Clothes

were hanging outside on the line; there were no broken windows. He wondered if scavengers had entered through the back door and were inside at that moment doing their unspeakable deeds. He expected to see windows shatter from the inside out.

But nothing like that happened.

He reached the entry ramp and placed a booted foot on it, timidly. Then he crept upramp, trying not to make a sound. The ramp squeaked with each step, making noises he had never noticed before. He reached the deck.

"Oh, there you are!" Sperl said boisterously.

Hiley fell against the wall. He had not been able to place the direction of Sperl's voice at first and now saw her at the base of the ramp, looking up at him and smiling. Apparently she had come around the aft of the dwello from the other side.

"Stamm's dwello was ransacked," Hiley said, standing up and moving to the railing. "You haven't seen anything unusual?"

"No. . . . Stamm. Isn't that your new friend?"

Hiley did not answer her query. "What about the neighbors?" he asked, drilling her with the intensity of his words. "Have you seen any of them running around or using their rotocars?"

Sperl shook her head. "Nothing like that," she said. Then, with a concerned expression, she said, "Come inside, darling. You're all worked up." She walked upramp and reached his side.

Hiley allowed her to guide him inside. He was weary, done in. "Stamm blames me for the break-in," Hiley lamented. "We were out looking for credits when it happened. A run of rotten luck. Didn't find a damn thing again."

"Scavengers in the morning? That's a first."

"Maybe not. Maybe the Holo-Cops gave out bogus information on scavenger habits." Hiley heard the inside heat-lock door close. The hallway and the doors to the various rooms were unfocused. "Maybe I've been taking huge risks going out. I thought it was safe."

"It's all right," Sperl said, guiding him toward the master bedroom. "You just need a little nap. You'll feel better afterward."

"They always blame me," Hiley said. "Maudrey, Stamm.

People don't like me. What is it about me that people, even my own family, detest?''

"Nothing, dear," she said. "You're a wonderful man. Just a run of bad luck."

Hiley sat on the bed and watched her unsnap his boots. "A lifetime of bad luck is more like it," he said.

"Nonsense." Sperl looked up at him lovingly. "We have a beautiful home. Plick and Ghopa are wonderful children. You gave me these things. Wonderful things."

Hiley scooted up on the bed and scrunched a pillow behind his back against the headboard. "Could I have a small bowl of tea?" he asked, putting on a sensor foke and pushing its lens out of the way over his forehead.

"I'll get it," she said, pulling a blanket over Hiley's legs and lap.

"Activate the dwello defenses," Hiley said. "Do it first. Are Plick and Ghopa inside?"

"Yes. They're watching plasmavision."

When Sperl returned ten minutes later with the steaming tea, Hiley was asleep in a seated position, his head slumped to one side. She pulled his legs to straighten him on the bed and made certain the blanket completely covered his body below the head.

Half awake, Hiley lifted his foke and said, "I love you."

"I love you too," Sperl said.

After his nap, Hiley sat at the living room window with a bowl of tea, drawing tea fumes into his sucktip and then releasing them into his sensor. Outside he saw an utwoman in her yard, shoveling rocks from a wheelbarrow. It was Sharci, the black-haired woman Hiley had met the day before. Her husband, Lome, stood nearby, talking with the taller, fair young man, Prabic. Hiley heard low, murmurous voices behind him, coming from the kitchen.

It was Sperl, speaking to Ghopa. "Go sit by your father," she said.

"Aw, Mom," Ghopa said. She sat slumped at the kitchen table, holding a love confession magazine.

"Do as I say!" Sperl said. "Show some concern for other people! You're so selfish!" *It's her age,* Sperl thought. *I hope she doesn't become like Maudrey!*

With a deep sigh, Ghopa put down her magazine and went into the living room. Under her mother's watchful gaze, she pulled a cushion next to her father and sat down. "That's better than my tea," Ghopa said, smelling the beverage's spicy, flavorful aroma.

"Yours is very good too," Hiley said. He glanced at his eleven-year-old daughter. "Almost equal, I'd say."

"You really think so?" Ghopa's olive-green sensor lit up brightly. It was the same shade as Sperl's and made Hiley wonder if Sperl had looked at all like Ghopa at the same age.

"I said so, didn't I?" Hiley heard a tinge of intolerance in his own tone and looked at her apologetically. "I didn't mean to snap at you," he said.

"That's okay."

"Look at those people out there," Hiley said, growing agitated. The three neighbors were still in the yard, and at the adjacent dwello two other women were talking while looking at a white-and-red, broadleafed plant. "Scavengers could attack at any second," Hiley said, "in broad daylight. Your mother told you what happened to my friend's house?"

"I heard you talking."

"I even suspect our neighbors. Anyone, in fact. The old guidelines are dead, Ghopa."

"Your friend's dwello is in a remote place," Ghopa offered. "Maybe that's why it was hit."

Hiley mulled this over for a moment. "Maybe," he conceded. "But until further notice, don't walk around outside. We'll go to the rotocar through the emergency roof hatch. Someone will always remain here to open the hatch when we return so we can get back inside quickly." *I'm assuming the old superstition that scavengers don't attack rotocars holds,* Hiley thought. *Maybe that's a fallacy, too.* He felt his fears closing in, about to overwhelm him.

"Okay, Daddy." In her mind's sensor, Ghopa envisioned a thousand scavenger rotocars on the horizon, approaching her while she and her father flew to class. They had to get to class, against insurmountable odds. Her vision faded.

"Do you think Maudrey was still angry with me when she died?" Hiley asked.

"I don't know. She wouldn't talk to me, or to any of us. Not even to Plick, who was always close to her." *I think she was mad at Dad,* Ghopa thought. *And I don't know how I feel about him, with all his ridiculous fears. I can't wait until I'm old enough to move out!*

"I didn't tell her husband to leave her," Hiley said. He heard Sperl in the kitchen, opening and shutting cupboard doors.

Ghopa grunted. She did not want to sit by her father. It was boring there, just sitting and talking. She wanted to get back to her magazine.

"Are you listening to me?" Hiley asked. Ghopa heard the demanding irritation in his tone. She knew his inflections well.

"Yes, Daddy." She tried to sound sweet, wishing to conceal her emotions.

"You never listen. Maudrey didn't either."

Ghopa felt all her anger against her father concentrating inside. He was beginning to pound her in the manner that used to make Maudrey crazy mad—using the same words. *Maybe I'll do something really crazy too,* she thought, *even if it scares me or worse. Just to get away from him, just to show him!* She knew Maudrey had done the same thing with games and rides, and in her impetuous, headlong marriage. These had been factors in her death. But it did not matter.

Hiley said something that did not register in Ghopa's brain. The words did not matter at that point. Her rage button had been pressed.

"You're always so sensible, Daddy," she said. "Telling us the safe things to do, the calculated things. Maybe we're getting a little tired of it." Then, venting her hostility: "Maybe we're sick of it!"

"Don't ever talk to me that way, you little—" Hiley held a sucktip tightly against Ghopa's arm.

"You're hurting me!" she said, trying to pull away. Tears moistened her sensor.

Hiley felt his own lifetime of frustration and anger. He was upset about many things and recalled striking Maudrey once the year before at a time such as this, when he had been feeling particularly low. It had been a too-hard and undeserved blow against the side of Maudrey's head that might have killed her—over some silly material possession of Hiley's that Maudrey had broken or neglected. He could not remember. But he recalled the heated argument with Sperl afterward. She threatened to leave him if he ever hit anyone in the family again. She pointed out—correctly, Hiley realized—that material things did not matter that much. Not as much as the permanent damage domestic violence could do to young minds.

Still holding Ghopa by the arm, Hiley came out of his thoughts and looked toward the kitchen. Sperl stood there in the doorway with her arms folded across her chest, watching and waiting.

"Your precious lists!" Ghopa screamed, trying to break away. "What about falling down and breaking your battery pack and then not being able to get to a fresh pack in time? Is that on one of your lists?" She had an I-know-your-secrets look on her face, the one Sperl sometimes used to great advantage. He had grown to detest that look. She was challenging him to strike her.

Hiley's sensor glazed over, and the colors around him blended together. He had the battery pack hazard on a list, and Ghopa acted as if she knew it. Such an obvious hazard. Ghopa had probably gone through his day pack, finding the spare battery pack there, or had read his lists. He felt uneasy about her knowing him so well. His grip on her loosened.

Ghopa broke free and ran past her mother out of the room.

In shock, Hiley watched his daughter. She seemed so angry, angrier even than he was. It did not seem fair—so many people misunderstanding him.

Sperl did not meet his gaze when he looked up at her. She stared at a bare spot on the wall by the window, shaking her head in dismay.

"What gets you won't even be on your lists!" Ghopa howled, from the hallway.

The comment hit home. Hiley realized his lists were incomplete, despite the time and thought he devoted to them. New hazards were forever occurring to him and finding their way onto one of the cello-pages. Only things he knew about were written down. He could not watch out for something he had not even considered! The death or maiming blow might come from anywhere, blind-siding him. Ghopa was right. But what did she mean by it?

Sperl turned without reacting to Ghopa's comment and went to her craft room. She had mentioned wanting to start a new color-by-numbers painting.

Maybe that's why Sperl was staring at the bare spot on the wall, Hiley thought, watching her close a hall door behind her. *She looked pretty disgusted with me, too.*

Something bumped in one of the other rooms. It was an angry noise, probably made by Ghopa.

What if it was a threat? Hiley wondered. But from an eleven-year-old, his own sweet baby girl? He had never even raised a sucktip against her. But she had been so hostile, so out of control. And Hiley had heard of such things happening in families.

He would add it to one of his lists.

Fourteen

Each basic Ut rule has dozens, sometimes hundreds, of subrules, subsubrules and subsubsub-
rules . . . all without explanation. The whole
setup seems quite remarkable at first, until one
examines his own life and society critically. Are
we really that different from the citizens of Ut?
Oh we have freedoms, to a certain extent? But
so do they.

> —Fasil O'Mara, *San Francisco Times*
> staff reporter, reflecting aloud about
> his Ut experiences

The next morning, Hiley took an ultrasonic shower, had a cup
of tea aroma, and filled his hollow legs with packets of money
and credits. Today he would attempt to visit Stamm to repay
him for his terrible losses.

Hiley got in his rotocar and took off. Since he was not
searching for credits, there was no requirement that he go on
foot.

I'm not totally responsible, Hiley thought, as the rotocar
approached the knoll between his dwello and Stamm's. *Maybe
20 percent, a third at most.* He watched the spinning tilt-rotor
on one of the craft's short wings, then pushed the black accelerator lever down slightly, slowing the speed.

I'll negotiate with him, Hiley thought. *It's the honorable
thing to do.*

When the rotocar passed over the knoll seconds later, Hiley

had increased his theoretical share of the blame to 35, maybe 40 percent. *Stamm never would have gone out if I hadn't urged him. He might have found a way to keep the attackers away had he been there.*

Stamm's one-story dwello was in sight now. Two police rotocruisers were parked on the galooflat near the dwello, and Stamm's rotocar was in its usual place on the roof. A Holo-Cop stood guard near the police ships, while two other projected light officers descended the dwello ramp, carrying a stretcher between them. A white sheet covered the stretcher.

Hiley's solar pulse raced, pushing blood through his veins at a rate that made him dizzy. It had to be Stamm! But what could have happened? He wondered for a moment if Stamm might have killed a scavenger, but something told him otherwise.

His friend was dead.

Hiley considered flying by, not wishing to talk with the police because of the Prussirian matter. Hiley had made his report by tell-all, but no one had been out to question him yet. He knew they would, eventually.

But the Holo-Cop guarding the rotocruisers pointed what looked like a handheld red light at Hiley. Larger red lights began to whirl on top of both cruisers, accompanied by sirens.

"Whirr-eee! Whirr-eee!" the sirens wailed.

"I'm ordered down," Hiley muttered. He moved the control stick forward and touched the three landing buttons that set the craft down. Hiley knew the light the officer had was not really handheld. It came from the light matrix hand itself and was a force beam, said to be powerful enough to knock a rotocar out of the sky at a distance of six kilometers. The utpeople had been told that one hand light meant the officer wanted to talk with you. Two lights meant the weapon had been activated. If you were ever unfortunate enough to see two lights, it would be the last thing you saw.

Hiley hurried to comply, setting the rotocar down near the officer.

As Hiley stepped out, all three Holo-Cops glided to meet him, training single red lights on him.

"Hiley OIV, three-six-five-oh-four," the officer said, having received accessible mother-beam data based upon the identification number on Hiley's rotocar. The officer also had verified the information visually by taking a sensorprint and bone vein scan on Hiley's body. "What is your business here?" the officer asked, gliding closest to Hiley. The voice was efficient, demanding.

Oddly, this officer was smaller than the others, with his box-shaped body coming up only to Hiley's shoulders. Hiley thought all Holo-Cops were the same size . . . and they were, before Mamacita started having projection difficulties. Unknown to Hiley, Mamacita was struggling with this officer's projection at that very moment. The black light lines toward Hiley glowed soft red as the officer concentrated his vision in that direction. Suddenly, the Holo-Cop grew larger, to normal size.

Hiley hesitated and considered stating he had just been on a recreational flight. Wisely, he decided to tell the truth, for Holo-Cops had verification methods. "I'm a friend of the dwello owner here. Stamm. He's dead? How did it happen?"

"I will ask the questions concerning this murder," the officer said, curtly. "When did you last see the victim?"

"Yesterday. I left around midday."

"There is more for you to tell," the officer said flatly. "I hear it in the inflection of your voice and see it in the perspiration around the roots of your skull hairs. You had a fight with the victim?"

"He became angry with me, yes. We went credit hunting yesterday morning, and when we returned to his dwello we found it had been ransacked. He blamed it on me, since I suggested the hunt. He thought I was tied in with a group of scavengers."

"Which you are not," the officer said. "There is something else, which I detect from your odor. You fear us . . . more than the normal fear."

"He has information on an unrelated crime, perhaps," one of the other officers suggested.

Hiley felt flush in the face at this comment. The word *crime* was all-encompassing, applicable to the serious and the not so serious. They would not necessarily arrest him.

"More just came in on my mother beam," the short officer said. "This one called in a fugitive report. Another officer is handling the matter."

Hiley stood transfixed, afraid to move or say anything.

"Your dwello location has been mapped," the short officer said. He motioned with his hand. "Just beyond the knoll."

"That is correct," Hiley said.

The officers glide-whirled in unison and left, taking the stretcher bearing Stamm's body with them.

Hiley stood for several minutes watching them leave. The police rotocruisers were profiled against the pale red sky as they flew off, passing to the right of the knoll. Soon they were beyond the range of his vision.

They called it murder, Hiley thought. *The scavengers came back.*

As Hiley flew home, he felt overwhelming sensations of loss, for both Maudrey and Stamm. How much of it had been his fault? He had been hard on Maudrey at times. And foolishly he had told the neighbors where Stamm lived, two days before when he met the trio on the galooflat.

They are scavengers! he thought. *I'm sure of it!*

Hiley imagined himself walking across the galooflats, holding out an infrared heat probe to check for scavenger traps. He imagined that the scavengers had developed traps that had no heat variance from the surrounding soil, making them nearly impossible to detect.

Why not? Hiley thought, returning halfway to reality.

Back in his vision, Hiley came to the realization that his heat probe was no longer any good. It should be discarded. Just then, Hiley returned to full awareness. He had touched the landing sequence, and his rotocar was setting down for a crisp landing in the middle of the galooflat.

Using a heat probe, he tested the ground before stepping on it. It was dry here, and the rotor wind had kicked up a little dust. He smelled it as he set foot on the ground. Suddenly, without thinking about it, he tossed the heat probe back in the rotocar cabin, following it with his belt-secured backup probe. His battery pack followed, despite the fact that the energy-giving blue sun was partially obscured by high clouds. He needed either direct sunlight or the battery reserve to survive. The reserve pack was in his daypack, which sat on the passenger seat.

A portion of hair-covered skin on Hiley's side showed through the clothing cutout where his battery pack had been. He took a step without the heat probe or any other gadget, setting a foot down softly. Then he let all of his weight sink in the dirt. The ground did not give way. He took another step, less cautiously this time. Then another. And another, in rapid succession. Soon he was running herky-jerk across the galooflat with no protection. The sun was totally obscured now, but he felt a Sudanna wind blowing beside him—an occult wind with a faint sensation of breeze. The presence reassured him.

Stamm should have seen this! Hiley thought. *And what would Sperl say? This is wonderful!*

Suddenly Hiley realized he was running across open land without a heat probe, without a battery pack, and out of the sun. He had no apparent source of energy. Panic struck, and he stopped in his tracks, afraid to take another step. The Sudanna presence had departed, leaving him at least two hundred meters from his rotocar.

How will I get back? he thought. *Am I going to die here? What have I done? Am I mad?*

He remained frozen, unable to take another step. Perspiration covered him, causing his clothes and solar hairs to stick to his body. He lost all concept of time. He may have stood there for ten minutes. Or it may have been an hour. Slowly, painstakingly, he tiptoed back toward the rotocar, looking for scuffed patches of dirt marking where he had touched ground before.

Hiley reached the rotocar safely and without apparent energy loss. He crawled into the pilot's seat, snapping his battery pack to the clasp on his belt so that the pack made contact through the clothing cutout with his solar collector hairs. He did not move again for a while as he regained his composure.

I won't tell anyone about this, he thought.

The sensation of running across the galooflat without protection and without caring if he lived or died had been stimulating, even thrilling. But it marked a breakdown in all the rigid systems he had followed during his adult life.

He was more frightened now than he had ever been before. He wondered if he might again be lured to an insane act. *No,* he thought, attempting mind-set. *It will never happen again! And no more morning credit searches. Too dangerous. We'll live more frugally from now on, making it on class and rule-quiz credits. We can do it.*

He recalled the year before, when he had become accustomed to wearing his headcap everywhere, out of fear that his head might tumble off. Then, at Sperl's insistence, he took a more "reasonable" course, only wearing the device during Flux. Hiley wondered now when his tendency toward taking chances had begun, and if he should revert to extreme measures. It would subject him to some ridicule, perhaps even warranted ridicule.

What's the reasonable course? he wondered. *The correct course?* He recalled a comment Stamm had made concerning people not being born with instruction booklets. Life seemed like such a lot of trouble to Hiley as he considered this. More trouble than it was worth?

Fifteen

Our sensors are downturned, brothers and
sisters, where once they turned up in broad,
happy smiles. We were a carefree and joyous
people, with dancing and Zuggy music! Do not
forget these things. Never forget them.

—words scrawled on the Great White
  Wall of Fortress 51 by an errant utwoman, just prior to her arrest

Wearing his long brown weight coat, Prussirian sat on a wind-
sheltered ledge to the side of the cave entrance, looking out
at the black lava landscape and listening to the wind as it
whistled, whooshed, and roared. His still-bandaged forearm
felt better. He had been up only half an hour and had been
sent outside by Crain so that the old utman could enjoy his
morning coffee aroma without contamination from the stench
of Prussirian's body.

I do stink pretty badly, Prussirian thought, deciding it
resembled the odor of something rotten and dead. The weight
coat pressed heavily on his shoulders, although Crain said he
would get used to it soon.

The scenery here was quite different, and Prussirian barely
recalled seeing it earlier. He had been ill when landing the
rotocar, and after that had been occupied with the three days
of sniffer reaction testing on his new body odor. None had
dye-marked him, thankfully. He did not want to endure
another skin scraping. He realized now that this was the morn-

ing of the fifth day he had spent with Crain, including that
first day, when he had been comotose.

The black rocks in this place covered virtually all of the
ground, with many splotches of galoo in sinkholes. Young
white grass and pastel blue and yellow flowers—all blown now
by the constant, clearly audible wind—grew in many places,
even on what appeared to be lava surface. The lava rocks
glistened softly, as if thousands of busy people—or an omni-
potent force—had buffed their tightly pored surfaces. Maybe
the wind had done it. And the shapes! Every rock looked different, with some resembling funny aliens and others looking
like common objects found around the dwello—chairs, tables,
a full bookcase. Some shapes reminded him of nothing in particular, but appeared beautiful to him all the same.

Prussirian was glad to be out of the sealed reading room. It
made him claustrophobic during waking hours, and he had
been unable to read there with sniffers present. They unnerved
and enraged him. A sniffer forced him to abandon Maudrey
and destroyed what might have been his last hope for happiness. They were horrid, ugly little creatures. Once, the day
before in a fit of rage, he had killed five of them in the sealed
room, smashing their little mechanical bodies with books and
a boot. He felt better after exacting this measure of revenge,
however inadequate it may have been.

As he sat on the rock thinking back, he wondered why the
sniffers had not retaliated when he attacked them. Could this
be a flaw in their design? Wouldn't anyone assaulting a sniffer
be a prime candidate for signal dye?

Whoever designed those things has a blind spot, Prussirian
decided, amused at his observation. *A weakness. And where
there's one failing, others are likely to appear.*

He had slept fairly well the previous night, the best since
leaving Maudrey's dwello. Crain was making Prussirian sleep
in the sealed room for a couple of weeks, until Prussirian's in-
duced stench weakened. The room was not such a bad place in
which to sleep. Prussirian felt relatively safe there, barricaded
from Mamacita's technology.

At the sound of footsteps in the cave behind him, Prussirian
glanced around. He greeted Crain.

Crain wore the new brown weight coat Prussirian had given
him and carried two Zuggernauts, one under each arm. The

long coat already had a number of dark spots on it, the old man not being particularly neat. His cave was not the cleanest place in which to live, either.

"We ran thirty-seven sniffers by you," Crain said, pausing next to Prussirian, "including the five you destroyed. You're safe now, young man."

"Good!" Prussirian said heartily.

"I brought our Zuggies out for a little celebration," Crain said. "You and I haven't had the opportunity to play together yet."

"Where's this tether you mentioned?" Prussirian asked. "I took a walk a few minutes ago and couldn't find anything resembling a tether—assuming I understand what the word means."

"You noticed the alloy cylinders on the rocktop above the cave?"

"Yes. I found the steps going up there. I saw what looks like a weighing scale topside, too."

"Come with me," the old man said, smiling gently. He led the way up steps that had been carved in the black lava.

It was warmer and wind-exposed on top of the rock, in full sunlight. Prussirian saw the scalelike thing again. An alloy platform large enough to hold two big rotocars, it had a short bank of solar cells and an instrument panel next to it. A long burnished silver alloy bar stretched at least fifty meters across the rocktop behind all of this. The substantial-looking bar ran parallel to the flat rock surface and approximately a meter above it. It was attached to the rock at each end, where the bar curved down.

"You don't see a tether, eh?" Crain said, glancing mischievously at Prussirian. Crain set the Zuggernauts on the platform and slid aside a heavy see-through cover over the instrument panel.

"I sure don't. I must be missing something."

"Permit me to have a little fun with you," Crain said, his voice crackling but full of boyish glee. His sensor was in full smile, and he fairly shook in anticipation. "I've only had a few opportunities to show off this equipment!"

"I can understand that." Prussirian looked around nervously as he watched Crain touch two switches.

"Step on the platform, please," Crain said.

Prussirian hesitated, then did so after Crain stepped on it himself. The wind moved their coats, but only a little because of heavy linings.

An orange glow lit the platform, Crain, and the two stringed flutes at their feet. Looking down at his own body, Prussirian saw that he too was aglow. He felt nothing and heard nothing, save for Crain's tiny, roguish laugh. It had to be safe, or the old man would not be laughing. Unless he was insane. He appeared to be near death, anyway.

"This is not a scale," Crain said. "It's a mass register, determining the mass of everything on the platform."

"What in the name of Sudanna for?"

The glow subsided, and Crain stepped off the platform.

Prussirian followed.

"No time to explain," Crain said. *Any second now,* he thought. *After the cylinders are loaded up there.*

A piercing, ringing noise touched Prussirian's sensor, coming from afar. To him it sounded like a large artillery shell fired over a long distance. After about a minute, the noise became tortuously loud, to the point where Prussirian closed his sensor and fell prone on the black lava. During the ensuing moments, he attempted a number of times to open the sensor, but each time found the noise too excruciating to bear. The rock shook beneath him—a rumbling, continuous movement that reached a crescendo and then tapered off.

Crain closed his sensor too, but remained standing. When he felt the vibrations subside, he opened his sensor and saw to his satisfaction that the tether had secured itself with a plaz-brass hook to the long bar—having traveled from a satellite at 22,000 kilometers to Ut, reaching a peak midpoint velocity of 345 kilometers per second. Attached to the thin black line of the tether was a large white passenger pod, which to a novice might have appeared too large and too heavy for the line. The pod swayed in the wind. A hatch on it slid open, revealing a rack of metal cylinders inside.

What technology! Crain thought. *Still working after fifteen million years! But this was Uttian originally. Why did the U-Lotans rebuild it to last so long? I've asked that question so many times.* He wondered if tether keepers preceding him had experienced similar thoughts. *The U-Lotans studied social orders. Social orders! Then why put so much money and ef-*

*fort into machinery? They studied people! People! Tether
keepers? Maybe that was it. Spying on tether keepers for some
reason . . .*

Feeling perplexed but glad the U-Lotans were long gone,
Crain gave the still prone Prussirian a nudge with his foot.

Prussirian opened his sensor and peered up at the old utman.

"The tether has arrived," Crain announced, proudly.

"Arrived?" Prussirian rose jerkily and saw it now. He
walked timidly toward it.

"No danger," Crain assured him.

Prussirian noticed that the black line stretched taut into the
red sky as far as he could see. It seemed tied to the roof of the
atmosphere.

Crain chuckled.

"How does it work?"

"There's a satellite at twenty-two thousand kilometers, in
SUO—synchronous Ut orbit. After receiving a reading on our
combined mass, it reeled out two thruster-boosted lines, one
toward us and another in the opposite direction—each carrying identical mass loads. This helps keep the satellite on
station. It's aided in that effort by frictionless, solar-powered
stationing engines that thrust continuously."

"What goes in that pod?" Prussirian asked, not particularly wanting to hear the answer.

"You and I . . . if you want to see the orbiting launch platform, that is. We simply remove the cylinders from the pod
and leave them here. They have a combined mass equal to that
of ourselves and our instruments. Then we get in the pod,
close the hatch, and step on a pedal to unhook the tether from
the bar. We're reeled up by motors in the satellite, and at the
same time the other line comes down to the satellite, from the
opposite direction."

"Equal and opposite forces."

"Right."

"Solar-powered reeling motors?" Prussirian asked.

"Right again. But no ordinary electric motors were installed
in that satellite. Those frictionless babies are first quality
U-Lotan, the finest in the universe. They'd have to be to still
function after fifteen million unserviced years!"

"I guess so."

"We'll go up rather slowly, without thruster boosting. That's only needed to get the tether to the bar in this windy region."

"Wouldn't the solar collector have to be huge for all that satellite's needs?" Prussirian asked, looking up. Deep red clouds moved briskly overhead, propelled by high winds.

"Twenty to twenty-five square kilometers, according to my calculations," Crain replied. "But that assumes our technology. The U-Lotans were way beyond us. That solar collector—incredibly—is only a few square meters. Don't ask me how it works. It just does, that's all."

Prussirian nodded, then watched the wind part thin strands of hair on Crain's head. "It must store energy in a big way," Prussirian said. Then: "I stink. Maybe we should go up in separate trips."

"I'll cover my sensor by playing my Zuggy all the way up," Crain said, laughing. "You'll want to watch the scenery the first time."

"Okay," Prussirian said. He looked forward to the trip and began formulating several questions in his mind. "Let's go!"

In Prussirian's dwello near Fortress 81, his sister, Tixa, sat on a hard plastic chair watching the round Lotanglas screen of her plasmaviewer. Holo-Cops in rotocruisers had been in the air above her neighborhood only an hour before, blaring by loudspeaker to everyone, "To your viewers, citizens! Watch the valiant assault team bring back Prussirian BBD!"

My own brother, she lamented, feeling shame. She was angry with Prussirian and worried about him at the same time. She wondered, too, how the case could be important enough to warrant an assault team—and if she would be thrown out of the kluss over it. Shriek assaults were unusual events. Tixa had seen only two previously on plasmavision.

The Shriek projecting an image to her stood on webbed amphibious feet at the rear of its brethren. All sixty-two Shrieks of Ut were there. To the right front, partially visible between the backs of brown-and-white Shriek heads, Tixa saw three neat rows of silver-and-green police rotocruisers. The image was clear, much clearer than the normal undersea view. She heard the low whine of Shriek sonar as they whispered among themselves.

A Holo-Cop hovered before the contingent of spider-bodied

Shrieks, preparing to speak to them. In actuality, he would also speak to the seventeen million utpeople huddled around plasmaviewers all over Ut. The Shrieks would perform their mission, dutifully as always—repaying the long-gone U-Lotans for rescuing them from a dead world. Prussirian used to marvel at the ages of these creatures. They were the original rescued group, making them millions of years old. "A Shriek does not live forever," Prussirian used to say, repeating an Uttian proverb. "But neither does a planet."

"I am Detective Nipp," the Holo-Cop said, getting Tixa's attention. "My fugitive, the lowly music criminal Prussirian BBD, is hiding in a remote region. He thinks he's safe there, but we have a little surprise for him! No one escapes justice!"

A hollow cheer rang out, followed by the grumbling sonar cheer of the Shrieks.

The image panned between Shriek heads to the left, revealing a Holo-Cop throng gathered in front of a rooftop fortress entrance—the source of the hollow cheer. Soft red glows moved among these policemen as they concentrated their banks of eyes in the general direction of Tixa's Shriek, then looked at other things.

"Fortress 107!" Detective Nipp shouted. "We're number one!"

Tixa did not understand what this meant, for the competitive machinations of police fortresses were never explained to the Ut populace.

More hollow, grumbly cheers ensued.

A Shriek in front of Tixa's projecting Shriek moved, blocking her view of Detective Nipp. She heard the detective's voice describing Prussirian's cave hideout and the manner in which he would be apprehended. She listened for something about what would be done to her brother, but heard no clue.

They'll kill him, Tixa thought. *Maybe that's best.*

She switched off the viewer, knowing the assault team would leave momentarily. She could not bear to watch.

From her classes and readings, Tixa knew that robot rotocruiser pilots would fly one Shriek apiece to the remote region. The robots would perform most of the police work, with the Shrieks as backups and broadcasters of the events on plasmavision.

They're making Prussirian into an example, Tixa thought. *It's not something I want to see.*

•   •   •

Detective Nipp hovered by himself on the nearly vacant rotocar pad, looking up at the squadron of rotocruisers filling the sky. They banked and proceeded east, following Robot Paleon's lead craft.

Refocusing his vision to look the opposite way, he saw a faint, hazy shadow on the concrete from his square body— a barely discernible, ghostlike image. *I don't cast much of a shadow,* he thought.

"Brave act," a Holo-Cop's voice said, from his side. "Everyone respects what you did."

The black light lines on that side of Detective Nipp's body glowed red as he looked at the speaker, the officer known as Detective Aviin. Identifiable by a particular configuration of triangular light matrixes on all sides of his body, this officer was the epitome of the Fortress 107 loser in Detective Nipp's opinion. Detective Aviin rarely did anything to warrant a mother-beam shutoff. He was a clever and gutless shirker— one who would never press the Assault Team Button himself, but instead would find devious methods of stealing part of the credit.

Detective Nipp groped for a suitable response. Then: *I won't even speak to him! Let him return to his lowlife hole!*

Presently and without further comment, Detective Aviin glided away.

Detective Nipp looked again at his own faint, ghostlike shadow on the concrete. He felt far superior to creatures like Detective Aviin—and had felt this way long before pressing the Assault Team Button. Now he had widened the gap.

But how significant is the difference? he wondered.

The Prussirian BBD assault constituted the biggest event in Detective Nipp's life, but on the full scale of things that might not be much. Mamacita could terminate his mother beam in a microsecond, creating a replacement in less time than it took to think about it.

He was highly expendable.

Extending this uncomfortable thought, he wondered how important anything on Ut could be. It was so tiny in comparison to the planet Sudanna. Maybe Sudanna was not all that significant. Maybe other bodies in the universe dwarfed it.

If this was the case, Detective Nipp realized, it made Ut even tinier comparatively and moved him completely off the scale.

I've got to concentrate on my police work, he thought. *These are not acceptable thoughts.*

He didn't allow himself to carry this thinking further, and reassured himself that his undertaking was both enormous and significant. He longed for a luxurious office with a long credenza, plush carpeting, and awards on the walls. He would be happy with such perks, and happiness was a very important thing.

When Prussirian stepped into the passenger pod with his Zuggernaut, he discovered the pod walls were not the opaque white they appeared to be from outside. He could see clearly through them. The pod swayed gently in the wind, moving him with it—then swayed more as the wind intensified and began to howl. He grabbed a white plastic chairback to keep his balance. The pod was spotless and probably smelled clean. He smelled nothing except his own rotten, decaying stench. Two other high-backed chairs like the one he held faced outward, one of them with a small instrument panel before it.

Crain brought his own Zuggernaut aboard and slid the hatch shut behind him, latching it and clicking down a double lock. He sat at the instrument panel, setting his Zuggernaut on his lap and securing a shoulder harness across his wide torso. Prussirian noticed a black rubber foot pedal on the floor near Crain's right foot.

Prussirian swung into the chair he had been holding and strapped himself in. The seat was hard and uncomfortable. He shifted in it.

"Ready?" Crain asked.

"Ready." Prussirian's own repugnant odor began to bother him. The quarters were tight.

Crain depressed the foot pedal, causing the pod to jerk upward. "We're free!" he said.

After the initial pull, the pod rose slowly and roughly, moving from side to side as winds buffeted it.

"Nothing to worry about," Crain said, feeling his chest swell with air in preparation for the Zuggernaut lying across his lap. Presently, he lifted the instrument to his sensor and wrapped wrinkled sensorlids around the sensorpiece. A haunting flute melody ensued, unfamiliar at first to Prussirian. Then, simultaneously, the sucktip on Crain's long arm strummed the black strings in the V of the instrument, producing a resonant, throbbing beat.

I've played that song, Prussirian thought, feeling a rush.

Through the floor of the pod, Prussirian saw the plaz-brass hook dangling, and far below that the rocktop with its long bar and mass register platform. He could hardly make out the line of the bar now, and soon it was entirely beyond the range of his vision. He focused on the platform next, until it too disappeared from sight—then on the cave rocktop itself, until it became indiscernible from its surroundings.

The pod rose through rust red clouds, making it impossible to see straight down any longer. Through an opening in the cloudcover to the east, Prussirian made out large rock formations and wondered if any of them could be Appa Crown. It was impossible to tell.

Crain's music picked up in cadence, to a happy, folksy tune. Prussirian recognized it instantly as another he had played himself.

Sudanna, Sudanna, Prussirian thought, feeling sun warmth in the pod.

With the view below increasingly obscured by clouds and too distant to be interesting, Prussirian let Crain's music dominate his sensor, to the detriment of his other senses. This temporarily reduced his vision, his sense of temperature and his sense of smell. He traveled in memory to a time long before on the planet Sudanna, when the breezes there played tunes in caves and high rock formations. The people listened and attempted to duplicate the sounds they heard with homemade, primitive flutes.

These were constructed of petrified galoo at first, and then of metal. Soon the people were approximating breeze sounds, pushing air through the flute pipes with their own internal winds. Shortly thereafter they developed the stringed flute, adding a new, creative dimension to their music. It went beyond what they heard in nature, to a realm of songs accompanying stories told about their lives. All of life's triumphs and tragedies were related in these story songs and were passed along to generation after generation.

Traveling on the same occult wind with Crain, Prussirian watched technology take its natural course, bringing with it creature comforts and the threat of war annihilation. In a nightmare of reality, the once peaceful planet erupted in righteous fury from eight sides, each mistrusting the other. One group fled to Ut—the survivors who spoke to Crain and Prussirian now. Prussirian beheld no faces in the vision, but met many people in ways that meant more to him than their appearances.

When Prussirian returned to the lesser awareness, he stood with Crain on the satellite's launch platform. They wore odd galoo shoelike fittings on their boots, which Prussirian did not recall having put on. He knew they were needed to stay upright on the zero-G metal decking. Crain might have explained it to him—or maybe Sudanna voices told him this, too. Crain was verbalizing stories now, telling of the ancient times Prussirian had already seen in his vision.

"I know those things," Prussirian finally told him. "I traveled with you as you played."

"Sudanna, Sudanna," Crain said.

The planet Sudanna was partially visible to Prussirian against the black, star-covered expanse of space—apparent hours early because of the satellite's altitude. Thick, black clouds partially obscured Sudanna's crater-mottled surface. A bolt of lightning flashed, sending a jagged orange line across the planet.

Prussirian knew other things. He understood how the platform worked, functioning as a base from which to hurl objects at the great planet. Tethers other than the passenger pod line were on this satellite, each capable of slinging objects at Sudanna with startling accuracy—objects encased in impact-bursting alloy cylinders that did not burn up in atmospheric entry.

Prussirian made no value judgment concerning the havoc rained upon Sudanna by his ancestors. He was glad to be descended from the victors, forgetting for a moment about the subsequent U-Lotan conquest.

After defeating their Sudanna brethren, Prussirian's ancestors chose to remain on Ut, fearing someone else might take the high ground if it were abandoned. But Ut was barren and ugly by comparison, and the people longed to return to Sudanna. After a century, the difficult decision was made by many to return—and construction was begun on a fleet of ships to carry them there.

The U-Lotans put a stop to this.

Prussirian realized as he stood on the satellite platform that his people would outlast Mamacita. It was an inevitable thing, an insuppressible longing that would remain as long as one utperson lived.

"Sudanna, Sudanna," old Crain said, barely getting the words out. He crumpled to the deck, with his sensorlids constricted all the way over his sensor. He lay peacefully on the floor for several minutes, clutching his Zuggernaut. Presently and painlessly, sensory deprivation took him. Even in death, he did not release his grip on the instrument.

Prussirian placed the old man's body and his beloved Zuggy in a large alloy cylinder, then tether-hurled it at Sudanna.

Prussirian remained on the satellite for many hours, strapped into a hard plastic control room chair. The small control room stood to one side of the launch platform, with tiny oval windows showing space outside—Ut in one direction, Sudanna with its braided ring in the other. Two parts in the jigsaw puzzle of his heredity. He could not see the wind or hear it from this place, but sensed its presence, with him as the third part.

And the fourth, he thought. *I am the fourth part. My physical being and everything I know.*

He considered many things, including whether or not he should hurl himself at Sudanna as a means of ending one life and beginning another. Or he could attempt to survive the trip in his present life state by designing a cushioned container that would not split on impact—one that would carry him safely to the new land.

What about a flying craft? he thought. *Will my Sudanna knowledge help me with that? I don't seem to know how to do it, but maybe it will come to me.* He tried to envision a container that would enter the great planet's atmosphere without burning up and would then open in midair (or change in midair) to a craft that would sail to the surface. Or maybe just a means of getting out of the container at precisely the right moment, so that he could sail down on his own flat Uttian body. He would need windows, or altitude indicating instrumentation . . .

This sounds pretty high-tech, he thought, *and Crain said he couldn't do metallurgy. I need to take a look at his shop anyway. Sudanna guide me!*

These things did not occur to Prussirian until late that night, when he sat in the reflected glow of the Sudanna moon. It was night as well on the black rock region of Ut, far below his geosynchronous orbital station.

Moments later, he located the control room lights and used the improved visibility to set two switches on a control panel. Then he stood with his Zuggernaut on the satellite's mass register. The orange glow came and went.

Soon he was back inside the passenger pod, this time strapped into the high-backed chair with the instrument panel and foot pedal. He touched the correct buttons, and the thruster-boosted pod screamed Utward. Prussirian felt G-forces, but they did not bother him. His body was an utperson's body, reputed to be one of the most durable encountered by the U-Lotans in their travels around the universe.

Just above the moonlit surface of Ut, an airborne Shriek assault team proceeded toward the same black rock destination at a slower pace. In the lead police rotocruiser, with a spider-bodied Shriek in the transport compartment behind him, Robot Paleon watched the shadowy galooscape as it passed beneath, looking for landmarks that had been described in the laser tick's special report. Robot Paleon did not need to be so attentive, for the coordinates had been programmed into his craft's computer system. He remained alert anyway, keeping in mind his forgetfulness about the burned-out message terminal light.

An internal learning circuit told him not to rely on mechanical devices.

Robot Paleon considered his own mechanical nature and laughed to himself. He had failed too, proving the learning circuit's point. But was he ultimately to blame for personal errors? Or were the Holo-Cops, Mamacita, and the U-Lotans? Were all of these entities mechanical—even the U-Lotans?

I could present an excellent case proving I'm never at fault, the robot thought. *Others should check and service me periodically. But I was programmed to report for servicing on my own and did so a little late. The programming error shouldn't be my fault! Others may not see it that way, though.*

In the transport compartment behind him, a motionless Shriek stared blankly ahead with its bright yellow eyes, sending Robot Paleon's image to millions of people gathered around their plasmaviewers. A Shriek in each of the sixty-one rotocruisers behind the lead craft projected images to the rest of Ut.

"ETA fifty-two minutes," Robot Paleon's cruiser computer reported in its sexless voice.

Imagining what it would be like if the computer had a feminine voice, Robot Paleon muttered, "Little Mamacita. That's what I could call you."

"I am not connected with Mamacita," came the reply. "Except as part of the enforcement system. Inappropriate name."

Robot Paleon paid no attention to this. He was thinking of something he had heard: *Mamacita is only as big as a Sucian eyeball.*

"Imagine that," Robot Paleon said in a barely audible tone.

"Repeat," the cruiser computer said.

"Nothing, nothing." Robot Paleon fell silent, remembering the mission and the plasmaviewers turned to him via the Shriek watching him at that moment.

Sixteen

Ut. A place where rumors travel like the wind.

—from an Oknos travel guide

With his sensor foke tilted out of the way above his forehead, Hiley lay awake on his back, thinking of the chances he had taken that day on the galooflat. *Oh, Mamacita!* he thought. *I ran hundreds of meters without a heat probe or battery pack! What got into me?*

Asleep beside him, Sperl stirred, shaking the bed and pulling the blankets away from Hiley. He jerked his share of the covers back.

Through the skylight directly over his head, Hiley saw part of Sudanna's braided ring, illuminated silver-blue this night. Clouds obscured the rest of the great moon.

I even enjoyed it! he thought, *knowing each step might be my last! It was exciting—frighteningly exciting.*

Hiley considered the addictive nature of thrills and tried to psychoanalyze each action he had taken, going back as long as he could remember. He began to see trends and punctuation points of action that swayed him one way and another.

Clouds covered Sudanna's ring now, and Hiley felt sleepy. His head sank deeper into the pillow as his muscles relaxed. His leg muscles went slack. He had not been aware of the tautness of his muscles until now and tried to concentrate on drifting off.

The clouds were an illuminated haze, and Hiley imagined

faces in them. As his muscles relaxed, he felt his entire body
sinking deep into the bed. He realized this was only his drowsy
imagination, but it was a peculiar sensation that consumed
him in softness. His sensor foke flipped gently down over his
sensor, making clear vision impossible. But he saw the clouds
again, dropping to meet him in his place of softness.

The clouds enveloped his dwello, then permeated its tiniest
openings, filling the master bedroom. One cloud became
Maudrey's face, and she pressed it against the plastic lens of
his foke.

"I'm all right, Daddy," she said. "Don't blame yourself."

Hiley struggled to awaken. He tried to reach for Maudrey,
but his arms seemed far beneath him and useless, having been
swallowed by the softness of his bed.

"Maudrey," Hiley said. "Are you coming back?"

"Tell Mama not to worry. Tell her I'm in Sudanna, where
we'll all meet someday."

Maudrey's face receded, and Hiley saw the cloud ascend,
seeping out of the room. It hung over the dwello for a moment, and through the skylight Hiley beheld Maudrey's face
once more, pressed against the skylight.

"I love you, Daddy!" she said. "Good-bye!"

Hiley felt himself rising from the paralyzing softness, and
one of his arms moved. He flipped the sensor foke out of the
way over his forehead and sat up.

Sperl stirred again, mumbling something and pulling the
blankets completely off Hiley's legs and lap. Sudanna was full
and bright in the skylight, illuminating the bedroom with a
low, silver-blue glow. No clouds were in sight.

Hiley swung out of bed in his pajamas and slipped quietly
from the room. He thought again of the addictive nature of
thrills. Despite this critical analysis he wanted to experience
another, different sensation. His stubby feet carried him
without argument into the living room.

Sudanna moonlight streaked through the prismatic Lotanglas around the rooftop solar cells, illuminating the 'glas case
on one wall with a dark rainbow. A stringed flute rested in
that case, and Hiley wanted to swing open the door. *Just to
touch it,* he told himself.

He inched closer to the case and touched the cool, moonlit
Lotanglas. There was no lock on the case—only a simple,
tempting latch that would slide to the right. He touched the

latch, then looked at the self-smoothing crystal strapped to his arm.

I can't do this, Hiley thought. *But I don't want a self-smoothing, either . . .*

He stepped back jerkily until he felt an armchair against his legs. He sat down in the chair, sinking into its deep cushions.

Hiley watched the dark rainbow of moonlight move away from the Zuggernaut, leaving it in shadow.

Prussirian descended to the Ut rocktop and saw the same Sudanna moon. But at his longitude it was only partially visible and slowly receding. Dawn would arrive soon.

He thought of Maudrey, and for a time he sat on the rocktop looking at the giant Sudanna fragment mounded along Ut's horizon. It was windy here, and cool against Prussirian's face—but his body stayed stable and warm in the long, thick weight coat.

Sudanna dropped below the horizon after half an hour, taking its illumination with it. Simultaneously, dawn pushed forth its first rays of blue sunlight in apparent exchange, from the opposite direction. Wearily, Prussirian clumped down the carved lava steps.

Halfway down, he remembered the tether had been left secured to the bar. *I'd better release it,* he thought. *Wouldn't want to keep tension on that line and snap it after all these years. I'm going to need that launch platform for what I have in mind.*

Prussirian took a mass register reading on the capsules he and Crain had unloaded from the passenger pod, then loaded them back in the pod and slid the hatch shut. He crossed the mass register platform to the instrument panel, where he touched two buttons. The tether hook snapped free and the hook, line, and pod ascended.

He noticed his body stench as he again proceeded down the steps. A wind shift had filled his sensor. He paused at the cave entrance to watch an approaching flock of birds, profiled against the eastern dawn sky.

Falcrows, he thought, turning to go inside.

But he looked back. Something struck him as peculiar about that flock. The whir-throb of rotors filled his sensor, telling him that these were not falcrows.

Prussirian scrambled back up the steps. *Rotocruisers! And I released the pod!*

The police cruisers were approaching fast. The lead ship reached the rocktop just as Prussirian touched the two instrument panel buttons to bring back the pod.

Expecting the screaming artillery shell noise of the tether, Prussirian leaned way over and closed his sensor. The rock shook beneath him, just as it had done before. Then it shook again, harder this time.

He opened his sensor and looked at the long alloy bar. The hook had not secured itself to it, and he saw the white passenger pod dangling and wind-buffeted at least a hundred meters beyond. Somehow the hook had missed its mark, and nothing in Prussirian's inherited knowledge told him why.

The rock shook violently, throwing Prussirian down on his back. He saw a sky full of police rotocruisers, flying in confused patterns and apparently hesitant to land. The tether's pod swung by, smashing against one of the rotocruisers and sending the cruiser crashing to the ground. The pod tore free from the tether and took a different course down, falling on the rocktop where Prussirian could see it. Prussirian did not move, for the disconnected pod could no longer take him anywhere.

The rocktop wrenched and cracked, throwing Prussirian headfirst against the instrument panel. It knocked him out, sending him into a nightmare of dream-world violence.

In his fantasy, Prussirian heard artillery noises, but knew they could not be from the tether pod. He knew he should not be able to hear such things, too, for his sensor was closed. Orange-and-red color illuminated his consciousness in an unsettling way. Pain colors, he realized. Had someone shot him? Was he dying? Something shook his body and threw him about.

Six minutes, he thought. *I must awaken in six minutes . . .*

When the first groundquake hit Hiley's dwello, he bolted out of the living room chair in which he had been dozing. Subsequent shocks rocked his dwello to one side, then threw it back upright. He slammed into the solar hearth, then against a table, injuring his left side. Hiley heard the children screaming and crying in another room and Sperl calling his name. A low, ever-present roar filled his sensor.

Clutching his side, which he saw was bleeding, Hiley careened down the hallway. The floor shook beneath him and he saw the walls rumple, worse than in any galoo storm he had experienced.

The snap-apart, he thought, recalling the rumor passed to him by Prussirian. *Could this be it?*

Sperl threw open the master bedroom door as Hiley reached it. A dark purple knot covered half of her forehead, and the expression on her face said without words, *The children!*

They reached the bedroom shared by Ghopa and Plick just as the dwello rocked and righted itself again. Hiley and Sperl bounced against the children's bedroom door, then fell into the room when Hiley pushed the latch.

Ghopa and Plick huddled in a corner, visible in low moonlight coming through the window. The children cried and clutched one another, and soon Hiley and Sperl were crouching over them—holding them and speaking reassuringly. The crying became whimpers and complaints over minor bruises.

"Brace yourself against the dresser," Hiley said to his wife. The dwello continued to move with the ground beneath it. The low, constant roar became louder, then subsided.

Sperl did as Hiley had instructed.

Exerting himself, Hiley pulled the mattresses off both beds and created a soft corner shelter around his family. He positioned the mattresses between the dresser and Ghopa's bed, both of which had been bolted down.

Using tens of thousands of Holo-Cop eyes connected to her on mother beams, Mamacita saw tremendous convulsions tear across the surface of Ut. Galoo, rocks, dwellos, and bodies flew in every direction. She despaired, knowing the snap-apart had come. With this realization, her circuits froze, going into the programmed protective phase known as "self-arrest."

Hiley's dwello flew through the air for what seemed like an eternity before crashing back to the ground. Still holding his family in the makeshift mattress shelter, Hiley saw night change to broad daylight. Then a hazy half-light came, and the dwello stopped shaking.

The dwello had landed right side up, but Hiley feared it would never be galooworthy again. He noticed part of the ceiling broken away, exposing what appeared to be a brownish-yellow galoo-swathed sky. Fragments of dirt floated in the air outside, and Hiley smelled the dull odor of Ut soil.

"Everybody seems okay," Sperl said. She held both children now, and the three of them looked at Hiley with wide-open sensors.

"I think it's over," Hiley said.

He herky-jerked to the door and opened it. The door stuck, but moved, scraping the floor with a deep gauge. With Sperl and the children close behind, Hiley walked carefully around debris in the hallway to the front door.

Both heatlock doors were wide open. The OIV family stepped outside to an astonishing sight. To Hiley, the planetoid appeared to have contorted itself in a most peculiar way, with the halves of its former peanut shape at right angles to one another. Where sky or the planet Sudanna should be along one horizon, there was instead more Ut, stretching up like a high, distant wall of galoo. The topsy-turvy scene nearly caused Hiley to swoon.

"Oh, my!" Sperl exclaimed.

"What happened, Daddy?" Ghopa asked.

"Get the children inside," Hiley said.

Six minutes, Prussirian thought, still repeating this to himself in unconsciousness. *I must open my sensor! Must!* His internal, instinctive sense of time told him he had only a few seconds remaining. The crack, crunch, and thud of artillery filled his hearing. Orange and red flashed across his brain.

Something moved beneath him—the ground, or someone pushing him. *Open my sensor!* Prussirian screamed in thought, to whoever might be there. *Help me!*

The violent noises and colors subsided, leaving Prussirian lying motionless and in darkness. *Is death taking me?* he wondered. *Not yet! Please, not yet!*

He thought he heard music—far-off, barely audible notes traveling to him on a whisper of wind. Other sounds, too. *Voices?* he thought. *Do I hear voices? Help me!*

The sounds became louder, definitely voices and music—and he felt the coolness of wind moving across his body, touching the lids of his sensor. The sensor opened slit-wide, then a little more. He found himself face down, looking at dirty black rock. He smelled the dirt.

Prussirian rolled to one side and with peripheral vision saw something massive and galoo-colored overhead. Startled, he looked at it full face in the available half-light, then attempted to escape by rolling away. But he could not flee from something so huge, and it did not appear to be moving toward him anyway. He no longer felt wind and heard no music or voices.

A sky full of galoo! Prussirian thought, sitting up and staring overhead. The sensation dizzied him, for it gave the illusion of sitting upside down on the sky itself, looking down at the surface of Ut. He took several quick glances at the rock-top beneath him to reassure himself that he indeed sat on solid rock.

With ground above and below him, it occurred to Prussirian that he might be inside a monstrous fissure. But glances in all directions showed this not to be the case. The shape above him resembled a great, galoo-smeared Sudanna planet, but was extremely close. Too close. He could make out topographical details there, even what appeared to be a Holo-Cop fortress far off to one side—and tiny objects near the fortress that might be dwellos.

He positioned himself so that he faced a place where the surfaces above and below seemed to meet. To his right and left, the red sky arched backward in giant sideways V's, with most of the red sky and light behind him.

As he concentrated on the apparent meeting place of the surfaces, he began to see a thin horizontal line of pale red light. The line widened, and soon he decided that the surfaces were in fact spheres, moving in relation to one another. The horizon of his sphere became distinct, with a slowly widening sky slice above.

He noticed as well with quick glances that the sky slices to each side remained somewhat constant, whereas the one behind him continued to narrow. The slices before and behind him were becoming equal, he judged. When he decided upon this, he saw too that the overhead sphere was getting very close to him. The wind was back, blowing his hair and weight coat—a cool, noiseless wind, unseasonably cool for spring.

That *was* a fortress on the other sphere—and those *were* dwellos near it. The spheres seemed to be either passing near one another, orbiting one another, or slowly colliding.

He hoped against the latter.

At the whir-thump of rotors from behind, Prussirian turned and saw two police rotocruisers approaching, hugging the rocktop. Resigned, Prussirian stood and watched them land. Two robots and two Shrieks were lifted out of the cruisers by mechanical arms next to the hatches. One robot appeared to be in charge—a round, silver alloy fellow who held an eternity pistol pointed at Prussirian.

"I am Robot Paleon," the leader said tersely. "Submit or die." He rolled forward.

Prussirian raised his unequal length arms overhead and walked toward his pursuers. He could see other rotocruisers parked on the black lava below the high rock, with robots and Shrieks milling around nearby. Some probably had gone inside the cave to search it.

"I'll go peacefully," Prussirian said. *Go in peace,* he thought. *Sudanna, Sudanna.*

Analyzing Prussirian's voice inflection and other factors used in truth verification, Robot Paleon satisfied himself concerning the fugitive's sincerity. The robot holstered his eternity pistol.

But as Prussirian walked to one of the rotocruisers with the robot, he was changing his mind about going peacefully. An escape plan formulated rapidly in his brain, involving that overhead sphere that loomed nearer and nearer. Would it pass close enough?

Prussirian broke away and leaped to the tail section of the nearest rotocruiser. Then he crawled to the highest point above the cabin and jumped high in the air, into the wind. A strong breeze caught his shield-shaped body like a sail, carrying him up, up, up. He heard music and voices again—stronger than before.

Higher, Prussirian thought.

The wind cooperated. Eternity pistols blasted away below, and Prussirian saw flashes of orange light on the two robots as they fired at him.

Then the robots, their Shriek companions, and the rocktop were above him, receding. The wind, music, and voices disappeared. Prussirian dropped gracefully to the surface of the other sphere, landing on dry galoo. He began running the minute he touched down—away from the fortress, which appeared to be nine or ten kilometers distant.

Moments later, an increasingly loud pounding noise caused Prussirian to stop and look up. All the rotocruisers from the other sphere were crossing the way he had gone, meeting no obstacle. Prussirian sat down to await the inevitable.

He wondered about the voices, the music, and the wind. They had helped him, and he thanked them in thought, adding: *I'll join you someday.*

Seventeen

LINE	UT DATE	SUBJECT	SEX	COMMENTS
194	15,007,220.179	Prussian BBD	M	Assigned to galoo raking crew 165-R. Sister not dependent upon him

—excerpt from the computerized
Smoothing Logs of Fortress 107

Seven days after Prussirian BBD's capture, Detective Nipp hovered before the desk in his sumptuous new lower-floor office, relishing the rewards Mamacita had bestowed upon him for the successful assault. His shiny titanium credenza stretched from one wall to another—the longest and costliest office sideboard available. Electron-particle photographs in bright gold and silver stand-up frames covered the credenza top—pictures of him posing by Mamacita's terminal screen, of his trusted robot assistant, of Shrieks, and of Detective Nipp hard at work studying cello reports on the case. There were even photographs of Detective Nipp's new hologram wife and children, for he had taken a bride the day before.

It was only a programmed marriage, performed by Mamacita through alterations to the memory circuits sent via his mother beam. He felt complete now in his career and could finally afford a family.

Mamacita will continuously adjust my memory circuits for the rest of my life, he thought, *making me believe marital experiences are occurring.* He understood how all of this happened, but it did not matter to him. Mamacita could make it work for him.

I feel good, he thought. *Better than ever before.* A warm, satisfied sensation permeated every black light line on his body. *I am number one. Numero uno. Numero uno? What does that mean? Where did it come from?* The thought troubled him, and he tried to discard it.

The lesser Holo-Cops in Fortress 107 had to share offices, for a glancing collision between Ut's other breakaway sphere and his fortress had done substantial damage. The upper-floor classrooms, half of the offices, and the entire rooftop rotocar landing pad were gone—demolished. He heard pounding, sawing, and grinding construction noises overheard—a new, lower landing pad was being built just two floors above him. New construction would begin shortly on what had been grassy, garden or unimproved areas of the fortress rock, creating low buildings that would not be hit by the next passing of Ut's other sphere.

In theory, at least, Detective Nipp realized. Acts of nature could not always be predicted.

There had even been talk of building along the sides of the rock and of moving the Good Thought moorages farther out in the galoo, with long lines or finger piers connecting them to fortress rock.

Many changes, Detective Nipp thought. *And more to follow.* He watched a little desk-mounted perpetual-motion machine Mamacita had given him. A spiraling slew on the device carried water to a spinning waterwheel, which in turn dumped water into a holding tank while forcing more water through a tube back up to the slew. It fascinated him.

Mamacita still functioned. Detective Nipp's very existence attested to that. But rumors were circulating among the ut-people, the Holo-Cops, and even the robots that many of her mother beams behaved erratically now—some problem caused by Ut's new configuration of two spheres orbiting one another in a peculiar cosmic dance. Word had it that many of the fortresses no longer contained holo-life, owing to disruptions in several of the projection-reflecting mirrors that had been concealed in clouds. Fortunately for Fortress 107, Mamacita's Sucian eyeball-size hardware had been installed on the same north sphere with this fortress, meaning that full-smoothings via Mamacita's fiber optic cables were still possible. Fortresses on the south sphere had been severed entirely from these cables and from the full-smoothing function.

One more matter to wrap up in the Prussirian BBD case,
Detective Nipp thought. *Punishment of that couple who failed
to turn him in promptly. Now what were their names?*

He rustled through a stack of disarranged cello-sheets that
hung over the edge of his in-basket.

Oh, yes, he thought, locating a sheet on the sister, Tixa
BBD. *Her too. Now the others. Where did I put those names?*

At sunset Hiley stood on the roof of his dwello, leaning way
over in the kneeless Uttian way while using a trowel to spread
a third layer of petrifying galoo over the long crack crossing
his roof. He looked up at the sound of rotors and watched a
police rotocruiser swoop low against a sky backdrop of
layered purples, oranges, and reds.

The cruiser's loudspeaker blared: "Report to Truthing
Sessions as usual! . . . Main floor, Fortress 107! No rule classes
there until further notice! An educational coordinator will
contact you!"

This last referred to the neighborhood study groups being
formed by the police to make up for the classroom crisis. In
the confusion, many citizens had not yet received the word. So
the rotocruisers returned each day with their message.

Hiley had seen Fortress 107 on a fly-by following the disaster, his rotocar being one of those still operating. Many of
the Fortress 107 floors had been turned to rubble. Everyone
knew why: Ut's spheres were orbiting one another only two
hundred meters apart. Anything taller than two hundred
meters on either sphere—a hill, a rock, a fortress—was being
knocked apart. The rumor mill said that half the fortresses
still remained intact through sheer chance, since they were not
located in close orbit sphere positions. But this would change,
the thinkers said. Rotational factors meant no two hundred
meter plus spot on either sphere would long endure. These
thinkers also said that eventually no point on either sphere
would be taller than ninety meters or so—just less than half
the distance between spheres—and that many places of any
height would be knocked down to galoo level, if a jutting
point on the opposing sphere got to it.

A lot of folks were doing a lot of figuring, and Hiley was
one of them. *Until things level out,* Hiley realized, *my dwello
could be destroyed by one of those high points.* He did not
bother to enter this hazard on one of his lists. Too much had

occurred for him to trouble himself with that sort of thing anymore.

At the moment, the sky looked normal from Hiley's vantage, with the Siamese south sphere on the other side of his and not visible to him. Gazing to the east, he saw the planet Sudanna poking its braided ring above the horizon, preparing to reign over the evening sky. Behind Hiley, the blue sun receded, leaving his backside cool.

Hiley's dwello had sustained serious, but not irreparable damage. He was glad he had gone to the trouble and expense of obtaining a triple-thick hull. The petrified galoo used in dwello construction was pretty tough stuff too, and he had found only surface hull cracks. He would have the dwello hauled out to check it over, with two crane company rotocars coming out the following week. His roof and walls appeared to have sustained the most damage, and already Hiley had done extensive repairs.

I've been luckier than a lot of people, Hiley thought, wiping his trowel on the lip of a small bucket.

As the police cruiser flew off toward nearby dwellos, Hiley heard other, approaching rotors, running roughly. A dingy, dented rotocar landed on the galooflat nearby, kicking up a little cloud of dirt. It was a galoo raker craft, with two unsavory-looking characters and their rakes, brooms, and other tools visible inside.

So many galoo rakers pestering me the last few days, Hiley thought. *Are they going to approach me now, with darkness coming soon?*

The galoo rakers stepped to the ground and looked up at Hiley. They talked between themselves and pointed at the fotta comprising Hiley's yard, apparently discussing things they saw to do.

Giving them a disgusted look, Hiley saw that the pilot was short and fidgety, with a full, unkempt brown beard. He wore patched and stained blue jeans and a torn red plaid shirt. His companion was taller, with gray-streaked black hair and a pockmarked, unshaven face. The companion carried a wide rake, and walked as the shorter man did, in the clumsy, shock-smoothed fashion of galoo rakers.

"Any work here, mister?" the taller man asked, his words slow and expression blank. He leaned on his rake. "We do good work."

Hiley shook his head. As he did so, he noticed hostility in the man's expression. Something familiar there, too.

"We need the work, mister," the shorter galoo raker said. "Things have been real bad."

"It's almost dark," Hiley said.

'We could come back tomorrow," the taller, vaguely familiar one said.

"We've all had it rough," Hiley said. He stared hard at the tall man's face. Someone Hiley had seen in class? . . . No. Then it hit him: *Prussirian!* The facial features were distorted and he looked older, pain-racked. But it was him, without doubt.

I should hate you, Hiley thought. *But I don't. What do I feel?* It was something, but not pity, fear or any other emotion on which Hiley could put his sucktip.

"What do you say, mister?" Prussirian asked, shuffling listlessly on his feet. He stared at Hiley with an inquisitive, "Do I know you?" expression, then passed the rake to his partner. Prussirian removed something from his own pocket and held it with one sucktip in front of his face. Something small and dark. A stone, perhaps, Hiley decided.

Prussirian stepped closer, his partner moving with him. "I almost went to Sudanna," Prussirian said. He held the dark object up, adding, "This is my moonstone. I got it someplace . . ." His expression vacillated between dullness and near exhilaration.

"Sudanna?" Hiley asked. "What do you mean?"

"I may not look like it to you, mister, but I've done a lot with my life! It took a whole Shriek assault team to bring *me* back!"

"And you remember that?" Hiley asked.

"Sure." Prussirian looked intensely at his moonstone, apparently trying to recall where he had obtained it.

"Do you remember anything else?"

"It's kind of dim. The Holo-Cop tried to get it all out of my head and must have thought he did. Guess I beat him, huh, mister?"

Astounding, Hiley thought. *An equipment malfunction, maybe, caused by the cataclysm?*

"Hey, mister," Prussirian said. "Our people can outlast them. Life can always outlast machinery."

His memory must have come back after they released him,

Hiley thought. *They'd have killed him before letting him go with such thoughts. Or maybe they can't even verify smoothings anymore. Imagine that!*

"Yeah," Hiley said. "I guess you did beat the Holo-Cops."

Prussirian beamed. Then his expression became dull, and he replaced the moonstone in his pocket.

"I'm sorry, fellas," Hiley said, "but I can't afford to hire you. Try those dwellos over there." Hiley motioned to his left, toward a group of moderately damaged dwellos.

As the galoo rakers clumped dejectedly back to their roto-car, Hiley identified the emotion he felt toward Prussirian. Envy. Prussirian had jumped from one sphere to another, try-ing valiantly to escape oppression. Some people in the neighborhood who saw it on plasmavision called Prussirian a hero.

A hero! Hiley thought. *And he married* my *daughter!*

To Hiley, Prussirian seemed like an old man now—a person who had experienced a rich life and could no longer recall the important details. *His fragmented memories are more than the things I have,* Hiley thought. *I'll go back inside my dwello now and continue my average little life. Is that what I'm going to do?*

Hiley thought of the Lotanglas-encased Zuggernaut on the wall of the living room belowdecks. *I'm going to play it!* he thought, watching the galoo rakers motor their rotocar along the ground to the dwellos Hiley had pointed out.

He considered Sperl, Ghopa, and Plick. *In the long run,* Hiley thought, *I'm doing this for them—and for others like them. If enough of our people resist the tyranny, especially now, when the Holo-Cops are having trouble, we'll be free. Free!*

Hiley knew he had to hurry, for the Holo-Cops might still question him over what he had done in the Prussirian matter. He scurried downramp to the entrance and tugged at the front door. It was sticking again, but opened. He slammed it shut behind him, stepped through the heatlock, and opened the in-ner door. The vibration and roar of a hundred police cruisers filled his sensor, and as he ran for the living room Hiley imag-ined that he too was leaping from one sphere to another.